DAVID H. KELLER, M.D.

LIFE EVERLASTING
AND OTHER TALES
OF SCIENCE, FANTASY, AND HORROR

By
David H. Keller, M.D.

EDITED AND
WITH A CRITICAL AND BIOGRAPHICAL
INTRODUCTION BY

Sam Moskowitz

HYPERION PRESS, INC.
WESTPORT, CONNECTICUT

Library of Congress Cataloging in Publication Data

Keller, David Henry, 1880-1963.
   Life everlasting and other tales of science, fantasy, and horror.

   Reprint of the ed. published by the Avalon Co., Newark, N. J.
   CONTENTS: Life everlasting.--The boneless horror.--Unto us a child is born. [etc.]
   I. Title.
PZ3.K281Li5 [PS3521.E356]   813'.5'2   73-13256
ISBN 0-88355-111-X
ISBN 0-88355-140-3 (pbk.)

Published in 1947
by the Avalon Company, New Jersey.
Copyright 1947 by David H. Keller, M.D.

Copyright © 1974 by Hyperion Press, Inc.

Hyperion reprint edition 1974

Library of Congress Catalogue Number 73-13256

ISBN 0-88355-111-X (cloth ed.)

ISBN 0-88355-140-3 (paper ed.)

Printed in the United States of America

CONTENTS

TITLE		PAGE
INTRODUCTION		9
LIFE EVERLASTING		
FOREWORD		34

CHAPTER		
I	FOUR FAILURES MEET	35
II	THE INITIAL EXPERIMENT	40
III	THE FIRST RESULTS	46
IV	THE EXPERT'S OPINION	53
V	THE RECIDIVISTS	62
VI	HIRAM SMITH'S BOY	68
VII	THE HUNGER STRIKE	77
VIII	THE AROUSED NATION	89
IX	CONGRESS CHANGES	99
X	THE SIX CONSPIRATORS	108
XI	FATE INTERVENES	117
XII	BIDDLE II AS A CALLER	123
XIII	THE PRESIDENT'S MESSAGE	128
XIV	BIDDLE EXPLAINS	134
XV	THE SCHOOL FOR UNUSUAL CHILDREN	142
XVI	LIFE IS DIFFERENT	151
XVII	HIRAM SMITH TAKES A TRIP	158
XVIII	THE ROBOT BABIES	168
XIX	THE WOMEN DECIDE	178
XX	OLD LIVES FOR NEW	187

CONTENTS

TITLE	PAGE
THE BONELESS HORROR	192
UNTO US A CHILD IS BORN	
FOREWORD	231
THE STORY	233
NO MORE TOMORROWS	248
THE THING IN THE CELLAR	268
THE DEAD WOMAN	280
HEREDITY	293
THE FACE IN THE MIRROR	313
THE CEREBRAL LIBRARY	325
A PIECE OF LINOLEUM	357
THE THIRTY AND ONE	364
BIBLIOGRAPHY	383
ACKNOWLEDGEMENTS	395

To Celia Keller

INTRODUCTION

AFTER consulting a number of standard dictionaries, I find there is a certain amount of overlapping in the definitions of the two words, *writer* and *author*. Just as irrefutably, there are certain meanings and added inferences that apply only to one or the other. Anyone can be a writer, conceding his education is sufficient to place understandable words on paper. An author, however, must, in addition, be a creator, an originator, and an elaborator. He must have something new to say, a novel way of saying it, and some definite reason for writing it. There have been periods in the life of David H. Keller, M.D. when, under the spur of necessity, he wrote as a professional writer, yet without ever "slanting" his stories toward a particular editor's viewpoint; but for the past fifty years, he has also tried to become an author.

For thirty years, he wrote simply for the pleasure of writing, with the definite objective of finding a satisfactory form of expressing his thoughts. This search finally produced a style, later noted for its simplicity and beauty, which became his trade-mark. While for many years he was the leading writer of *science fiction,* he never produced a trend, no one being able to imitate successfully either his style or the authenticity of his human understanding.

In an interview published in *Science Fiction Digest,* July, 1933, Doctor Keller thus sums up his ambition to become an author:

"I like to write beautifully—to string words together like a necklace of pearls, each word having a definite relation to the word before it and the word following, and all together forming a well balanced sentence; and when I write this way, I have nothing in mind except the pleasure of writing."

It is generally accepted that only authors write literature. Since most great literature is about people, then the more fully a man has lived, the closer his association with, and understanding of, people, the deeper his emotional experiences and the more he has traveled, the greater is his chance of creating a genuine masterpiece of literature. However, in addition to all these, he must have at least some degree of literary talent.

Throughout the ages, scholars have plumbed the most intimate depths of the lives of writers who have become acknowledged authors. They have searched through rare sources for facts concerning background, heredity, environment, emotional stresses, and, in fact, any information which would explain the source of the vital spark of divine fire that gave to the author's writings the shape of permanency.

The life of David H. Keller, M.D., is as interesting a one as can be found in the annals of literature. Born and educated in Philadelphia, he practiced medicine for ten years as a horse-and-buggy doctor in a small country town. In 1915, he became interested in psychiatry, which specialty he practiced until his retirement in 1945, after serving as Assistant Superintendant in state hospitals for the insane in Louisiana, Illinois, Tennessee, and Pennsylvania. In May, 1917, he became a First Lieutenant in the Army Medical Reserve, serving through both World Wars, being retired after twenty-eight years of commissioned service with the rank of Lieutenant Colonel. During these years, he gradually accumulated a variety of interesting experiences which interpenetrated everything he wrote. Although many of his stories wear the guise of fantasy, few are of the stuff from which dreams are made, and most of them have a basic foundation of personal adventure; for to him all life is adventure. Thus, often he wrote about the actual life of real people. If a man has lived largely and richly, it is unnecessary for him to draw on his imagination for plots, though he may embroider them as he will. The elements of his life provide enough literary wool to weave *kelleryarns* until eternity.

In a small glass-doored bookcase in Doctor Keller's library, in his spacious home at Underwood, in

South Stroudsburg, Pennsylvania, are two rows of unpublished novels and stories. Many of these will, perhaps, never be published, at least not in his lifetime; and yet they are, in a way, more interesting than his printed work, for they tell in a most intimate manner the story of one man's life. As a psychiatrist, he found that the personal analysis of life, as he had lived it, was extremely interesting. This study he incorporated into many of his novels, and made no attempt to publish them.

It has been my privilege to read many of these books, such as "Shadows and Realities," "Wanderers in Spain," "The Lady Decides," "Through the Back Door," "The Fighting Woman," and his published book of poems, *Songs of a Spanish Lover*. Of these personalized stories, "The Fighting Woman" is, to me, the most interesting, because it reveals the answer to many questions that can be asked about David H. Keller. In sheer reading entertainment, this novel is exceptional, but it is far more than entertaining. It tells the story of three generations of the Keller family, as scientifically evaluated by a well-trained, mature, psychiatrist.

Until David H. Keller reached the age of six years, he talked little English. His language could be understood only by his sister, eighteen months older. When she died at the age of seven, the little boy lost all verbal communication with the world. This part of his life was the basis of Doctor Keller's story, "The Lost Language," in the January, 1934 issue of *Amazing Stories*. In the story, the question is raised as to whether the factor of ancestral memory could be considered as the origin of the jargon he used as a child.

At the age of six years, he was sent to public school from which he was sent home the first day as being language-deficient. His mother, a proud woman, realized for the first time that this retardation might cause her son to be considered mentally defective, so she began intensive efforts to teach the boy to talk English. For years of her daughter's life, she had been completely absorbed by and with this lovely child, doing only those things which were absolutely necessary for the son whom she did not consider an integral part of her life. She had failed to either care or understand that nearly all children have a language of their own; and because it was easier for his sister to translate his thoughts than for her to spend time trying either to understand or teach him, he was now, to her amazement, a potential disgrace.

For three years, this indomitable woman supplemented his private schooling, so that when he again entered public school he had a vocabulary far in advance of other children of his age and grade.

The great importance of this childhood experience lay in the fact that he had to be taught English as a foreigner would. Every new word learned represented a magnificient victory, bringing ever closer an easy medium of expression. He came to understand the value of simple words and short sentences. Thus in later years, when he began to write, his compositions were distinguished by an exemplary economy of bi-syllable words and a use of short sentences. This resulted in a literary style which has never been duplicated by any other science fiction writer.

Many of Doctor Keller's stories deal in some form with the conflict between the sexes in which the men often lose the battle for supremacy. In his novel, "The Eternal Conflict," which will be published in a few months, he sums up in a magnificent allegorical fantasy, his life-long conclusions concerning the never-ending strife between man and woman, which he feels has existed from earliest times and is becoming more aggravated in the present. This novel is the master thesis repeated in part in "The Feminine World," in which society becomes completely dominated by women, and only a few men are saved by the unwillingness of some women to destroy their own beloved men. "The Feminine Metamorphosis," published in *Science Wonder Stories*, August, 1939, tells of an international group of women who scientifically change themselves into males with the purpose of destroying male supremacy. Fortunately, Taine of San Francisco, Doctor Keller's counterpart of Sherlock Holmes, is able to defeat their purpose.

The women in most of his stories are not pleasant companions. They seem dominated by an inferiority complex compensated for by a determination to destroy those they love or envy. In his fantasy, "The

Golden Bough," is shown the inability of the husband to satisfy his wife. She strangles him with her hair, and then follows the demi-god, Pan, to her destruction. The story ends with Pan's comment:

"These mortals are never happy. They always try to gather moonbeams, and even I cannot do that."

In "Bindings De Luxe," a beautiful Spanish woman lures male book-binders to her home, drugs them, tattooes their backs, and uses the skins to bind her *Encyclopedia Brittanica*. Fortunately, her twenty-sixth visitor turns the tables and binds the last volume in a skin of a more delicate texture. In "Seeds of Death," the woman feeds her admirers seeds which grow inside them, and when these plants flower, the men die. In "The Tiger Cat," the woman blinds her would-be lovers, chains them in her cellar, sings to them, and beats them until they applaud her.

It is, however, in "A Piece of Linoleum," that this feminine dominance reaches a climax. This is not a tale of beautiful dæmons in faraway lands, but of a very ordinary woman who, through years of commonplace married life, so thoroughly dominates her husband that he finally escapes through suicide. Not all husbands seek such release, but every man seems to understand the story.

Judging from these tales, it would appear that David H. Keller does not like women. Perhaps it is because he is basically afraid of them. It may be that the answer to this pronounced complex can be found in his unpublished novel, "The Fighting Woman." It seems evident that he was early conditioned by the unflagging efforts of his mother to completely dominate, control, and possess, his every thought and act. A brilliant woman, she either dominated everyone in her life-sphere or eliminated them forthwith. Not until he became a psychiatrist, could he fully understand the conflict between mother and son. This may easily have been the cause of his distrust of all women. Later, in state hospitals for abnormals, he always served on the female wards, and there he met women who, because of their psychoses, had lost all repression, becoming completely primitive. This gave him keen insight into the multitude of tragedies women brought into the lives of their men folk.

This viewpoint is one of the most powerful influences evident in his writing, expressing itself subtly or forcibly in dozens of his published stories, though occasionally, as in "Life Everlasting," softened by his deep compassion for any human in distress, regardless of sex.

David H. Keller entered the Central High School, Philadelphia, at the age of fourteen. Here he wrote his first science fiction novel and many short stories. The original long-hand manuscripts remain in his collection, but will probably never be published. They show little except the desire to write.

As a medical student at the University of Pennsylvania, this urge to write continued. Some of his stories were published in the college paper, the *Red and Blue,* and in the religious journal, the *Presbyterian.* While in college, he joined a group of literary-minded juveniles, and with them produced seven issues of a magazine patterned after the *Black Cat,* and appropriately called the *White Owl.* Five of Doctor Keller's stories appeared in this magazine under the pen-name of "Henry Cecil." The stories are not important, but the experience made a lasting impression. He has never refused a request from an editor of a science fiction fan magazine who had nothing to offer in payment except thanks.

Doctor Keller has written largely of his ancestors, the Kellers from Alsace, the Hubelaires from France, and the Cecils from Cornwall. In all the stories woven around these families, especially the *Cornwall Stories,* it is evident that he is the hero reliving some fancied adventure of a long-dead ancestor. Some might call this "wish fulfillment," while others may feel it is the inherited memories dug up from the subconscious. The fact is that whether he is writing of life in the twelfth century, or in the year 1947, David H. Keller enjoys writing about himself, and when he writes thus, he writes well. If anyone doubts this, I would advise their reading *The Devil and the Doctor.* No one knowing him and talking to him at his home at Underwood can doubt who is the hero of *The Sign of the Burning Hart,* the retired army officer in his new novel, "The Homonculus," or the book lover in "The Gentle Pirate."

All the quarter morocco bound novels and stories in his library are credited to "Henry Cecil." This is also true of his privately printed book of poetry, *The Songs of a Spanish Lover*. His personal volume of these poems is illustrated in exquisite water colors by a patient of his, a lovely paranoiac, who believed she was the rightful heir to the Spanish throne. In this book is a letter in Spanish, and those who read that letter can gain insight into the reason for the writing of these poems.

In his published stories, the lead character is often named Henry Cecil. It appears in "The Thirty and One," "The Life Detour," "The Key to Cornwall," and "The Doorbell." In this latter tale, he uses the pen-name, "Amy Worth," a name under which he wrote many stories for *Ten Story Book*. This story is one of unique horror. Fish hooks, very small, are placed in capsules. The victims are given these capsules by an innocent doctor who cares for his patients in a small infirmary. On the floor above, directly over the bed, is a large magnet. When the doorbell rings, the magnet begins drawing the fishhooks; certainly an unusual use of accredited scientific machinery, and a unique method of continuing a feud between two Southern families.

As a horse-and-buggy doctor, David H. Keller found life something far different from his boyhood fancies. There were years of struggle to support the family, in course of time increased by two daughters. After ten years, satisfied he was facing financial failure, he accepted a position as Junior Physician on the staff of the Anna State Hospital in Illinois, and thus began his life as a psychiatrist. One published story, "The Bridle," tells of the little town he served for those hopeless years. The real story, however, is told in his "Wanderers in Spain," an unpublished novel.

Doctor Keller's experiences in mental hospitals are detailed in his unpublished autobiography, "Through the Back Door." In this work, he shows the impression such an environment made on an essentially sensitive personality. He studied thousands of abnormals, lived with them, in some strange way became their friend. Each of his patients had a story, ever new, always fantastic in novelty and horror. This close observation of, and association with, the abnormal mind with its indelible background of sheer terror, could not help but condition the physician. Undoubtedly, his writings were influenced by this association. There is an underlying horror and morbidity in much of his writing, after he became a psychiatrist. Even as he strove to write beautifully, as in "The Sign of the Burning Hart," "The Golden Bough," "The Eternal Conflict," and "The Thirty and One," an actual under-current of insufficiently repressed horror flowed through. This element was not the manufactured bogy, part and parcel of the stock in trade of the weird tale hack, but part of the man's mental outlook; at times, barely noticeable, at other times, ominously surging toward the surface and held in check only by a counter-balance of deep understanding of, and sympathy and love for, humanity, gained through the years of service to the unfortunates of life.

In no *long* story that Doctor Keller has written, has horror predominated over human understanding and humor. It was not in him to maintain the gloomy face overlong or look at the sorry aspect of life forever. But in his short stories there have, on occasion, been instances where sheer horror predominated. This type of horror can only be developed by an experienced psychiatrist pressing relentlessly on the basic emotional centers of the brain. Such a story is "The Thing in the Cellar," which has often been called "the greatest horror story in the English language." The simple phrasing and disarmingly leisurely pace of the story lead to a culmination of truly shocking impact. Many thousands of words have been written speculating on the real meaning of this thriller, questioning as to the reality or lack of reality of that *thing* in the cellar of an old English home. Few critics have considered that this fine terror tale carries behind it a grim, psychological truth based on hundreds of case histories studied by a master-psychiatrist. The moral is simply this: *Our own fears will destroy us, if we permit them.*

Some critics believe that "The Dead Woman," first printed in *Fantasy Magazine,* and then reprinted in the English anthology, ***Nightmare by Daylight,*** surpasses in terror "The Thing in the Cellar."

Its tempo is slow, but the story gains in intensity of feeling. At the end, only the psychiatrist realizes that the husband has been psychotic for many months. The man is definitely without realization that he has done anything wrong. At the conclusion, he asks:

"What would you do, Doctor? What would any man have done who loved his wife?"

Examine the art of this author: Superficially there appears to be a story told only for its own sake, but the slightest research reveals an ever present strain of allegory. There are lessons in human behavior to be learned, and Doctor Keller is teaching them. A near perfect state of the future may someday be devised as in "Unto Us a Child Is Born"; but it will not make people happy if it ignores the basic human emotional needs simply for the sake of maximum utility.

In the lead story of this anthology, "Life Everlasting," America is granted eternal life and health, but in the end the women do not want it because the price is sterility, and the American women want to know what is the value of additional years, if they could not become mothers.

When Doctor Thomas S. Gardner, one of the country's leading Gerontologists, informed Doctor Keller that due to inspiration from the story, "The Boneless Horror," he had experimented with "royal jelly," a food eaten exclusively by queen bees and which seemed responsible for their long life-span in contrast to the short life of the worker bee, and that in experiments he has been able to greatly prolong the life of fruit flies by feeding them this food, Doctor Keller simply asked, "What will the fruit flies do with these extra days of life?"

This should not be considered an anti-scientific attitude on Doctor Keller's part. His tales again and again show a heartfelt admiration for scientific research, and the aid it has given to humanity. His fight is against the effort to change man into a precise scientific instrument. He believes all such attempts will end in tragedy. Science, he believes, should be an aid, a help, constructed to serve, not command obedience from man. No scientific advancement merely for the sake of science, but for the sake of man!

It was with stories based upon that conception that David H. Keller first appeared in print in a science fiction magazine with "The Revolt of the Pedestrians" in 1928. For long, long years, Doctor Keller had been writing to please no one but himself. In his spare time between hospital duties, in the evenings, he had written incessantly, injecting into his stories the experiences and knowledge accumulated through his own life. He wrote such books as "The Fighting Woman," "The Adorable Fool," "The Sign of the Burning Hart," "The Stone Fence," and "Deepening Shadows"; over five thousand pages which he never expected to sell. Of these, he sent only one to a publisher, "The Sign of the Burning Hart." *Harper's Magazine* offered to buy this if he would explain what it meant. The Doctor refused three times to do this, saying, "I will not draw a blue print of the story. The humming bird is beautiful alive; but dead and dissected by an anatomist, it loses that beauty."

This lofty attitude of the "artist" called for radical change when the growing daughters demanded a college education. To finance this, he turned to writing professionally, and received an enthusiastic reception from the readers of *Amazing Stories, Science Wonder Stories,* and *Weird Tales,* where his efforts were accepted and published. While others wrote of rocket ships, ray guns, bizarre monsters, interstellar flights, and fourth dimensions, he wrote only of ordinary people and the problems they might conceivably encounter in the more highly specialized, scientific world of the future. The people in his stories lived; they were the men and women next door, experiencing and expressing the same manner of human behavior. In "Free as the Air," he showed a world where even air space was rented, and commercialism threatened to place a bounty on breathing. "The Psychophonic Nurse" told of a robot nurse that mechanically cared for babies (predicting a device that would register when diapers became wet, which is now used in Russia.) The story tells of inter-relations between parents, a child, and a robot nurse. In still another story, "White Collars," he wrote of the eventual uprising of a starving white collar class in a world where a man who worked with his hands was socially disdained but well paid, and thus showed a flaw in our social set-up that drove many of our high school and college students into an overglutted field that paid more in prestige than in salary. "Stenographer's Hands" had a gigantic corporation found a community of men and women with training so specialized that it affected their health until finally psychic-epilepsy destroyed their usefulness. This plot is not far-fetched, for the Pullman Company, in its early history, constructed an entire town completely controlled by one man. The whole life of the workers were subject to his rules. Depression and cuts in salary finally ended his domination. But today, in Hershey, Pennsylvania, the existence of an entire town centers about the creation of chocolate bars. In the coal regions, miners live in company houses and buy supplies from company stores with company scrip for money.

Such subject matter was the basis of the *kelleryarn*, as his tales came to be called; and year after year, he won first place in popularity in the readers' columns and in specifically conducted polls of science fiction readers.

When he sold his first story, he was 47 years old! The tales of a man who wrote himself and his experiences into many of the stories he created were bound also to show this influence of age. Examine most Keller stories, and you will find that the hero, often named Jacob Hubler, is frequently middle-aged, somewhere between forty and sixty. That is the case in "Life Everlasting," for instance. Jacob Hubler, hero of "Unto Us a Child Is Born," is virile at sixty years of age. The likable lead male in "The Adorable Fool" is middle-aged. This, it may be noted, does not necessarily preclude romance. Jacob Hubler's women must accept him as he really is and not in any polished idealization, and this they usually do.

Stroudsburg, Pennsylvania, is the Keller family's ancestral home since 1736, and there, at Underwood, the Doctor is spending his riper years. Many of his stories are located around his home. There Taine of San Francisco solved his problem of "The Cerebral Library" and saved the community a second time from the dangers of enlarged cancer cells raised by an erratic scientist in the story, "Wolf Hollow Bubbles." "Creation Unforgivable" is located in the rear of the garden at Underwood. Part of the action of "No More Tomorrows" takes place in Stroudsburg. In writing about the town and its people, the author writes with incisive knowledge. In "The Devil and the Doctor," he tells of families who have lived near the Kellers and Buzzards for over two hundred years.

The bond of friendship, between Doctor Keller and the editors of the early science fiction and weird magazines, was very strong. Hugo Gernsback, original publisher of *Amazing Stories*, and later founder of *Science Wonder Stories*, was so impresed with his work that stories were often accepted on virtually little more than the strength of the title. T. O'Conor Sloane, Ph.D., renowned scientist, who, at an advanced age, was the editor of *Amazing Stories*, would have liked nothing better than to publish Keller's entire morocco bound library of stories, if he could have contrived to explain in some manner their lack of the scientifictional element to the readers. As it was, no author in this writer's memory has ever evaded magazine policy as successfully as Doctor Keller. Many of his published stories had not the slightest tinge of fantasy, being best designated as off-trail. Strangely enough, the readers rarely complained. Farnsworth Wright, of *Weird Tales*, always particular about what he published, had, nevertheless, nothing but praise for the first author in the history of the magazine to win first place in popularity with the readers for each of the three parts of a serial, "The Solitary Hunters."

It is common knowledge that Farnsworth Wright suffered from a very serious nervous disease contracted while serving with the armed forces in France during World War I. When the opportunity came to marry a very fine woman, he turned to Doctor Keller in desperation for advice concerning the wisdom of marriage and the possibility of a child inheriting his disability. Without an opportunity for close study of the situation, the Doctor staked his reputation and urged the marriage. The birth of Robert Wright, physically and mentally exceptional, vindicated his decision. When I informed Doctor Keller that Mr. Wright had told this story to me, he was amazed; for, during the years, he had never divulged a word of it, believing that Farnsworth Wright wanted the actual facts concerning his marriage kept an absolute secret. Actually, Farnsworth Wright had released the information earlier, and it had seen publication in the science fiction fan press.

In addition to his fiction, Doctor Keller wrote many scientific articles. All told, over seven hundred scientific articles from his typewriter have seen publication in dozens of diverse scientific journals and popular scientific magazines.

A family history, *The Kellers of Hamilton Township, a Study in Democracy*, was privately published while he was living in Louisiana. This history is so thoroughly documented that it has been accepted as a reliable source book by the Daughters of the American Revolution, an honor accorded to very few such histories. A companion book, tracing his maternal ancestors, "The George-Whitesell Families," has been typed, but never published.

Early in World War II, Colonel Keller was asked by the Army Medical Corps to organize the first school for illiterates and foreign language speaking soldiers. Feeling the need for adequate training literature, he wrote a primer and first reader, using a basic English vocabulary of 370 words. It was not till two years later that Winston Churchill, in his address at Harvard, proposed the adoption of a similar basic vocabulary. He felt that the adoption and use of this would promote harmony among the peoples of the earth. David Keller knew at the time and Churchill found out later, that something more than a simple vocabulary was needed to perfect the brotherhood of mankind.

In the foregoing, then, may be ascertained the elements of Doctor Keller's phenomenal popularity in the science fiction world. In addition to a simple story-teller's writing style which could phrase simple words into messages of extraordinary power, he possessed a vast knowledgs of humanity, absorbed from his long years as a physician, and was able to supplement this with a background of unimpeachable scientific knowledge.

It should also be observed that Doctor Keller never fabricated a weird tale about werewolves, ghosts, vampires, or other common plot-props of the terror tale writer. Actually, his horror stories were harbingers of the psychological novels and movies so popular today. The science of the mind, as displayed by an expert psychiatrist, was just as authentic as any of the science in his tales of future scientific development. Therefore, his horror stories are rendered with the same full effective power as his science tales.

There is commonly found in kelleryarns a wry, whimsical, and often grim, type of humor. Satire is often revealed as simple pleasantries in the context of the story, but, occasionally, as in "The Flying Fool," we find the author almost chuckling sardonically at the behavior of his characters. Examine "No More Tomorrows," and you will find a strong element of this characteristic. It peeks out from "The Thirty and One" when least expected. Taine of San Francisco, in "The Cerebral Library," is not above drollness. "A Piece of Linoleum" has humor which makes the horror more terrible. This story could be called grossly exaggerated were it not based on real life, as are a great many of the author's seemingly most fantastic yarns.

We deduce from this that, through all adversity, through the multiple tragedies and suffering of human beings he had witnessed, Doctor Keller had, perforce, to see some humor in the situation or go mad.

To appreciate the whimsical humor of the good Doctor, it is compulsory that you read *The Devil and the Doctor,* published by Simon and Schuster in 1939. In this work, the author sets out to prove, with the aid of devastating allegory, that the Devil is a real gentleman who is responsible for the bulk of progress up to the present time, and whose fair name has been besmirched by his brother, who assumes the name of God. The brother is actually the culprit behind the misery and suffering of mankind, but has used through the ages a clever, subtle, form of propaganda, not to mention brute force, to cover up his faults. So convincing is this argument that Mr. Tim

O'Brien, a writer for the religious magazines, stated in his review of the book before the Eastern Science Fiction Association, that, in his opinion, "it was enough to turn the head of a priest."

Publication of this title gained Doctor Keller considerable favor among the literary critics whose assiduous eyes were quick to recognize that a very human type of personality had written the book. But others did not like the book, for after a single advertisement, the publishers became silent about it. Later, several hundred were sold at a low price. It is a question whether religious pressure was not brought to bear on the publishers, on account of the character of the plot. How much greater might have been their distress, if they had only known that, when recalled to duty for World War II, David H. Keller, with the rank of Lieutenant Colonel, served with singular distinction as a professor at Harvard University where it was his responsibility to instruct more than six thousand chaplains of all denominations in their duties in the armed services.

Like Edgar Allan Poe, David H. Keller found literary acceptance sooner in France than in his own country. When a group of Frenchmen founded a literary publication titled *Les Premieres*, it was with the purpose of "presenting to the cultured French a comprehensive view of literature by living authors." Regis Messac, formerly Professor of Literature in Montreal, Canada, was asked to determine the greatest living science fiction author. Messac selected David H. Keller, M.D., by-passing no less a notable than H. G. Wells in the process. As a result, "Stenographer's Hands" was printed in French. This was followed by other stories and a book of three stories titled *La Guerre du Lierre*. *Les Premieres* was publishing his novel, "The Eternal Conflict," in serial form when World War II forced them to suspend publication.

At present, the Colonel, nearly sixty-seven years of age, shares his ancestral home, Underwood, in Stroudsburg, with his charming wife and a little dog. While his army rank is permanent, it is probable that he will see no more active Army medical service.

His most fervent group of supporters are still the science fiction and fantasy fans who first recognized the superior quality of his prose style. In recognition of their loyalty, he semi-annually gives hour-long addresses before the leading science fiction organizations. These addresses reveal an old man who refuses to age. His intellect remains crystal clear, his memory phenomenal, and his entire approach kindly and human. He is a master orator, full of wit and human understanding, and his guest appearances before these literary and scientific organizations is always regarded as the year's stellar event.

The literary creatorship that has brought pleasure to many remains unimpaired. Only recently he completed a fantastic novel, "The Homunculus." This story tells of the effort of Colonel Horatio Bumble to create a son after the method of Paracelsus. It is not difficult to identify Bumble, his charming wife, and his Pekingese dog.

In a recent letter, Doctor Keller tells me that he has finished his last long novel, "The Abyss," and that he will write no more. Personally, I doubt that statement. It is my opinion that when he has something to write, he will write it. He says that he is becoming a philosopher, but I know he cannot help writing any more than he can avoid breathing. He said as much in his interview in *Science Fiction Digest* for July, 1933:

"I look forward to death as the Great Adventure. If after death comes nothingness, what a wonderful rest it will be, for I have been tired for many years. And if there is another life, I will go further, see more, spend less, than I have on any trip so far. The first thing I will do is to hunt up a good library. I am afraid that the Heavenly one is rather well censored, and I may have to go to the asbestos library of Gehenna to get the books I want to read. Then I am going to start writing. My idea of Heaven is to have every story accepted by an appreciative editor."

I have personally selected the material for this anthology in the hope that it will show the work of a man who has lived fully and bravely; a man who has slowly, after fifty years of writing, made for himself a definite place in literature. It is my belief that the evidence contained in this volume will convince many that, in David H. Keller, America has produced another important contemporary *author*.

—Sam Moskowitz

Newark, N.J.
September, 1947

FOREWORD

A REAL *science fiction* story should be written about realities of life, concerning which all the readers are familiar. The most commonplace things of life can become the most wonderful, if handled in the proper manner. So, in writing of sickness, crime, poverty, starved and twisted bodies, life everlasting, radiant happiness, riches, leisure, marriage, divorce, and babies, the author feels that he is dealing with material with which the everyday man and woman is well acquainted. Given the supposed discovery of a wonder-working serum, the rest of the happenings seem to be most natural. Though the following tale will be considered a fairy story by some and a sermon by others, it is in reality a science fiction tale of the most classical type. And if, in addition to furnishing pastime amusement to thousands, it makes a few readers think and live and love better in an effort to make this a more beautiful world for our babies to grow up in, the efforts of the author will be well rewarded.

—*David H. Keller, M.D.*

LIFE EVERLASTING

CHAPTER I

Four Failures Meet

SALLY was sweeping the stairs. When she was not doing this, she spent her time making beds, scrubbing pots, and washing windows. Life in the cheap boarding house was just making dirty things clean, as far as Sally was concerned.

From her babyhood, she had suffered from poverty and asthma. These twin afflictions had stunted her body and warped her mind. When she was not conscious of the struggle to breathe, she was keenly aware of the fight to earn the necessities of life. The dual conflict left her no time for the finer things in life. Fortunately, she was only dimly aware of their existence. Days of work with nights of respiratory anguish dulled her soul, till she only had one pleasant anticipation, the pleasure of an early death. At twenty she was aged and worn, an old woman who had never been loved since the day her

mother had taken the baby girl in her arms, cried a
a little, and died.

As she swept the steps, perfumed youth passed
her. Mary Casey she had been called in Shamokin,
Pennsylvania; but now, as a jitney dancer in the
Moonland Dance Hall, she was called Valencia
Moore. Her body was formed of curves, and her
mentality was slightly above that of the adenoid
moron. Her parents, alternating between love and
hate, had procreated her in lust, and raised her in
an environment that would have mired the whitest
lily. She grew up to be unmoral rather than im-
moral. Wanting clothes, perfume, and a good time,
she commercialized her sex appeal by spending her
days in bed and her nights in the arms of anyone
who would pay ten cents for a one minute dance.

For six months she had passed Sally, the scrub
woman, several times a day without speaking to her.
Sally was only conscious of her as one of the pieces of
dirt that someday would be swept out of the house.
The two girls had nothing in common except that,
anatomically, they were both females.

As one girl swept up the steps leaving behind her
a cheap perfume, and the other swept down the steps
leaving behind her just dust, Harry Wild crabfooted
down from the third floor back and passed both of
them. He had a hump on his back the size of the
regulation football, a right leg that was four inches
shorter than the left leg, a twisted face, strabismus,
and a clear conscience. For years he had made a

good living selling papers and smiling at his patrons. On the street, he had friends from every walk of life. In his room, he read books, fed mice, and dreamed of a day when some woman would love him. For two years he had written daily love letters to Sally, and so far had never had the courage to do anything with them save put them in his trunk. Sally knew him, adored his smile, hated his mice, and kept his bed clean.

The third floor front held the mystery of the house. He was a man with a steady income, and no occupation. John Jones was his New York name. Every two weeks he received a letter with a check. He was clean, bald, and old. He spent a little of his income for food, more for clothes, and the rest in the cheap dance halls of New York. He danced one third of the dances and rested the other two thirds, and never gave a hostess more than one ticket. He hoped that some night he would find the woman he was looking for. Since he was hunting one with the intelligence of Minerva, the body of Venus, and the kindness of the Mother Mary, his quest was doomed to failure. So he danced, and twiddled his thumbs, and wished that his heart muscle and his moral code would allow him to spend ten dollars on one woman instead of ten cents each on many. He had danced with Valencia Moore, but did not know that she lived on the floor above him.

Jones bought his newspapers from Harry Wild, and occasionally danced with Valencia Moore. Wild smiled on the other three, and dreamed of loving Sally. Valencia paid no attention to any one of them; they simply did not enter her plan of life. Sally kept things clean for all of them, and fantasied a life free from dirt and asthma.

Singly they might have been interesting to the sociologist; as a quartette, they made a harmonic failure. From the animal viewpoint, they shared certain biological urges. They slept, ate, and moved, as necessity demanded. Spiritually, there was no contact. Even had Sally known of the letters the newsboy was writing to her, she would have reacted with a confused negativism. That any man should love her was a thought so impossible that it never entered her consciousness.

These four were failures, and all of them through no fault of their own. Heredity, environment, disease, the inhibitions of a false standard of morality, had twisted and warped them mentally, spiritually, and physically, till they were caught in a web of fate from which there was no escape.

The metropolis could have furnished a hundred thousand foursomes as badly assorted, unharmonic failures, as these. In fact, there was no reason why they should have been selected as the experimental basis for a scientific study that was destined to change in every way the life of the human race. There were thirty others living in that boarding house, any four of whom might have served equally well. But the scientist selected these four. His decision was not exactly a haphazard one. He wanted a beautiful woman who was bad; a good woman, sick and soulless; a gentleman whose body was shattered; and an old man who was trying to be young.

The scientist found what he wanted in these four failures.

CHAPTER II

THE INITIAL EXPERIMENT

HARRY ACKERMAN had something, and he was not sure what to do with it. For five years, he had used a serum on the lower mammalia, had checked, rechecked, and double checked his results, and continued to doubt his own observation. No matter what animal he used for his experiment, the results were the same.

His results were so uniform, the method so simple, the final analysis so weird and unusual, that he simply could not believe what he saw. It was impossible to confide in any of his brother scientists; they would have considered him insane. He refused either to be laughed at or to spend the rest of his life behind the walls of a hospital for psychotics. In addition to this, he wanted to have the sole credit for his discovery, and this selfishness made him become an antisocial hermit. It was not a question of selling his brainchild; he neither needed nor wanted money, but he did want recognition leading to fame.

Now at the end of five years, he was ready to begin human experimentation. That, after all, was to be the crowning effort of his years of work. He felt that he knew what he could do with the body, but when it came to the mind, he was not so sure. It was difficult to properly imagine the results; it was more nearly impossible to determine the size or the number of the doses. It was one thing to feed the panacea to crickets or mice, and another to inject it into the veins of a man. Too little would be tantalizing, too much, dangerous. He could not keep his subjects in cages as he did the little monkeys.

Yet he realized that, sooner or later, he had to face the issue. It would not take him more than one minute to inject five cubic centimeters into a human vein. Once that was done, all he would have to do was to wait for the results. If he failed—why, other men had failed before; if he succeeded, life would be changed; not just one life, but the life of the Genus Homo.

For the present, the last thing he wanted was newspaper publicity. A cleverly worded advertisement would have given him experimental material by the hundred, but it would also have brought unpleasant notoriety. For the present, he had to work in secret. That is why he came to New York, where a man can be lost quicker and more completely than he can in the Sahara Desert.

At times, he had contemplated giving himself

an injection of the serum. That would have been the easiest way and the simplest. But he was not sure of the results, and he could not face the thoughts of an accident—not on his own account, but for the sake of his son. The last ten years of his life had been spent for the good of the boy. Otherwise he would not have had the courage or the vision to go on with the work. If he took the serum and died, as some of the animals had died in the early years of his study, there would be no one left to love the little fellow, and though he rarely saw him, he felt that love was very essential for the welfare of Harry Ackerman Jr.

There was no special method in his selection of a boarding house when he came to New York. He simply picked out a cheap one in a poor neighborhood, paid a month's rent in advance, and started to become acquainted with his fellow boarders. From those he met he selected the four failures; and, much to their surprise, asked them to spend a Saturday evening with him. The hard part of the programme was persuading them to accept his invitation. Each required a different approach, and, with the exception of Harry Wild, none of them would have come had he known the others were to be there.

Sally came because the landlady ordered her to be nice to a star boarder. John Jones came because it was the first time anyone had been kind to him in New York without charging him for it. Valencia saw a chance to do some fancy gold digging; and besides, a twisted ankle kept her from the dance hall. But Harry Wild had found a man who knew more about mice than he did, and that was enough for him.

Of the five at the party, only the scientist was at his ease. Sally was breathing hard, and wondering how soon she would become a dope-fiend. Adrenalin did not help her much nowadays, but morphine made the hell of breathless life a heaven of comfort in fifteen minutes. Wild kept thinking of those love letters never sent, and wondering if Sally was looking at the "Roger's Group" or at his twisted spine. The dancing temptation could not understand why the guy had asked the rest of the crowd, when she could have given him seventy minutes of pleasure for every hour he was willing to pay for. The old man could not keep his eyes off her curves, but he knew that his myocardium could not stand the strain. Besides, her English was impossible.

Ackerman turned on the radio, passed the candy, cake, and cigarettes, and tried to be the perfect host. Socially he was a failure. The party was nothing more nor less than five incompatibles meeting in a test tube. He shut off the radio just as the "Quarrelsome Quartet" gave place to the "Malted Brew" advertising.

"I want to talk to you people," he began, "and I am going to try to be as brief and as plain as I can. There is a serum I have been working on for some time, a medicine, you understand. In some ways I am a physician, and I have tried to discover something that would help people get well. It is something new, and I am not sure how much good it will do, but I am sure that it will not hurt the people I give it to. I am not in regular practice and so I cannot give it to my patients. That is why I have asked you here tonight. I believe that it will help Miss Sally Fanning's asthma, improve Mr. Jones' heart trouble, and make a different man out of my friend Harry Wild."

"What do I get it for, Old Nut?" asked Valencia Moore.

"You get it for anæmia of your pocketbook. In other words, it means just one hundred dollars to you to take one dose."

"Attaboy," she laughed. "Now you are talking my language. For a hundred bucks I would take a dose of any poison. Give it to me quick."

Sally Fanning, breathing harder than usual, looked at the dancing fool and then at the stranger, and then she gasped:

"I do not understand you, Mr. Ackerman. Do you really mean that you believe that you can cure my asthma? And if you can, will the same medicine help Mr. Jones? Perhaps it will, but what has that to do with Miss Moore? Or Mr. Wild? They are not sick."

"It is hard to explain to you, Miss Fanning," answered the scientist, and there was a tone of patient kindness in his voice. "This serum I am going to use is a most peculiar one. . It has, or at least I think it has, many different kinds of actions. There are different kinds of sicknesses, you know, and I hope that all of you will be benefited by the injection. I am not promising anything definite, but I honestly feel that it will help everyone of you, and I am sure it will not hurt you. When I told Miss Moore I would give her a hundred dollars, I really should have said that I am going to give each of you that amount, because you are all helping me in a study that is very important to my future. If you are ready, I will begin, perhaps first on Mr. Wild. He knows me better and trusts me more than the rest of you. Will you take off your coat and roll up your sleeve on the right side, Mr. Wild? There, that will do very well. Now you can all watch me. First the tourniquet, then the needle goes into the vein, and I slowly inject the serum. It really does not hurt at all. Who will be the next one?"

"I will," announced Valencia, "but first give me my hundred."

CHAPTER III

THE FIRST RESULTS

"GOOD MORNING, Miss Fanning. How is the asthma?"

Sally, the scrub, looked up from the brown stone steps she was cleaning. Ackerman was smiling down at her.

"Your medicine helped me," she answered simply. "All my life I have taken Green Mountain Asthma Cure, and lately adrenalin, and even morphine, and everything else that anyone advised. They all helped for a while and then I was as bad off as ever. Of course, having to work for a living made it hard for me. Perhaps your medicine is the same as the rest, good today and no good tomorrow; but it certainly helped me to sleep, and this morning I feel strong and rested. If I felt this way all the time, I might amount to something, have courage to try to do something different; might even go to night school and get an education. I read in the paper once, that even if a woman was ugly, it helped if she knew something."

"But you are not ugly."

She laughed bitterly.

"You must be blind. Look at my neck! And my hands, my hair. Dead, every bit of me. Work all day to earn an honest meal and a decent bed, and then work all night for the right to keep alive, every breath a battle. How could a woman be anything but ugly?"

"But you are going to be better. Suppose I told you that in a little while you would be well—that your body would grow beautiful, your hair radiant? How would you like to sing as you work—to have people tell you your voice was lovely, your soul a thing of charm? What would you do then, Sally Fanning?"

"I would cry, Mr. Ackerman. I would be so happy—I, who have never been happy—that I would cry for the joy of it. I would brush my hair till it came alive, and wash myself, and put on clean clothes, and go and sit in the park, in the sunshine, and just breathe deep. It is a terrible thing to fight for every breath, as I have all my life. I used to dream of being a bird, flying high in the sky, and yet having enough air left in me to sing; but always would come the waking and the asthma."

"Perhaps the dream will come true," replied the scientist. "Have you seen my friend, Harry Wild, this morning?"

"I always see him in the morning. We always

see each other early at dawn. We are the first up and out, he to sell his papers, and I to do my cleaning."

"How did he feel?"

"He was smiling."

"But he always smiles."

"Yes, that he does. But this morning he said he felt better. You know he has trouble with his back—never speaks much about it, but the pain is there, where the hump is. This morning he said it was gone. Of course, he meant the pain. There is nothing can untwist the body of him. I guess he smiles to help forget his legs and his back."

"I like him," said Ackerman, quietly. "He is kind to the mice."

"They come to him," explained Sally. "Wherever he is, the mice gather. They used to be all over the house, and now they all live in his room. Of course, he feeds them, but there is something more than that."

"Do you suppose they know he loves them?" asked Ackerman.

The girl frowned:

"If I don't get to work on these steps, they will never be cleaned. But I will say this about Mr. Wild. He is a nice young man, as nice a young man as I ever cleaned after, and there would be more than mice loving him if his back was straight and his legs even. But he was born that way and cannot help it, any more than I can my having asthma."

"But suppose that would all be corrected? I mean, suppose he would get well and be like other men?"

"Suppose you go and ask him? His stand is just around the corner. Suppose you stop talking to me about the moon, and heaven, and singing birds that never waken? You know, and I know, that just as he is now, so he will be till they place pennies on his eyes."

"I am not so sure of that," retorted the scientist. "At least I will go and buy a morning paper from the lad."

Harry Wild was singing as he handed the lurid sheets to his regular customers.

"Happy?" asked Ackerman.

"You said it! No pain. Slept all night and woke as fine as could be. Turned on the radio and took my exercises. One—two—three—four! Great stuff. Old twenty-three used to be hard to do, but this morning everything was easy."

He lowered his voice:

"Did you see Sally this morning?"

"I did, and she was breathing with the ease of an opera singer. She is a nice girl, Harry, only she lets herself be discouraged."

"It would be fine if things were different, Mr. Ackerman. Just suppose that she didn't have asthma, and suppose I was like other men—big and strong, and easy walking. Just suppose that! Say, that would be great stuff, wouldn't it?"

"You are going to be, Harry. First the pain will leave you, and then your short leg will get longer, and your back straight, and even the mice won't know you any more."

"Quit your kidding. Still, it sounds nice. Think there is a chance that the girl will get over her asthma?"

Ackerman took a deep breath:

"You are going to get well," he whispered. "All four of you. Strong, and well, and sane, and good. You are going to be the first of a new race. It is too soon for me to be sure, and too wonderful for me to see clearly; but if that medicine works, Harry, you will soon be able to love something else than just mice."

"Quit your kidding," blushed the boy. "But it would be nice, Mr. Ackerman, it would be nice."

In the next twenty-four hours, the inventor saw and talked to the other two of his experiments. He visited John Jones in his room, and found a puzzled man who did not wait to be questioned.

"Two years ago," he began, "the doctors told me I might die at any moment, so I came to New York. They said that I would die on my feet, and I made up my mind that I would learn to dance, and die with a pretty girl in my arms. After you gave me the serum, I went to sleep. It was the first night I missed going to a jitney dance hall. This morning things look different. I know now that I am not going to die that way. In fact, I feel so well that I am not sure I am ever going to die."

"That is an interesting statement," said Ackerman. "Suppose you kept on living, and growing stronger and younger? What would you do? How would you pass your time?"

"I would write. All my life I have wanted to write. There is nothing as fine as putting a piece of white paper in a machine and pounding out your thoughts on it. But for years I was too busy; had to make a living; lots of people depended on me for the necessities of life. I had lots of things to write about, but never any time, and when I did have the time, the strength was lacking. Then my heart went bad after influenza. The doctors tried to be kind and lied to me at first. They called it post-influenza asthenia. Later they told me the truth."

"So you tried to kill yourself dancing?"

"No. I tried to die while dancing. But it was not the dancing I was after. I wanted love. And no one is going to love an old broken man. So I took the best substitute. But not one of them gave me rest. Did you ever hear the girls talk in a dance hall, Mr. Ackerman? It is just too bad. I think everyone of them is feebleminded. And all they are after is a man's money. If a skeleton was worth a million, they would pretend to get hot, rubbing the wire that held his bones together. Just one night was enough for me to find that out. I told my first partner that I was enough of a healthy Vulgarian to enjoy holding a pretty woman in my arms. For ten minutes they fought with each other for the next dance. I finally asked one of them what they were excited about, and she said that the first girl had spread the news that I was a wealthy Bulgarian. Of course they had never heard of the Vulgate Bible."

"What do you think of Miss Moore?"

"She is as pretty as can be, and as soiled as man can make her. If she were disinfected and educated, and had the evil burned out of her, and I were young, I think I could love her and be happy."

"Have you seen her this morning?"

"Yes."

"How is she feeling?"

"Said her ankle was ok. She must be worried; she forgot to paint her face. She does not know it, but she is prettier without her makeup."

"I think she is going to change," commented the inventor.

CHAPTER IV

THE EXPERT'S OPINION

ACKERMAN waited for three weeks, and then decided that it was time to check up on the results of the serum. Before giving the four injections, he had anticipated waiting at least six months; but two things had happened to make him change his mind.

In the first place, Harry Wild had a number of friends. Not the kind to invite him to dinner, but interested enough to go out of their way, and buy papers from him, and slip him a fiver at Christmas. Some of them had known him for years—from the time he had been a ragged, but smiling, street urchin. They noticed the change in him. Variations in the health and conduct of the other three might have come and gone without any one knowing or caring, but with the crippled man on the corner it was different. Men talked to him, and he did not hesitate to talk back to them. One man believed.

That night Harry Ackerman had a visitor. In

fact, three: a man, a woman, and a little child. The man lost no time in stating his business. He was the kind of man who had made his millions in Wall Street by taking an opportunity quicker than the others. His name was Hiram Smith, and the woman was his wife.

"And this is our son," he continued, "our only son. Does that mean anything to you?"

"It does," said the inventor. "I have an only child and he—well, at any rate—I know what you are thinking."

"Good. This little boy is bright, nothing wrong with his mind, but he cannot walk; he cannot even feed himself. He was born that way. Can you cure him?"

"I am not a physician."

"No. But you are the man who helped Harry Wild. I have known him for years. Financed his first news stand. He knows about my boy, and he told me about you. During the last week, I have had Harry to see three specialists. They have examined him in every way known to the medical world. They took a series of X-rays of his back and legs. They did not understand what happened, but say that in a few more weeks he will be a perfect man in every way. Now the boy says you did it. Did you? Can you do the same thing for this boy of mine? If you can, I will give you one million dollars. And I am not saying what I will do, if you can and refuse."

"There are other boys and girls in the world," whispered the inventor. "Your boy is not the only one who is not normal."

The woman carried the boy over, and gave him to his father. Then she went over, and knelt beside Ackerman, and looked up at him. In her youth, she had been a beautiful woman.

"I am not threatening you," she said, "and I am not bribing you with a million; but I am telling you this: I can never have another child. My husband loves me, but he says that he must have a son who can carry on the family tradition. That means another woman in his life. I have a son. Make him well! Do it for the sake of your wife."

"My wife is dead," said the man. "Take his coat off, and roll up his sleeve—the right one."

He prepared a dose of the serum, and injected it into the boy's vein.

"I am promising nothing," he cautioned, "but I am asking two favors. First, I do not want any publicity. Second, there are three other people who have had the serum besides the newsboy. They live in this house. I will give you their names. I want you to take them to these specialists and have them examined. I also want their intelligence determined, their morals, and viewpoint on life. I want an analysis made of their metabolism, the number of calories it takes per day to keep them in health.

When they are finished, bring me the four reports. It might be interesting to have your son examined now, and again in a week, and at the end of a month. I am leaving New York today. I will give you my address. Keep it secret. You can pay the expenses of the examinations, otherwise you will owe me nothing."

"My boy is asleep," commented the woman.

"He will sleep. The first effect of the medicine is complete freedom from pain, which brings relaxation. Good night."

The man stood up, holding the sleeping boy close to him.

"I cannot let you do this for nothing. Dunn and Bradstreet rate me as one of the rich men of America. I pay my debts."

"Wait!" almost commanded Ackerman. "Wait till you see what happens to your son. If he is helped, you will be given a chance to pay the debt. I am not forgetting that there are other sick children in the world, and I am not going to let you forget it either."

The visitors gone, he started to pack his bags. Frowning, he had to leave his work and open the door. A woman entered; glasses, tailored suit, a notebook, told her occupation. She handed the man a card. She was Betty Farday, star sob reporter of the *Purple Flash*, New York's latest, and most startling, tabloid.

"I am asking for an interview, Mr. Ackerman.

When any worth while events take place in this city, the *Purple Flash* gets the news first. Who are you? What are you doing in the city? What kind of serum do you use? What did you do to Valencia Moore, who used to be Mary Casey of Shamokin, and who, for many months, has had the reputation of being the worst taxi girl in the dives of the city? What did you do to her and how did you do it?"

"Did I do anything wrong to the young lady?" parried Ackerman.

"No. That is just it. I heard a rumor that there was something big going on, so we looked up her record. That girl has been bad enough to satisfy the cravings of a dozen girls and several thousand men. She has not been satisfied to burn the candle of life at both ends, but has turned herself into a pin wheel of fireworks. She was diseased in every way—morally, spiritually, and physically. In one more year, she would have rested quietly on a marble slab at the Morgue. Now she is quite different in every way. Her talk, her thoughts, her life. She does not even paint anymore, and I'll tell the world that she is ok without it. One of the most beautiful dames I ever saw, and don't forget that the men all know it. And what does she tell them? 'If you want me to think kindly about you, go and make someone happy'—Pollyanna stuff. I have seen her, and she talks freely. To use a good word of the psychologists, she has insight. She knows she has changed, and gives you the credit.

Says that one night you gave her a hundred dollars and a shot in the arm, and since then she has been different."

"Talked too much," commented Ackerman. "Changed her, but could not take the eternal feminine out of her. Listen to me. Ackerman is not my real name. I am leaving the city tonight, destination unknown. You can give me all the publicity you want, but you cannot identify me. You find out all you can from Miss Moore, and then you interview a girl by the name of Sally Fanning, and two men: Harry Wild, the newsboy, and John Jones, a retired gentleman. They all live in this house. Get their story. Study it, but please do not put it in the *Purple Flash*. Write it as it should be written, and sell it to the *Times* or the *Sun*. If it is true, they will pay you for it."

"Where are you going, and what is your real name?"

"No!" said the inventor, returning to his packing.

The reporter looked at him, and she smiled:

"You are probably a wise man," she commented, "but you do not know very much about newspapers and nothing at all about the *Purple Flash*. We are like the Canadian mounted police. We always get our man. If the news you represent is as important as I think it is, we will get it. As far as the *Times* is concerned, I used to work for it. The

Flash tripled my salary to get me. Now will you tell me what I want to know?"

"No. It is a two letter word beginning with an 'N' and ending with an 'O', and it means negation. Use it in your cross-word puzzle, and let me finish packing."

"Did you, or did you not, on the night of the third, give a dose of serum to four people?"

"I did. I told you that. I told you their names and the fact that they lived in this house."

"What was the serum? What was it supposed to do to them?"

"I have no answer."

"Did you, just before I came in, give a dose of the same serum to a little boy carried by Hiram Smith, the Wolf of Wall Street?"

"I have no answer."

"Let me tell you something. Two days after you gave Harry Wild his serum, the *Purple Flash* knew about it. We paid him to keep quiet, at least as far as reporters are concerned. We have had six men on the case ever since. We know all about the Fanning girl, and her asthma, and John Jones, and his cardiac trouble. We have made an independent X-ray examination of Harry Wild. In the office, there are over twenty thousand words ready for release. We know that the newsboy told Hiram Smith, and that Smith had him examined. We know about Smith's son. And here is something to make you smile. We know who you are. Don't ask how.

None of your friends betrayed you, but you left a trail that was easy to track.

"Five of the greatest scientists in the United States have been under the employ of the *Purple Flash* for the last week studying the four people you gave the injections to. It is their opinion that, if you have a serum that will work on them, you have something that will revolutionize the entire social and economic status of the human race. We are not interested in the first four, except in regard to their relation to the next four million or four hundred million. If you have what they think you have, it is too great a secret for one man to hold. It should belong to the nation; in fact, one of the men said it should belong to the world.

"Suppose you should die? Or develop insanity? Don't you see what a priceless secret would die with you? And how are you going to use it? What price are you going to ask for it? Are you going to give it free, like the man who discovered insulin did? What will it do besides curing asthma, heart disease, and making twisted bones straight? Will it change the personality, make bad people good?"

Ackerman shook his head:

"I do not know. That is one of the things that I came to New York to find out, but you people are making it too uncomfortable for me. I hate publicity. It never occurred to me that any paper, especially one like yours, would go into a mystery so thoroughly. Why did you do it?"

"To increase our daily circulation, which is already over five million. Come on, Mr. Sidney Biddle, give me a break and talk."

"No. But you tell the owner of the *Purple Flash* that when the time comes for me to talk, when I have something to say, I promise to give you the first interview. But not now, not till I am sure."

CHAPTER V

THE RECIDIVISTS

SIDNEY BIDDLE, alias Harry Ackerman, went back to his laboratory, and worked and waited for two weeks. At the end of that time, he received the reports promised by Hiram Smith. In addition, there were several preliminary reports concerning the Smith boy. It was all very interesting, and made Biddle feel that he had every reason to be confident in his discovery.

But he was too much of a scientist to be a gambler. He knew that the experiment had to be repeated a hundred, a thousand, even a million times, before the results could be taken as definite and conclusive. Yet he was sure that the time had come for work on a large scale. He went to see the Governor of Ohio, a man who was so devoted to the interests of his people that he was lovingly called Welfare Watkins. The Executive listened for over an hour without interrupting, and then said:

"I suppose you have had sufficient vision into

this matter to understand what it means to the nation if you are correct?"

"I think so."

"It must be thought over very carefully. The consequences are so revolutionary that I am afraid I will not sleep tonight thinking of them. Do you realize that with one step you are going to wipe out the employment of large masses of our citizens? Some of these groups have carried on an honorable existence for centuries. They will no longer be needed. Of course, taxes will be lowered at once, but unemployment will be increased. It is a complex subject. Perhaps we had better wait till your experiments show that you are absolutely correct. Of course, I will give you permission to go to our prison. In fact, I will go with you. The Warden is a fine fellow, but he has been a penologist so many years that at times I am afraid he has ceased to remain a humanitarian. A personal command from me will be better than a letter. Have you enough of the medicine with you?"

"Yes. Seven hundred doses. I understand that the prison population is slightly over fourteen hundred. I wanted to hold half of them as control cases."

"We will go at once. I will tell my secretary to announce that I have left the State for Washington. We will make the trip to Farview in my personal airplane."

Two hours later, a group of men sat in the Warden's office at Farview. These men were the Governor, the Inventor, the Warden, the prison Physician, and the prison Chaplain. The Governor introduced Sidney Biddle as a scientist who wished to make an experiment on the prison population. He ended by asking the Warden to make a statement concerning his charges.

"Farview was built," the Warden replied, "to take care of the criminal who could not be reformed. There are fourteen hundred and thirty here at present, and we have room for twenty more. It is the only prison in America that is not overcrowded. The men average twenty-four years of age, a population of mere boys. Every one has had at least four convictions for felony or worse, and not a man here is up for less than twenty years. Sixty-five percent are here for life. They have committed every crime known to the criminal records of mankind. Some of their crimes are absolutely new. You see, with the advent of the machine and the electrical age, new ways of being bad developed, and that gave my boys an advantage, even over Nero. So far we have never had a riot. We may have one the next hour."

"How is their health, Doctor Yardly?" asked Biddle.

"As good and as bad as would be expected.

Syphilis, epilepsy, tuberculosis, hold up the death rate. A lot of them are insane or near it. You see, they have no hope, and that makes it hard for them to want to live. We try to make their life worth while, give them sports and talkies; but I guess that only adds to the mental irritation of their hopelessness."

"Their mental attitude is difficult to combat," interrupted the Chaplain. "You see, Mr. Biddle, they have been so poisoned by their past life that many of them have not only lost hope in the present, but also in the future. A large number of them do not believe in a God."

The Governor frowned.

"In a way, I do not blame them. Are your records up to date? Do you know your men, Warden?"

"I think so."

"Then pick out seven hundred for Mr. Biddle. I suppose the mere giving of that many intravenous injections will not take long, but at the same time I think we had better call on the Department of Health for a few physicians to help. I am going to send in thirty-six men. They ought to be here tomorrow. Take care of them. I will have a stenographer for each man. One of my private secretaries will be here to organize the office force, and help with the records. Let me see, I want twelve physicians, twelve psychiatrists, six lawyers, three hard-headed business men, and three of the clergy from different denominations. Get me the Department of Health on the phone. Also the State University. Do we need anyone else, Mr. Biddle?"

"There should be some psychologists, though most of that fraternity are so technical that I am afraid they will block the work; and there should be someone to take charge."

"I am going to do that," replied the Governor.

"Welfare Watkins," said the Warden, with a smile.

"I'll take that for what it is worth, Warden," retorted the Governor, "and it may be that it is not very much. I am the Governor of this state, and the people trust me. This experiment of Mr. Biddle's is too important for me to ignore. I will spend most of the month with you as your guest. Will you stay, Mr. Biddle?"

"No. Not after the seven hundred doses are given. I do not want to influence the findings of your experts in any way. All I want is a written opinion from you personally at the end of the month."

The Warden frowned:

"Just what do you expect, Mr. Biddle?" he asked.

"I will answer that question for him;" interrupted the Governor. "He has talked this over with me, and we are not going to tell anyone what he does expect. As far as you know, it is simply a new treatment for ringworm of the feet. What we are going to do is to have a short, concise record of these men now, and a month after they have their injection. There will be a statement concerning each prisoner. Complete, but concise. If a man is blind, I want a short, nontechnical statement as to why he is blind, and the condition of his eyes at the end of thirty days. All you have to do, Warden, is to run this prison as you always have and furnish every possible help to these specialists."

"I will have to have more guards. The prisoners won't understand it, and whenever anything happens they do not understand they get ugly. I ought to have at least fifty additional men."

"Ok," agreed the Governor. "You understand their psychology better than I do. Now suppose we get busy. I want to go over your files with Mr. Biddle. There are some of these prisoners I am interested in, and I want to get all of them on the list."

After three days of hard work, Sidney Biddle left the prison. His part of the work was done. There was nothing to do but to wait for the end results.

CHAPTER VI

HIRAM SMITH'S BOY

BIDDLE went from Ohio back to New York. He wanted to see the newsboy and Sally, the scrub, but changed his mind at the last moment and went right down into Wall Street to the office of Hiram Smith. There he was met by the usual obstacles confronting anyone who wants to see, without appointment, one of the financial overlords of America.

"Your name, please, and your business. Have you an appointment? Perhaps you had better fill out this card," purred the manicured and marcelled doll at the outer barricade.

The inventor smiled, and wrote on the card.

"YOU OWE ME SOMETHING; BUT, AFTER ALL, NOT PUBLICITY.

HOW IS JUNIOR? I WOULD LIKE TO SEE HIM. ACKERMAN."

"See what happens," he advised the doll. "Better rush it through."

In less than a minute, the Wolf himself came out, barking.

In less than another minute, the two men were

in the most private of all the private offices in the building.

"Well?" asked the inventor.

"I should say so!" laughed the Wolf. "You would not believe me; but the boy is actually walking, and using his hands. Of course the specialists say that the impossible is happening, but suppose it is? What difference does it make so long as it happens? It is my opinion, though of course I am not a doctor, that in another two weeks he will be just as good as the average boy of his age. And you ought to see the wife. She is ten years younger. Wait till she sees you. Talk about a woman worshipping a man! I have had lots of cause for jealousy. Can you come out to the house? I hope you did not register at a hotel, but if you did, it makes no difference. You cannot stay anywhere but with me."

"You seem to be excited over it," laughed the scientist.

"After all, he is my boy. Think of the mess I was in. Only son a hopeless cripple. Finest woman in the world my wife, and actually thinking of divorcing her and marrying some other woman just so I could have a real man-child; and then you came along and make a healthy, robust lad out of a twisted monstrosity. Of course I am excited. The last time I had him tested, the psychologist told me the lad had an intelligence quotient of one hundred and thirty-five. And you ought to see him run and jump. Learning to swim. Come on, and let's go. No more work for me today."

The two men went aboard the private speed boat that was the pride of the Wolf and which he used on his daily trips to the city. Thirty minutes up the Hudson, and they arrived at a wharf. From there they walked to the house. It was a Revolutionary relic hidden in a forest of oaks. Nearing the lawn, they saw a man, a woman, and a boy, playing ball. The boy, recognizing Smith, came running.

"That's him," explained the Wolf. "Look at those legs! No wonder the orthopædic surgeons were flabbergasted."

"Looks like a real boy to me!" exclaimed Biddle.

By this time, the adults had caught up with the boy. Biddle looked at them. He felt he ought to know them, but somehow he could not identify them. The man smiled, and then he knew him.

"Harry Wild! And can this be Miss Fanning?"

"Call me Sally," cried the woman.

Biddle looked at the woman—a wonder-woman, beautiful, radiant, glowing with health, vitality, happiness. He looked at the man, as fine a man as any male would want to be.

"Are you really Harry and Sally?" he asked.

"None other," laughed the Wolf. "They are living out here with us. They meant too much to me to let them stay in the city. The other two are here also."

"And we are all well!" cried Sally.

"Well in every way!" agreed Harry.

"And the kid is doing fine. We are teaching him everything."

"You teaching him?" asked the inventor, doubting his ears.

"We are indeed. You see, something happened to our minds as well as our bodies. Of course Harry and Mr. Jones knew a lot to start with, but Valencia and I never had much of a chance to learn so we are just reading all we can, and it is no trouble at all to remember everything we read. You would be surprised if you knew just what the four of us are doing for you."

It was not till after nine that the Wolf and the inventor were able to have an hour to themselves. Everybody was happy and excited. Mrs. Smith cried, but they all understood why. They all talked during dinner, all except Biddle. He just sat, and listened, and looked. He tried to remember the night he had invited these four to his bedroom, and explained to them what he wanted. Were these the same four? Jones did not look a day over thirty. Wild could have held his own as guard on a football team. Sally was lovely and Valencia charming, and they were both as fine young women as you could find anywhere. Sally always had been wonderful, but Valencia was now pure gold with all the dross burned out.

In the library, the Wolf turned and faced his guest:

"You have something," he said. "What are you going to do with it?" he demanded.

Biddle threw out his hands in a hopeless gesture.

"I am not sure," he replied.

"You know what this means?"

"Partly. I have just come from Ohio. You have heard of the Governor, Welfare Watkins? He was good to me. I have just finished the injection of seven hundred recidivists, a group of men who would be considered hopeless by every known method of analysis. Watkins is in personal charge of the experiment. I am simply waiting till I see the results."

"Suppose the sick ones get well, and those who are bad become good? What are you going to do about it?"

"What is there to do? What will Watkins do? Seven hundred sick men, imprisoned for life, become well in every way. What is the answer?"

"My answer is this. If you can do it for seven hundred, you can do it for every criminal in the States. If you can do what you did for my boy, you can do it for every little child who needs it. *If you can cure Sally, and Harry, and Valencia, and Jones, you can cure everyone who is sick. That is my answer. Can you? Are you going to? And how? What kind of machinery will you place in operation? You are going to change humanity. Before you do it, you must be sure of your control."*

Biddle walked silently up and down the book-lined room.

"I am going to wait," he said at last, "till I have the monthly report from Farview Prison. If that is favorable, I am going to give a guarded statement to the Press."

"What paper?"

"The *Purple Flash*."

"You are true to your promise."

"How do you know?"

"I ought to know. I am the owner of the paper. My reporter told me what you had promised her. We are just waiting for your word, and then we are going to have the greatest story any tabloid has ever sprung. By the way, do you know what those four patients of yours are doing? They are writing a book; trying to imagine what the world would be like if everyone were given a dose of your medicine. I am working on it with them at night. I give them ideas concerning business. Of course so far, it is only a dream."

"Yes, just a dream."

The two men sat in silence. Suddenly, the Wolf whispered:

"Have you given yourself a dose of the serum, Biddle?"

"No."

"Why not?"

"You see, I have a boy. That is what I have had in mind all these years. I wanted to do something for him some day, and it did not seem fair to let him go last."

"He—is sick? Like my boy?"

"Worse."

"And you were willing to help my boy first?"

"Yes. You see, I had to be sure. I could fail with others and keep working—have hope—but if I gave it to the boy and failed, I would have to stop."

"I understand. Well, you cannot stop. You have something that is so wonderful that it does not belong to you. Understand, I am not asking for anything for myself. I could sell that stuff for you at a million dollars a dose, serum you have been giving away to diseased convicts. But I am not doing that. I am not even asking for a dose for myself. You gave me a real son, and I am yours to command for the rest of my life. But you have something in that serum that is dynamite. If it goes off at the wrong time, it will devastate the world. And if it does not go off, it will rob the world of something the human race has a right to. Suppose you were killed?"

"Who is going to kill me?"

"The doctors and the lawyers ought to, but I suppose you are safe from them. They rank rather high. There are business men who are going to be wiped out, but I doubt if they would try to kill you.

But how about the bootleggers and the underworld? Those who traffic in vice of every form? I have talked to Valencia. She knows all about that life; but now she is clean, clean as a hound's tooth. She says she deserves no credit for her reformation. She just decided suddenly that she did not want to be bad any more. The criminal lawyers may smile when their living is taken away from them, but how about the criminals? And I am not sure of the politicians. They fatten on vice; it is a source of their power."

"Let's wait," answered Biddle. "I want to be sure of myself, and then I will have a message for the American people."

"Will they be ready for it?"

"That is a point well taken. Would it be best to take them into my confidence, or wait till the number of cures was so great that no one could doubt?"

"You cannot keep it a secret," declared the Wolf with a twisted smile. "My reporters, who have been trying to cover the work in Ohio, tell me that there are two hundred reporters at the Farview prison. If the Governor had not quarantined the place and called out the National Guard, they would have broken into jail to find out what was going on. So far, they cannot say anything because they do not know anything, but when the governor of a state goes into a prison for one month with a large staff of specialists, that's news, my son, that's news, and those reporters are going to do everything possible to find out what is going on."

"I guess we will let Welfare Watkins take care of that."

Hiram Smith went to the phone and called up the night editor of the *Purple Flash*. After listening carefully, he said:

"Watkins has told the newspapers that he has nothing to say."

CHAPTER VII

THE HUNGER STRIKE

SIDNEY BIDDLE decided to stay on as the guest of the Wolf of Wall Street. He wanted to think. Some of the questions Hiram Smith had asked were enough to make anyone think. Biddle was a scientist, not a sociologist; an inventor, not a financier. When he started his studies on a serum that would help mankind, he was thinking in terms of his son rather than in terms of the nation. His experiments up to this time had been done only to make sure of his discovery, rather than to help the human race in its toilsome staggerings towards the stars. The thought that it would revolutionize the life of the world was something new to him. He decided that he had to think it over.

His position in relation to his discovery was not unique. The first man to tame fire, Tubal Cain hammering the first piece of iron, the discoverer of gunpowder, of movable type, of the telescope; Newton with his apple, Watts with his steam kettle, Morse with his telegraph, Wright with his gliding machine—none of these had a clear consciousness of what his discovery would do to the life of the world. But those who were benefited knew. The man, warmed and protected by fire and by the iron tipped rod, the man reading the first Bible, looking at the moon through a lens, riding on a train, sending messages first over wire and then without wire, the man chasing birds through the air; these men knew what the discovery meant. Sally Fanning breathing lustily, Harry Wild standing erect, Valencia Moore cleansed from the desire to sin, John Jones made young again, the crippled son of the Wolf chasing rabbits through the woods; these had a far clearer vision of what had to happen in the world through the use of the serum than the man who had spent years perfecting it. And Hiram Smith, sensitized through years on the Stock Exchange, knew perfectly well what stocks would boom and what stocks would break when Wall Street heard the news. Already he had sold all of his holdings in the United Drug Company, a ten million dollar concern he had helped organize.

Biddle wired his address to the Governor of Ohio, and spent the next week in long conversations with the guests of Hiram Smith. He was especially interested in talking to Mrs. Smith. She was a woman, college educated, club cultured, and devoted, through the illness of her son, to charities for children of underpriviledged people. In her joy over the changed condition of her only child, she could not forget that there were other children who were warped, twisted, and bent. She could not forget them, and she could not let the inventor forget. He listened to her pleading; he looked at the pictures of the little lads and lassies in the homes for the incurables in which she was interested.

"You are a peculiar inventor!" she exclaimed. "Most of the breed I have met have made things out of metals or devised new uses for electricity. But you work with living things, and so far you have not uttered a word or mentioned in any way the financial side of your undertaking. What are you doing it for? What are you going to gain from the development of your secret serum?"

Biddle simply smiled:

"I have a son," he replied. "I invented several processes and sold them. Now I am spending that money. What is money, anyway? What thing that is worth while can it buy for you? What good did your husband's wealth do you? In the end, the thing you were willing to pay millions for was given to you like the sunshine—like the air you breathe."

"Are you going to let the world enjoy it?"

"I do not know. Just now, I am interested only in my son."

On the evening of the eighth day of his visit, he received a telegram from the Governor of Ohio urging him to return to Farview Prison as soon as possible. No explanation was given. He showed the wire to Hiram Smith, who simply asked him for permission to take him to the prison by airplane.

"Something big must be happening there, and I want to go along and see what it is," he explained. "You know I am interested."

"The Governor might have something to say about your entering the prison."

"He might," agreed the Wolf, "if he knew who I was, but you can simply introduce me as your secretary, or a fellow scientist, or even your valet."

"Ok," agreed Biddle. "Let's start."

Morning found them at the prison. It was closely guarded by several companies of the National Guard. The few hotels of the neighboring town overflowed with newspaper men who were rapidly going insane over their inability to find out what was going on behind the mammoth granite walls of the prison. Biddle, once he was identified, had no trouble in entering; and the Wolf went with him as his private secretary.

"What's wrong?" the scientist asked Welfare Watkins, as they met in the Warden's office. "Has the serum failed?"

The tired executive shook his head:

"On the contrary, it has succeeded too well. The change in the seven hundred who received the injection has been rapid and in every way satisfactory. Especially so to the men who were treated. Men who were almost dead from tuberculosis started to recover; syphilitics cleared mentally as well as physically. Every man developed a new viewpoint on life; they started to sing, whistle, laugh. The utterly vicious and hopelessly desperate changed almost overnight."

"The representative of the National Committee of Mental Hygiene told me that he had never seen anything like the difference between the men before and after the serum. The specialists spent one half of their time saying that such changes could not happen to the human body and the other half finding new causes for astonishment.

"That part of it is all right. The serum has started to act in exactly the way you said it would. Not a single failure. But the news spread to the other half of the prison population. How? Don't ask me. In a few days the other seven hundred knew that something great and wonderful was happening to their mates and not happening to them, and they did not like it; and, in a way, I do not blame them. Suppose you were in the hospital of the prison rotting to death and in the next bed was a man sick as you were and from the same disease. Suppose you saw that man recover, almost over night, and you just kept on dying? What if you remained hopeless and your cell mate hopeful? The men who received the serum gained the idea, I do not know how, that they were going to get well in every way, and when they did I was going to pardon them. They were filled with hope.

"Naturally, the rest of the men wanted the same thing to happen to them. They were not sure what it was, but they knew it was something, and they wanted it. So they have gone on a hunger strike, seven hundred of them, and they swear they will not eat a bite till they get what they call fair play. So far there has been no violence, but Hell is likely to break out at any moment. And the men who are getting well are sympathetic. They are saying that the medicine ought to be given to all of the prisoners."

"If you are willing to do so, Governor," replied Biddle, "we will do that. It will not take long for me to get enough serum from my laboratories, and, with the physicians we have here, the work can be completed in a very few days. That ought to satisfy them."

"It will, and I think you had better send for the medicine. But I am afraid it will not satisfy others. We have five prisons in the State. And then there are the reporters. I am actually afraid to leave the prison. They feel that there is something big happening, and they want the details. What can I say to them; and if I say it, will they believe me? You have started something big, but how is it going to end? And what shall I do with these men after they have turned this prison into a paradise? Are they still guilty?"

"What does the Warden say, Governor?" asked Biddle.

"Of course, he is a penologist. He has looked on this type of human behavior as hopeless. Even now, he says that they are suffering from some type of group hysteria, that in reality they are just as wicked and just as sick as they ever were."

"What do the physicians say?"

"They are talking their heads off, and working twenty hours a day studying their pets. Each man has seen some impossible condition change for the better. One man was almost dead from cancer of the throat. From hour to hour they expected the disease to rot into a large blood vessel and the man to bleed to death. Now they say the man is going to recover. Of course they say that occasionally a cancer will do that, but they feel that too many things like that are going on at the same time. First they talked of coincidence, and now some of them are talking of omnipotence. They swear they are going to do something to you, torture you, if necessary, to make you tell them what it is you injected into the veins of these seven hundred degenerates. Something has to be done."

"We will do it. You announce to the prisoners that I am sending for some more medicine; and that, as soon as it comes, every man will receive a dose, and the medicine and the dosage will be the same as was given to the other prisoners.

"You can tell the doctors and specialists that at the proper time I will make an announcement to representatives of the ethical medical societies of the United States; and when I do that, I will give the secret free to the nation. In the meantime, explain to them that they have had a wonderful opportunity to see the drug tested on over fourteen hundred cases and that it would be a good idea if they would prepare a report to the American Medical Association so that, when the time comes, that body of physicians will not think that I am some kind of a charlatan.

"As far as the reporters are concerned, tell them that in twenty-four hours you will have a statement to make giving them the bald facts of what has been going on in Farview Prison. I will help you prepare that statement. Now I guess that ought to please everybody."

"But you said that it would take thirty days before the full effects of the drug could be observed."

"That is true. And we will not make any extravagant claims at this time."

"And you will send for the seven hundred doses at once?"

"Yes. My private secretary is here in his airplane. I will ask him to go to my laboratories, and

THE HUNGER STRIKE 85

have the drug rushed here. I will start him at once."

The Wolf of Wall Street had overheard all of the conversation. Biddle took him to one side, and gave him a Philadelphia address.

"You will have to take a letter there for me. They will give you the package, and you can send it back by special messenger."

"But how about me? I heard you promise to release the news to the papers in twenty-four hours."

"Well, what of it? I did not forget my promise. You have your plane. When you leave here get to the nearest big city. Take over a private line, and burn the news over to your city editor. Tell him anything you want. Right at this minute you have, or at least I think you have, over twenty thousand words typed and ready for the press. In a few hours, you can bring that news up to date, and have the special edition of the *Purple Flash* on the streets. You ought to have at least twenty hours lead on every other paper in the States. More than that, you have a rather clear idea of what it means. You can use all of your information except one thing, and that is my name. Now I will write the letter, and you can start. Better not let those boys outside the walls learn who you are. If they do, you will not get far."

"This is wonderful, Biddle," whispered the secret owner of the *Purple Flash*. "It will put my paper at the head of all of them, and increase the circulation by five million. Could I speak to a few of these doctors, and sign them up for some future articles?"

"No. The last thing in the world I want is for them to find out who you are. All I want is for you to keep quiet for a little while."

Once Hiram Smith was safely up in the air, Biddle returned to the Governor. He said:

"Suppose we start writing that statement for the papers?"

"I think that would be a good idea," assented the Executive. "What do you think we had better say?"

"Not too much and not too little. Something like this:

> *For the last two weeks Governor Watkins has been personally supervising the giving of a new form of medical treatment to all of the inmates of Farview Prison. The prisoners treated have been under the care of medical and sociological experts who at the end of thirty days will make a preliminary report.*
>
> *For the present, all that can be said is that the health of the prisoners is excellent. One half of the prison population were treated two weeks ago, and the other half will be treated in the next thirty-six hours. The Governor intends remaining at Farview till the expiration of thirty days, at which time he will permit the medical experts conduct-*

ing the experiment to make whatever statement they wish. Till that time, no statement not signed by the Governor can be considered trustworthy.

Signed: Watkins

"That ought to be satisfactory, Governor," said Biddle.

"Sure. Just enough to finish their insanity."

"Do you want to tell them the truth?"

"I would if I were sure, but suppose the Warden is right? What if they are not well, only think they are?"

Biddle shook his head:

"I think I know how you feel. I have used this serum on hundreds of animals. I saw its effect on five people in New York before I came to you. I think I know what it will do, but even now I am not sure. If I were sure, I would give a dose to my son. You see, he is, well, not actually sick; but abnormal in some ways. I do not want to give it to him till I am sure. So I am waiting. I hoped that after this prison experiment I could go ahead with him. Now, if I feel that way, what is to keep you from doubting? Suppose we get something to eat and then spend the rest of the night seeing some of your cases. I want to talk with them, especially some of the psychopathic personalities and mental defectives.

I am a little more interested in their minds and souls than I am in their bodies."

"You think they are going to change—that way?"

"Yes. The serum seems to work in any kind of sickness, and after all a bad man is simply a sick man."

CHAPTER VIII

THE AROUSED NATION

WITHIN the next twenty-four hours, the *Purple Flash* gave to the nation, and incidentally to the world, the first of a series of articles on the new serum. The paper was being sold on the streets of New York one hour before the signed statement of the Governor of Ohio was handed to the impatient reporters surrounding the prison. They could each take that statement and embellish it as they saw fit, but pratically all they said was pure imagination. Meantime, the *Purple Flash* was giving to the world thousands of words, well written, and apparently so authentic that all of those who read were forced to believe.

There were millions of American citizens, however, who only had access to the twisted, garbled accounts written by reporters who had little but fancy to draw on. Half truths are worse than whole lies; and at once a tangled fiction spread, especially through Ohio, as to just what was going on at Farview Prison. A Chicago paper, driven to despair by the success of the *Purple Flash,* started to publish a series of articles in which the direct charge was made that Ohio, forced to balance its budget, was experimenting with a new form of enthanasia, whereby thousands of its criminals, abnormals, and defectives would rapidly die and thus relieve the State of their financial care. The fact that many states were having difficulty in providing for their Welfare Departments made this slightly plausible. In addition, the personal attendance of the Governor of Ohio, his secreting himself in Farview Prison for several weeks, his calling out the National Guard, his employment of additional prison guards, the use of Medical experts, the definite secrecy, the quarantine, the peculiar and somewhat ambiguous statement given to the Press; all this could mean only one thing, and that was something so terrible that it could mean just that Ohio was starting to free herself of the burden of life care of the hopeless criminal class.

The *Chicago Freepress,* carefully avoiding the libel law, became eloquent in its defense of the forgotten men, the lifers in the Ohio prisons. After all, they were human beings, made in the image of God. Though sentenced to life imprisonment, deprived of their citizenship, without homes, family, or hope, they were still worthy of help.

The *Freepress* pointed out that, if this condition were encouraged, there would be nothing to prevent other states following the example of Ohio. It showed how much Illinois, New York, California, could save by the immediate destruction of all of its criminals and abnormals. It asked whether there was any real difference between the slaughter of the Innocents at the time Christ was born and the slaughter of the criminals at a time when His teachings were being forgotten by a mob of politicians driven to impotent fear by the mob of taxpayers at their heels.

In some way this paper obtained the names of the inmates of the Farview Penitentiary. It hunted up their relatives, the wives, mothers, and children, of these men. The reporters told them that their beloved men were being killed in the name of science, and then obtained their pictures, and took their statements, and recorded their tears. It made wonderful sob stuff. Other papers followed the example of the *Freepress*.

Charges were made that the *Purple Flash* was being subsidized by the Ohio Governor to give a false account of the experiment in order to deceive the public. Soapbox orators addressed the unemployed on every street corner. For a few days, the issue tended to become a national one. Fraternal organizations paid the expenses of the families of the criminals to Farview, where their hands, held at the wrists, by agitators, knocked without avail on the steel gates of the prison.

Everyone talked of the serum. Those who knew the least about it talked the most. It was discussed from the pulpit, the radio, and the stage. Meanwhile, day after day, the *Purple Flash* continued its series of articles, which were so impossible that no one believed in them. At the same time, all read them.

At last, the excitement became so acute that the President of the United States determined that it was his duty, as the head of the nation, to make a personal investigation of the matter; and, irrespective of what the real truth was, to give it to a nation fast growing hysterical. Without parade or publicity, he made the journey from Washington to Farview, and was inside the walls of the prison twenty-four hours before the group of experts were ready to give their statement to the papers.

The first interview with Welfare Watkins took place behind closed doors in the Warden's office. Sidney Biddle was the third member of the conference.

"I suppose you know why I am here," began the President. "There has been such a hysteria shown over the news from Ohio that I felt it my duty to come here and make a personal inquiry. I trust, Governor, that you will not feel that I am doubting you and the work of your State, but—you have read the papers."

The Governor smiled at the President, as he replied:

"That is all right. No apologies needed. If you had waited another day, my specialists would have given you their report, and when that report is given to the Press, some of the papers, especially those in Chicago, will be rather ashamed of the tommy-rot they have been feeding the gullible public. There is only one thing we have been doing with these convicts and that is helping them; restoring their health, apparently burning the evil from their personalities, making real men out of them. Have you read the articles in the *Purple Flash?*"

"I have. The terrible side of their method of deceiving the public is the fact that they are so well written that they seem to be the truth."

"Suppose we have Mr. Biddle answer that. You should understand, Mr. President, that Mr. Biddle is very much interested in this experiment. He knows more about it than anyone else. What do you think of the truth of the articles in the *Flash?*"

"The main facts are all true. Of course, the editors had no real scientific information concerning the composition of the serum used. Their guesses of the future use of the serum may seem to be science fiction; but the premises are correct, and their conclusions may be equally correct. The secret owner of the *Flash* is vitally interested. His son was one of the first five human beings to receive the serum."

The President looked at Biddle in astonishment. At last he said:

"There must be a mistake somewhere. My personal physician, Rear Admiral Sloane, went over the account of those first five cases, and he told me that no medicine could accomplish what was claimed. He said that it would have to be a cure-all, a panacea."

"He should have said that there was no known medicine that could do it," was Biddle's calm reply. "But now that you are here, why not see the prisoners? The thirty day period will be up for half of them tomorrow, and it has been about eighteen days since the other half received their serum. I suppose, Governor, that there will be no objection to the President seeing the men?"

"None at all. Suppose I have them line up on the parade ground? I could have you interview the Prison Surgeon and the Chaplain. I could have the various specialists and the psychologists tell you about the changes that have taken place in these fourteen hundred men, but I guess it will be best to have you see them as a group first. Do you know what the usual collection of life term prisoners look like? Are you acquainted with the prison pallor? Can you identify the look of hopeless hate, the insane eye, the lustful cunning, of the psychopath? Do you know how a man feels when he knows that he will never leave a prison till he dies?"

"I have been in a good many prisons," acknowledged the President.

"Then you will be able to detect the difference between the average lot of prisoners and these men we are going to show you. I will give the order, the men will fall in, the band will start playing, and the men will pass in review. We have done a lot of drilling lately. The men are feeling so well that they are keen for all forms of exercise. I will call the Warden, and in ten minutes we can go out and watch them. They have a setting-up exercise that is especially fine. They strip to the waist for that."

Fifteen minutes later the reviewing party saw over fourteen hundred men pass in review, in perfect time, beautiful formation. They marched with the sure step and certain time of well drilled soldiers; and back of every movement was glorious health, the joy of being alive and well. Later they took off their coats and shirts, and went through a complicated series of setting-up exercises. The President broke his fifty minute silence:

"No prison pallor there," he exclaimed. "Those men are sunburned athletes. Where are your sick men, the hospital cases?"

"That is not sunburn," replied Biddle. "For some reason not clear to me, the serum turns the skin a beautiful golden tan. The two women I gave it to have the most wonderful complexion you ever saw. In regard to the sick men, those who were in the hospital dying from cancer, tuberculosis, syphilis, and every possible result of vicious living, they are out on the parade ground. There has not been a death in the prison this month, and at the present time there is not a single patient in the prison hospital. Physically, they are well."

The President shook his head:

"But the Chicago papers said that you were experimenting with a new form of euthanasia; that you were going to kill them?"

"Doesn't look like it, does it?" answered the Governor. "And these men are not only well physically, but there is a change mentally. Just wait till you hear the sociologists, psychologists, and psychiatrists report on the changes in their mentality, their personality, their viewpoint on life, their moral sense. It raises a very serious question. Biddle and I have talked about it. We do not know what we ought to do with these men."

"They are all old offenders, are they not?"

"Yes. But suppose we show that they were sick when they broke the laws, and that now they have recovered from their sickness and won't break any more laws. Shall they be punished for being sick?"

"I don't know," admitted the President, "but I want to talk to some of them. I want to see for myself, and I want to talk to some of the doctors who have spent the month here, and I think I want to talk with the Warden. After that, if what appears true is true, I feel it my duty to issue a statement to the American people. Tell me one thing. Who discovered this remedy? Does the man know the full extent of its power? What is he going to charge for it? Can the nation buy it? Is there a chance that he will become worried over the publicity, and go and sell it to a foreign power? How is he going to act...?

"What?—this man Biddle the inventor? Then I must talk to him first."

The President of the United States was a man who was close to the common people. As far as the nation was concerned, he was as welfare minded as the Governor of Ohio. He was not an intense isolationist, but he did feel that the good of his people was more important than the good of a dozen nationalities of Europe and Asia. While he was not a socialist, he believed in equal opportunities for those who were equally capable of profiting by them.

During the three years he had served as President, he had seen the national debt grow, taxes increase, and unemployment become more prevalent. While he had watched the convicts on parade, he had been impressed by their glorious bouyancy, their apparent health. He knew with a fair degree of accuracy what the Federal prisons were costing the taxpayer; and whatever may have been the route of his thinking, he rapidly reached the point where he saw that the wealth of the nation would have to improve with the health of the individual. The prevention of crime was secondary, in his thought, to the cure of diseases which otherwise were forcing the nation, the commonwealths, and the large cities to spend an ever increasing percentage of their funds on hospitalization.

In the cure of hookworm and in the fight against yellow fever, malaria, smallpox, and tuberculosis, the nation had ever been active in association with various foundations. It was natural for the Chief Executive to feel that if a new drug, a startling medicine, a universal panacea, were discovered, that it should belong to the nation. Laws would have to be made for its use, machinery devised for its distribution; in every way it would have to be protected and guarded against the attacks of the unscrupulous who would wish to commercialize it or to make its use possible only to the wealthy, the pampered favorites of fortune.

He wanted to talk to Biddle.

The result of that conference had ramifications neither dreamed of.

CHAPTER IX

CONGRESS CHANGES

THE PRESIDENT worked at intense pressure for twelve hours, and at the end of that time issued the following statement to the Press:

I wish to announce that I have personally made an investigation of the health programme of the State of Ohio as practiced at Farview Prison, and feel that it has been to the definite advantage of all of the inmates. All have been greatly benefited and nothing has happened to any of them that in any way can be considered as prejudicial to their health, happiness, or future, should they at any time be pardoned and restored to their former citizenship.

Signed: Richard Caldwell

And, exactly twelve hours after this statement was broadcast to the nation, the general report of the specialists who had been observing the work of the serum was likewise released to the Press. After that there was a rapid exodus from Farview Prison. The seal of secrecy being broken, a wide expression of universal opinion was given. These men were all specialists in their line, men who knew so much about a little that some of them had reached the point where they knew everything about nothing. For thirty days they had lived in an atmosphere of the fantastic and impossible, they had seen the impossible happen, every belief of theirs shattered. It was almost necessary for them to reconstruct their scientific world. Under ordinary circumstances, most of them would have doubted and remained silent, but now they had to talk; and as talking was very profitable, they gave their opinions to the world.

The majority believed that the treatment was highly tonic, to a great degree stimulative and restorative, but it could not be any thing permanent; and the marked improvement could only be considered as a temporary change. Only the future could determine whether other doses of the serum would be equally potent. All felt that nothing but benefit had resulted from the first dose, but several raised the point that it might result in drug addiction. Would the individual be able to live without a constantly increasing dose?

The President went back to Washington, met with his Cabinet, and, as a result of that conference, invited one hundred of the leaders of American politics to come to Washington. This list included Senators, Representatives, Governors, Mayors of seven of the largest cities, and six of the silent advisors of the Administration. The selection was carefully made. Not a man was invited who was not in absolute control of his district, and not one of the hundred was in good health. They ruled now; but in ten years the majority would be dead, merely historical names fast passing into oblivion.

The invitation was carefully worded. The President invited them to meet with him to consider a matter important to the economic welfare of the Nation. Up to the time he began to address them, the majority of his guests believed that the subject to be discussed was purely of a financial nature. He lost no time in telling them the real reason.

The meeting was held in the Green Room of the White House. Present were the President, his Cabinet, Vice President, the one hundred invited conferees, and Biddle, the man of mystery.

"You have all been reading," began the President, "of the work done at Farview Prison, Ohio, by the Governor of that State. Over fourteen hundred prisoners were given a single dose of a serum, and the effect on their general health and mentality studied by a carefully selected corps of experts. As you know, I made a trip to Farview Prison, and personally investigated this experiment. As a result, I conferred with the inventor of this serum, Mr. Biddle, and secured from him a promise that he would neither perform any more mass experiments, nor capitalize his discovery till I had a chance to consider it from a national standpoint. It appears that the maximum improvement is reached in thirty days following the giving of the serum. My thought was that one month from today I would call a special session of Congress to provide for the control of this discovery, provided we can make satisfactory arrangements with its owner. Up to the present time, every great discovery leading to improvement of the lives of our people has passed into the control of private corporations. I am told that, for three generations, the obstetrical forceps remained the secret of one family, and during that time, thousands of women died in childbirth who would have been saved had every physician known the use of the forceps. Steam, electricity, the telegraph, telephone, and radio, are all controlled and operated by private capital. Insulin was given to the diabetics of the world by its discoverers, but that is one of the few exceptions to the rule.

"I am going to bring the entire problem to the attention of Congress. In the meantime, it is of importance to us, as leaders of national thought, to have a first hand observation of the use of the new drug and its powers. Only by this method can we properly determine the matters pertaining to its universal use in this nation. I have asked you here, not only because you are leaders of your communities and can sway public opinion, but also because I have reason to feel that you are all sick men. My advisers tell me that few of the men in this room will be alive at the expiration of ten years. Thus you are admirable subjects for demonstrating the power of this drug. Mr. Biddle has everything ready to give all of you an intravenous injection. I am not offering you something I am afraid of myself; I am not asking you to do a thing I will not do.

"Gentlemen, I am giving you a secret that, unless something is done soon, will no longer be a secret. Grant died of cancer, Cleveland was operated on for cancer, and I have been treated by radium for over a year for cancer. It has been a discouraging year. A week ago, my medical advisers told me that, at the most, I would die in six months. At Farview I saw a case similar to mine who was considered to be completely cured thirty days after he received one dose of the serum.

"You are all sick men. I am not asking you to give the diagnosis. This is going to be a gift to you, and not a cold-blooded experiment. You know what is wrong, and you will know if you are benefited. I am suffering from cancer, and I am going to ask Mr. Biddle to give me the first injection. I am going to have him give it to me in front of you. There will not be, as far as we are concerned, any secrecy. After I am treated, I am going to have a dose given to my dear friend, the Vice President. After that, the line forms on the left. You can take it or leave it. Think it over, talk it over, come to a decision. All I ask of you is a gentleman's promise of secrecy. It will not help the stock market to know that I have cancer, and that the Vice President has angina pectoris and may die at any moment. Mr. Biddle, will you proceed? Which arm?"

There was an air of resistance in the group. Whisperings of disapproval and negativeness. Ignorance of medical matters made the average man fear the procedure. The thought of allowing an unknown drug to be introduced into the veins was a difficult one to face. Biddle had given the serum to the President and Vice President, but no one stepped forward to be the third. Suddenly, a little dog walked slowly up to the table leading a blind man. The dog was a seeing friend; the man, Goresome, the sightless leader of Montana.

"Was there a blind man among those convicts?" he asked.

"There was," Biddle answered.

"What happened to him?"

"I will answer that," interrupted the President. "I saw the man. I talked with the eye specialist who studied his case. He had perfect vision by the end of twenty days."

"That is enough," replied Goresome. "This little guide of mine kept urging me to move. For twelve years he has guided me, and not made one mistake. I was born blind. I would like to see the sunshine before I die. Give me the needle."

"No man from the West has any more courage than a New Yorker," exclaimed a Senator from that State. "I have been only half a man since I had my stroke. I want to be the next man after Goresome."

That started a general movement. At the end, only six men remained untreated. Silent, critical, cool, determined, they refused to be swayed by the group movement.

"Come back to Washington at the end of thirty days, Gentlemen," concluded the President, "and let us at that time determine what is best for the Nation."

"One minute, Mr. President," shouted one of the untreated six. "What does Mr. Biddle get out of this?"

"You answer that, Mr. Biddle," whispered the President.

"Nothing!" said Biddle. "If the serum is of any value, I am willing to give it to the nation."

"Why are you doing this?"

"I have a sick son."

"Have you given him the serum? Have you taken it yourself?"

"The answer to both questions is NO."

"Why?"

"I do not care to discuss that. It is personal."

"Are you sure you know what the serum will do?"

"No."

"What do you mean by that?"

"I mean that I am not sure of all it will do. I only know a part of its power."

"Be honest with us. You say it makes the blind see, the criminal an honest man; it cures cancer, heart disease, and every disease man can have. You admit that. If it can do all that, what else can it be asked to do? What other powers do you think it might have?"

"I do not know."

"Have you any suspicions?"

"Yes, but I will not say what they are. Anything else?"

"No. You have said enough."

"Just one word more, Gentlemen," said the President. "If Congress, in the special session, passes the legislation I will ask for, Mr. Biddle has promised to address a joint session of the Senate and the House, and at that time explain the theory of the serum and give the formula to a selected group of scientists and physicians. He tells me that it is easily and cheaply made. He assures me that he wishes to make a gift of it to the nation. But he feels that its general use must be safeguarded by wise and effective laws. I want to thank those of you who have helped me by personally giving Mr. Biddle a chance to demonstrate the merits of his serum. I am not in any way blaming the six gentlemen who refused to experiment with an unknown drug. Good night, and good luck to all of you."

CHAPTER X

THE SIX CONSPIRATORS

THE SIX who had refused to take the serum met that night in a Baltimore Hotel. It would be interesting if it could be written into the record that these six were powerful but corrupt politicians, that they were the recipients of large sums from the racketeers of the underworld, that they saw in the serum of Biddle the destruction of all forms of vice. But such was not the case.

The six men were clean cut, respectable, hard-headed business men who considered political office simply as a necessary adjunct to their business. They were the majority stockholders in some of the largest corporations in the United States, and their main interests were life insurance, accident insurance, drug manufacturing, bonding hospitals, and the higher education of the youth of America. One of them was the president of a large university.

The reason for the meeting was not too much disbelief in the experiments of Biddle, but too great a belief. They saw, perhaps more clearly than any other six men in America, what the general use of his serum would result in. They sat around a table with their coats off and their shirt sleeves rolled up. They wanted to think.

The University man started the discussion:

"I will imagine that I represent the higher education, not only of one university, but of the nation. We pay much of our expenses from the income on our endowments. That money is invested mainly in life insurance companies and railroads. The railroads have been hard hit. If the life insurance companies collapse, every college in America will have to close. There would hardly be enough money to pay the janitors, let alone the professors. I am not going to do your thinking for you, but I am going to ask each of you to imagine what effect the general use of the Biddle Serum will have on the business of the life insurance companies. Also the companies who are doing accident insurance.

"And here is the second thing I ask you to think about. What two departments of every university are the best attended after the plain A.B. or B.S. groups? The answer is law and medicine. Why do our young men study law and medicine? Because they expect to make a living. Now one more question: Suppose the Biddle Serum works the way the inventor thinks it will, what will happen to the practice of law and medicine?

"I do not like to admit it, but the practice of law depends on the weaknesses of men's souls, and the practice of medicine depends on the weaknesses of their bodies. That must be evident to all of us. There are over one hundred and forty million persons in the United States, and every day millions of them break some law and have to have the help of lawyers, and every day millions of them break some law of health and have to appeal to the medical profession. I tell you that thirty days after the Biddle Serum is given to all of these people, the income of these two professions will cease, and the lawyers and doctors will be on the streets selling apples and holding out tin cups for sweet charity. No one will want to be a student of these professions. Our law and medical schools will close their doors. Who will want to study medicine for ten years at the cost of fifteen thousand dollars when any disease can be cured by a single injection of a simple serum that can be made by the barrel by any manufacturing chemist? The millions invested in our hospitals will not yield one cent of income. Every drug company in America will go out of business over night. There will be no more surgical instruments sold. It looks bad to me."

The other five remained in stolid, stodgy silence. At last Winston Manning almost cracked the spell of quiet thinking. He had been Secretary of the

Treasury under a former President. He was said to be one of the ten richest men in America.

"I guess that is all so. At least, the conclusions are correct once the premises are granted. There is another thing that is disturbing me more than the tottering of our universities.

"Our Government is essentially one that is ruled by the classes for the masses. It is highly political. Ever since it was founded, the common people have supported it in taxes, and the rulers have lived on those taxes. At times, the farmer, the little laborer, the poor white collar man, have had a hard time to get along; but so far they have not done much because they have had no great and outstanding leadership. If they had the right kind of leaders, they would tear the present political machinery to pieces; and out of the ruins they would build a government that was sympathetic to the little man, the forgotten man, who does little except work like a dog, live as best he can, and pay taxes.

"Keep that in mind. For the time being, forget the cases of cancer and blindness and kidney disease that are said to hive been cured by the Biddle Serum. Think what it has done to the souls of the people who have taken that serum, think of the changes it has made in their personality. Take the case of the taxi dancer in New York City. Of course, the *Purple Flash* did not give her right name, but I bet the facts concerning her are absolutely true. Then consider the reports of the psychologists and sociologists who studied those fourteen hundred convicts in Farview. Take the simple statement of the hard boiled Warden. Take the strong words he gave to the press. *'I have known many of these men for years. Since the giving of the serum, they have changed so for the better that I would trust any of them in any way. I am seriously considering approaching the Governor of Ohio with the suggestion that these men be released from prison and given one more chance to rehabilitate themselves.'* Does it not seem that in some way this serum enables men to think more clearly, to live more cleanly, to follow more accurately the teaching of the *Golden Rule?*

"Today you saw over a hundred of the leading politicians in the United States step up and take that serum. I know those men. You know them. Outside of Welfare Watkins, who is an emotional, idealistic, assinine sort of a person, I would not trust one of that bunch with a five cent piece. They would take the pennies from a dead man's eye, and rob a starving infant of his bottle of milk. They have had charge of the Government Cow for years, and they have milked that cow dry. They know every trick to deceive and rob the public. And in their way, they are as criminal as the men of Farview ever dreamed of being, only they were too smart to be caught.

"They took the serum. The President was smart. He wants to come up for another term. He thinks that if he gives the populace free health they will vote for him. He never said a word to those men about curing their souls, but he was very anxious to give them healthy bodies, so they could repay him with their gratitude. Perhaps they will. He may have overlooked what the damned drug would do their souls. But I tell you this: *If the serum works on those politicians in the same way it worked on those criminals, they will come back to Congress representing the common people, and having the interests of the forgotten man at heart; and at the next election both the Democratic and the Republican Parties will be killed, and the country will cease to have a political rule, but will be governed solely in the interests of the people. That will mean the death of every large corporation in America.* Laugh about that if you can."

Again the sextette remained quiet. At last, a Bishop broke the silence. He was a combination of priest and politician, and once had swayed a national election by an appeal to religious prejudice.

"Biddle knows more about this serum than he is saying," the clergyman whispered. "You have talked about the fall of universities and political parties, but there is something more serious. Suppose he is right in his claim of being able to cure the bodies of mankind? Suppose the sick became well and the well stay well? How are people going to die? Are they going to die? What is going to happen if they don't die? Every religion in the world is based on the fear and hope of eternity—the fear of Hell, and the hope of Paradise. But how can there be a future, if there is no end of the present?

"Our religious life will smash, our churches close, the contributions to the support of the clergy come to an end."

"You take it too seriously, Bishop," laughed the university president. "Biddle never said he could give the people immortality. He does not think so, and no one else thinks so."

"I know he did not say so," argued the Bishop, "but he did say that he was not sure just what power the serum held. Even suppose that death does come. His serum robs the world of sin, and I cannot see how the Church would function were it not for sin. I understand his subconscious thought, and it is one I have had to combat for years; the idea that there is no sin, only disease, and that all crimes are simply symptoms of an abnormal body or mind; that if the disease could be discovered and cured, the symptoms would disappear and the patient cease to be a criminal. I have had an army physician argue that a cocaine fiend was simply a sick man, like a case of typhoid fever. Now, if all wickedness in the world can be done away with just by giving every person a dose of the Biddle Serum, what is going to be the future of the Church?"

"It is growing late," growled one of the men. "What is the answer? We cannot get anywhere by talking about the immortality of the soul and the philosophy of crime and religion. What are we going to do about it?"

"We have to see Biddle, and buy the secret of the serum from him!" demanded the Bishop.

"Suppose he won't sell?"

"He will, if we find out his price."

"But he may be honest."

"Then there is only one thing to do," sighed the university professor. "We will talk to him kindly. We will show him where he is wrong. We will persuade him that the best thing is to form a company for the manufacture and distribution of his drug. We will tell him that he can be president of the company. Tell him anything. Pay him anything he asks. Money, power, reputation, a trip to Europe to demonstrate the drug.

"We will do that little thing. If he refuses to listen to us, we will have to take him out for a ride!"

"Why, Professor!!" exclaimed the politician.

"And," continued the president of a noted university, "Congress can then meet. The blind Goresome may see, our beloved President may be cured of his cancer. They will wait, but they will wait in vain for the arrival of Biddle, the philanthropic inventor of the cure-all serum. There will be a lot of talk, and then the people will laugh and call it one of the greatest bluffs of the age. They will say that Barnum died too soon, but left worthy followers in Welfare Watkins and our great President."

That was the final decision of the six conspirators.

CHAPTER XI

FATE INTERVENES

THE SIX lost no time in making contact. It was thought best to have the negotiations opened by the Bishop. He went to Philadelphia, located Biddle, and called on him in his laboratory. His name, his position in society, made the door to the scientist's office open rather easily, in spite of the fact that the man was guarded, and every move he made was carefully watched by Secret Service men. The President did not want anything to happen to the maker of the serum.

The Bishop thought he knew his man.

He had an idea that honesty would be the best policy; at least sufficient honesty to convince his listener that he was honest. Without loss of a second he opened the conversation:

"Mr. Biddle, I represent five other men besides myself. When I name those five you will recognize them as being leaders in everything that is traditionally great in America. They stand for culture, education, stability, and the best things of life. We have met and given serious consideration to your discovery. We believe in you and the value of your serum. But we are not convinced that the plan of the President of the United States is the wisest and best one. To our minds, there are several objections. As I understand it, you propose to make this medicine available to every one, rich and poor, wise and ignorant, and irrespective of color. Am I right?"

"I really do not know. It may be that there will be some restrictions. That is up to Congress."

"Would it not be better to have at least an educational limit? You are giving unlimited health to the world; would it be wise to give it to all? Should it not be limited to those who can use and appreciate such a blessing?"

"You think that to those who have shall be given and those who have little shall lose their all?"

"Not exactly."

"Then what do you think?"

"Just this. The man who receives your serum will be endowed with wonderful health. He will have a great advantage over his fellows. To use that advantage to the greatest good, he should have a corresponding intelligence, be of a good family, have a background of culture. Your experiment with the criminals was all right as an experiment, but we cannot approve of it as routine practice. Do you intend to restore healthy bodies to the underworld, the insane, the mentally defective, and turn them loose on society to continue to be a burden, and an additional one because of their vigorous bodies?"

"I hoped that there would be a change in their minds."

"That is impossible. Can a leopard change his spots?"

"Perhaps not. At least, even with his spots he will be a happier leopard, if he is a healthy one."

"All right. But how about Europe? Asia? Those nations owe us millions, even billions, of dollars. Are you going to give them universal health? I feel that they are waiting for the time to come when they can crush us. If you make a public announcement of the formula, every country in Europe will start making the serum at once."

"It will be a fine thing for their sick."

"Oh! I admit that, but think of our country. Would it not be better to keep it a secret and sell them the drug? If you do not want to profit, let a corporation be formed with a large percentage of profits going to the Government. That would lower taxes and at the same time keep the secret as a national possession. Would you do that?"

"No."

"Will you sell it to us?"

"No."

"What is your price?"

"I have none."

"What do you want? Wealth? Power? Fame? Office? Name it. We are in a position to give you anything you ask for, if you go in with us."

"I do not want anything."

"One more question: Why did you want to make a serum like this?"

"I have a son."

"Have you given him the serum?"

"No. Now Bishop, I feel that we understand each other. My time is valuable. Will you excuse me?"

"Five hundred millon?"

"Go. If you do not, I will have to have you removed."

The Bishop left.

Biddle sat down and in longhand wrote a confidential report of the entire conversation, and sent it to the President. He felt it was important. So did the President.

The Bishop went back to the powerful five.

"I know a man," said the politician, "who can do this little thing for us. He takes pride in his special abilities. Of course, his price for Biddle would be high. The inventor has become a national personage. But this man would do it for a million."

"Put him to work," said the Bishop. "I hope he has better luck than I had."

That night a sleek little man, nicely dressed and carefully manicured, called by invitation to see a powerful politician. He listened to the man's story.

"A million is a lot of cash," he at last commented, "and this guy Biddle is worth it, and maybe more. It can be done, but I do not want to take all the grief. Who is back of this?"

"Do you have to know?"

"I should. I want to feel sure that they have power enough to take care of me. The matter need not be talked about. Just have a supper in a quiet place and invite me. I know most of the big guys; and then, after I have a chance to look them over, I will give you my answer and my price."

"I am not sure they would come."

"Then I am sure I won't do it."

"I'll see them."

"Better make it tonight, and get a quiet place, and a back room. How about meeting at Tony's place down on the Avenue? He is a friend of mine, and knows how to keep his mouth shut. Ten tonight, and the six of you had better be there."

Seven men sat around a small table at Tony's place that night. Six of them ate little, and talked less. The sleek little man ate and talked for the rest of them. At last he wiped his mouth.

"You want me to take this man Biddle for a ride?"

"Something like that," whispered the politician.

"How about two million?"

"We will pay it in gold," said the university

president. "No bank notes and no checks, and no publicity."

"Ok with me. But with your education you ought to know that two million in gold is a lot of metal. You better arrange to give it to me in negotiable government bonds. Suppose one of you meet me here tomorow night with them. I'll be going now. I don't want to be seen leaving here with you. I have a reputation to preserve."

He went out of the room. Ten minutes later the six men left Tony's place. On the sidewalk they were greeted by a blast of machine gun bullets. They were dead before they knew what happened to them; dead before the auto with the closed curtains was a block away.

CHAPTER XII

BIDDLE HAS A CALLER

TWO DAYS after this Biddle had a visitor. He was none other than the President of the United States. He came without notice, and so secretly that his arrival in Philadelphia did not reach the attention of the papers till he was ready to return to Washington. He asked for a private interview with the inventor.

"I received your letter," he said to the scientist. "In a way, I was not surprised. Those six men have been persistent in their efforts to block every effort of mine to have legislation passed that would in any way be of benefit to the people. They were intelligent, and felt that they had a sacred trust, and that was the preservation of special interests. They felt that in some way the general use of your serum would be injurious to the various corporations they represented. In refusing to take the serum themselves, they paid you a high compliment. They evidently wanted to go the limit in blocking any plan leading to its general use. Have you seen the papers?"

"I have not seen a paper for four days. I have been busy working out my plans for the manufacturing of the serum in bulk."

"Then you do not know what happened to the six?"

"Oh! That? Yes, I heard about it."

"Did you have anything to do with it? I know that is a hard question for you to answer, but I must know. Their antagonism to my future plans must be known, and their being killed in front of a New York speakeasy has already raised all kinds of gossip. I feel that the administration can weather the storm, but I would like to know the facts. Would you mind giving them to me?"

"You do not think I killed them!"

"No. You do not impress me as a gangster, and this was that kind of a murder. But you had every reason to fear them, and I feel sure they intended some harm to you; probably not murder but certainly kidnapping, or blackmail. As soon as I received your letter I made arrangements for your protection, but evidently it was not necessary."

"No. It was all taken care of."

"Do you know how it was done? Who did it?"

"Yes, but just within the last two hours. In fact, I just said good-bye to the source of my information about thirty minutes before you arrived. My visitor was none other than Silent Sincox. Perhaps you have heard of him. He is a rather powerful force in the various rackets of New York. He came to see me.

"Life, Mr. President, is a rather peculiar thing; millions of people acting, and interacting, and reacting on each other; millions who are swayed this way and that way by the tides of life, with no clear perception of where they are going or why they are doing what they are doing.

"Something of all this happened in regard to our six leaders. When they found they could not bribe me they decided to kill me. I suppose they had the right idea, and I am not sure that we can blame them. They were a little careful in the way they went at it; at least, they secured the services of a man who was never known to double-cross a customer and who never failed to earn the price of taking a man for a ride. He was so clever that the police so far have absolutely failed to pin a single murder on him. Of all the killers in America, they could not have selected one who was more to be trusted in a matter like that.

"But Silent Sincox did not come from Italy. He came from Shamokin, Pennsylvania, and his right name was Peter Casey. He had a sister he loved dearly, and her name was Mary. He tried to make her behave, but made a failure of it. She came to New York, changed her name to Valencia Moore, and was one of my first cases. The serum made a rather remarkable change in her morals. The case was one of those detailed in the *Purple Flash,* but the name was changed. Of course, the brother knew of the change. He knew that in some way I was the one who was responsible for it. Rather a coincidence, was it not?

"You would think that was enough. But it was not the only odd feature of this story. Silent Sincox had a friend, a boy he had known since childhood. The friend committed murder, was caught redhanded, and sentenced to life imprisonment in Farview Prison. Sincox used to go and visit him. He was dying from tuberculosis. Death was just around the corner. He was one of the convicts who received the first injection. Sincox knew about that. He was not sure of my name, but he made it his business to do something for me. He told me that his first thought was to buy me a diamond ring. That was coincidence number two.

"Now of all the killers in America these six men had to go to this man and ask him to kill a person by the name of Biddle. He knew there was more than one Biddle, so he did a little stalling and learned that the specific Biddle he was being hired to kill was the man who had reformed his sister and cured his friend. So he arranged matters, met the six men, walked out of the speakeasy ahead of them, gave the signal to his helpers, and that was all there was to it. There was no way at all to show that he was in anyway connected with the murder. He paid all the expenses, and the men who did it are now on their way to Italy in a private seaplane.

"But he felt that I ought to know about it. If some men wanted to kill me, there might be others. He wanted me to be on my guard. So he called on me and told me the story. He will never kill another man."

"How do you know?"

"I gave him a dose of serum just before he left."

CHAPTER XIII

THE PRESIDENT'S MESSAGE

THE SENATE CHAMBER was filled with Senators and Representatives. The visitor's galleries were jammed with the aristrocracy of America, and ambassadors and consuls from foreign lands. The pressboxes were filled to overflowing. The President was going to personally open the special session of Congress and read his message.

The Chamber rocked with applause as he walked in followed by his Cabinet and governors from over three-quarters of the States. When the applause died away to silence he began to read:

"To the Senators and Representatives of the Congress of the United States:

"I have asked you to meet in Special Session to consider a matter of vital importance to the interests and welfare of every citizen of this country.

"At a time when the economic foundations of our country are being shaken, when the deficit is growing, and in spite of all our efforts to balance the budget, the nation is rapidly falling into bankruptcy and no system of taxation appears possible, new hope is given us by a scientific discovery that may be of such value that it will revive our entire economy and make us again a prosperous and happy people.

"I refer, as you probably know, to the discovery of a serum by a scientist named Biddle. This serum has been given to five persons in New York City, to over fourteen hundred convicts in Farview Prison, Ohio, and lastly to over one hundred of the leading officials of this country including your President and Vice President.

"In every case, the giving of the serum has been attended with changes so decisive, so far reaching in the healing of disease and the recovery of the patient, that the medical experts feel that a new force has been isolated which will revolutionize the life of the human race.

"For several decades, the commonwealths of our country have been increasingly burdened with the care of the abnormal. The care of the insane, the mentally deficient, the epileptic, the criminal, the psychopathic personalities, has become one of the main costs of our national life.

"In addition, there has been an increasing demand that the state or nation care for the tubercular, the cancer cases, and other forms of incurable disease. Add to all this the hospitalization of our ex-service men, and the entire country is loaded to the saturation point simply with discharging its responsibility to its sick and disabled citizens.

"Crime also adds to the cost of government. Remove crime and you lessen the work of our Judiciary to a minus point, and also empty our prisons.

"The general use of the Biddle Serum promises all this and more to our nation. He has offered to give it as a gift to the country, if we can assure him that it will be wisely and properly used. He feels that its use should be available to everyone in this country, irrespective of their race, wealth, or social position.

"I have, therefore, prepared a law to be known as the *Serum Bill*. I am asking you to pass this law with such amendments as you see fit. If you can assure Mr. Biddle that the main features of the law, as we have framed it, will be preserved, he has promised to address you at once and give to the representatives of the medical profession who have met with us at my invitation the formula of his serum, full directions as to its use, and his opinion as to just what benefits the country will derive from his gift."

His message delivered, the President turned and sat down. Instead of applause, there was a buzz of conversation. The Vice President rapped for order, and said:

"I am going to call on Senator Goresome of Montana."

Down the crowded center aisle walked a little

dog leading a man. The sight was a familiar one. For years, the blind Senator had been lead by his faithful dog. Reaching the rostrum, the dog sat down and looked up at his master and friend. The man turned, bent over, and patted the animal on the head. The dog wagged his tail.

"My friends," began the Montana Senator. "We have all received printed copies of the legislation called the Serum Bill which the President asks us to consider, and if we see fit, make a law. We have read the bill, and approve of it. I have been in conference with the leaders of both Republican and Democratic parties, and they assure me that action will be taken as rapidly as is consistent with the rules of our respective bodies. Mr. Biddle need have no doubt as to our intentions in this matter. Both the House and Senate pledge themselves to support this legislation.

"Now I wish to say something that is purely personal. I was born blind. For the last twelve years my little dog has lead me through the dangers of this world, and has lead me safely. We have become inseparable friends. I think that, if he discovered that he was no longer a necessity in my life, he would die of grief. Some weeks ago, I received an injection of the Biddle Serum. I recovered my sight, and now have perfect vision. It may have been a coincidence, but I feel that the serum gave me something I was sure I could never have. But in gaining my sight I saw that I might cause my little friend much suffering. He is growing old, and will soon die. For the little while he lives, I am going to pretend I am still blind, just to make a little dog happy.

"Mr. Biddle, a man who was once blind but who can now see wishes to thank you for his sight. The world he now sees appears to be a very beautiful one. When I realize that the same gift I received can become the heritage of every blind person in the United States, I am filled with awe and wonder. Sir, you are but a human being, but in your invention of this serum, you have been inspired by a Power that is divine.

"In the future, you will receive due praise for your work. Your name will go down in the history of the nation as one of its greatest benefactors. But I cannot wait for the future. I wish to take this opportunity of voicing the thought of a nation that has not yet awakened to the gift you have given them. In the name of every man, woman, and child, every one who is sick or afflicted, I thank you. If, at any future time, a grateful nation can do anything for you, Mr. Biddle, all you have to do is to come to this Chamber and ask it for help. Again, a blind man who can see thanks you for the blessing of that sight."

He turned to walk back to his seat, the little dog leading him. There may have been an uneasy murmur when the President finished his message, but now there was wild applause. The legislators, the audience, the Press, rose and gave the greatest personal tribute to an individual, that the Senate Chamber had ever seen. Goresome and his little dog and his simple speech had touched the human heart more than any flight of oratory could ever have done. The audience was cheering Biddle, the inventor of the Serum, but they were also adding their tribute to the great leader who could, in his moment of happiness, think of the happiness of his little dog.

Biddle stood up and bowed in response to the insistant clamor of the cheering throng. He went over to Goresome and took his hand. Just a handshake, and not a word from either of them.

CHAPTER XIV

BIDDLE EXPLAINS

AN HOUR LATER, the scientist met twelve physicians in the President's office at the White House. The President was there, a stenographer, and one representative of the Press.

The physicians had been carefully selected by the American Medical Association. Each was a specialist, and one was, in addition to being a physician, a noted chemist. After introductions, Biddle began his explanation of the Serum. He talked at length concerning the one-celled animal; showed how man was simply a collection of such cells. He called their attention to the fact that under favorable circumstances the isolated cell could live indefinitely, whereas, in large masses, as in the body of a man, they rapidly died, could not reproduce, starved from lack of proper nourishment, and ultimately produced such a poisoning of the system that the entire mass died.

He explained that his thought, years ago, had been to improve the circulation in such a way that the individual cell would live longer. Later, he found that within the cell was a mass of energy capable of activating life indefinitely, provided it could be liberated. He was not sure what this energy was. It might be some form of radiant vibration; it might be energy obtained from the splitting of the hydrogen atom. He had worked for some years on the problem of the release of this energy, and had finally solved it. Even with the solution, he was very much in the dark. He simply knew that the injection of a certain serum, or solution of chemicals, gave an extra function to the individual cell, and enabled it to release this energy just as well when it was in combination with millions of other cells of the human body as it could when it was isolated and detached from all other cells.

Even here he was in doubt as to whether he was simply restoring a lost power to the cell or giving it a new power.

He had experimented with this solution on many forms of multi-cellular life. In all instances, the effect was the same. It made a sick plant or animal well. Five years ago, he had started experimenting with sick mammals, and had cured various diseases. His work with the higher apes had been most interesting. At last, he had felt justified in beginning his work with the human animal. The results here had been identical with those he had seen in the lower types of animal life.

It was more and more clear to him, he explained, that all conduct that was selfish and antisocial was simply the result of sickness. He hoped that future work with the serum would make this thought a definite scientific fact. If it were true, then all sin and evil in the world could be wiped out; and man, following the Golden Rule, would leap upward toward the stars.

In his work with animals, he felt that he had been able to prolong life. That would have to be considered. At present, all that could be said was that the expectancy of life would be increased. How much would be added to the span of human existence would have to be determined by years of observation. The question of a second dose would also have to be experimented with. Personally, he felt that the maximum result would be obtained from one dose of ten cubic centimeters.

He hoped that there would be an improvement in the intelligence of the nation. He was sure there would be some advance. Certain of the convicts had shown a remarkable increase in their intelligence quotient. That also would have to be studied.

But even if nothing more resulted than the improvement of the physical health of the nation, it would be worth while. He advised that the serum be made in at least a dozen laboratories and distributed free to every reputable physician. He understood that the Serum Bill would provide for pensioning the medical profession in return for their services. They would need some pension because, when the entire population was treated, there would be little or no work for either the physician or surgeon, except in accident cases. Even in severe accidents, a dose of the serum would perhaps cure without an operation.

He ended by giving the the composition of the serum, and the manner of its preparation. It was not a true serum, but rather a water solution of certain well known chemicals. He had called it a serum because that name was best understood by the laity. When he finished he asked the chemist if he understood and would be able to make it.

"Understand? Make it?" asked the chemist. "Why it is so simple that anyone could follow the directions and make it. It is too simple. I wonder why no one thought of it before?"

"Columbus and the egg," remarked the President. "And now, Gentlemen, have any of you any questions to ask Mr. Biddle? He is very anxious to leave the city."

"How about the diet?" asked one of the doctors.

"Anything at all will do, but the person will eat less and less food and drink more and more water.

He may use the hydrogen atom in the water. I am not sure."

"I think," said the President of the A. M. A., "that I have never met a man who knew more about a thing and was less sure of that knowledge. At the same time, it is not necessary to know how the drug works so long as we are sure of the fact that it does. I feel that Mr. Biddle has done his share. It is now our duty, as members of the greatest, most sacrificing profession in the world, to begin the work that will ultimately make us all hunt for another job. You are not sure, Mr. Biddle, how much life will be prolonged?"

"I cannot answer that. Certainly some years."

"Do you think there is a chance that after a person lives a long time, we may gain the impression that he cannot die?"

"I do not know."

"Have any of the animals you have experimented with died?"

"None of them have died a natural death. Of course, I killed a number of them for microscopic study."

"Have you considered the great increase in population, if the span of life is greatly prolonged."

"Yes, but I do not think we need worry about it. Wealth will greatly increase. Life will be easier, happier. The healthy man will find new methods of socialization. In addition to all this, there will be a decrease in the birth rate."

"What makes you think so?"

"I do not know. I just feel so. Perhaps man will be wiser."

"You evidently do not want to discuss this point. Why not?"

"Because I know so little about it."

"Have you anything to tell us? To advise us?"

"Yes. I would first concentrate on the abnormals—those who are definite charges on the State. Empty the hospitals, and then see to it that every citizen of the United States receives his dose. You will have to be careful of the criminal class. They will probably try to escape. There is one thing I think that the medical profession should go on record as in favor of. In regard to the prisoners, we should feel that every so-called bad man and woman was a sick man and woman. Once he has recovered from the sickness, he should be given his liberty. You know my argument. The legal profession, the penologists must accept it. In fact, I had it written into the Serum Law, but you must educate the public to the point where they will be willing to follow out that provision."

With that, he prepared to leave the room. He went into the President's private office for a last word.

"I forgot to ask you, but perhaps it was not necessary. How is your throat? The cancer?"

"Cured! At least, that is what my specialists tell me."

"Good. That is fine."

Just then one of the private secretaries came into the office:

"The British Ambassador is here. He is demanding an interview with the President and Mr. Biddle."

"You know what he wants, Biddle?" asked the President.

"Certainly. He wants the formula so he can send it over to his country. He is just the first to ask for it. In the next twenty-four hours, the world will be knocking at your door."

"I have been afraid of that. How would it be to effect a compromise? Tell them they can have the secret, if they promise to disarm and sign a treaty of everlasting peace."

Biddle smiled; it was a rather timid, frightened smile.

"I do not think that will be necessary. I think we should tell them how to make it, and advise them to give it to their entire population. If the serum works the way I think it will, there will never be any more wars, treaties or no treaties. After all, war is simply insanity and a form of sickness. The serum ought to help. I believe it will. Of course, it is a big idea, Mr. President, and it is so big I am a little afraid of it; but I would advise you to talk frankly with the various ambassadors, and give them the formula without restrictions. And now, I must be going."

"Won't you stay for supper? I would like to give some of my friends a chance to meet you."

"No. My work here is over. I have a son. I want to go and see him."

CHAPTER XV

THE SCHOOL FOR UNUSUAL CHILDREN

THE Mary Gregory School for Unusual Children was one of the first of its kind in America. In the past, the super-rich had built libraries, endowed museums, financed foundations for the eradication of disease, and even built monuments to their family fame in the form of wide roads across an entire state.

But Mary Gregory, left more millions by her family than she or any other woman would know what to do with, built a school to care for fifteen hundred unusual children; and after it was built and completely furnished, she employed the best personnel in the country to go there and work. She also set aside an endowment sufficient to provide a thousand dollars income for each child per year. Then and only then she gave the entire school to the State of Maine. When she was criticised for giving it to Maine rather than New York, she simply smiled and said she felt that the children of Maine needed it.

At the head of the School she placed a man who for years had worked with the abnormal child. For twenty years he had studied them, cared for them, laughed and cried with them, and tried to make them happy. He was a great man who in his simplicity believed that in another twenty years of study he would begin to understand how to care for the unusual child.

Dr. Bonchields motto for the entire school was "happiness first." He believed that if the children were happy, the other essentials of life could be easily supplied them; provided, of course, there were money and intelligence.

Slowly, fifteen hundred children were admitted to this school. They were all mentally deficient, of all grades from the lowest idiot to the highest moron. But each child, irrespective of his intelligence quotient, was to be given an opportunity to advance to the limit of his ability. They were to be given academic education, occupational therapy, moral instruction, athletic diversion, and emotional outlet.

When Biddle left Washington, he went directly to this school. Here he met by appointment Mary Gregory and Dr. Bonchields. Both of them knew him as he made occasional visits to the school. Mary

Gregory was growing old, but was still alert mentally.

"It appears," she said as she greeted Biddle, "that you have become a personage of international renown."

The scientist smiled:

"It seems that way, and that was the last thing I wanted; but certain things had to be done, and in doing them, people had to find out who I was. Now that it is all over, I want nothing more than to sink back into obscurity. I have a little work to do here, and then I intend to go to Canada. I have a country place up there that I believe is safe from reporters."

"Up here in Maine," interrupted Dr. Bonchields, "we are very much in the backwaters of life. Of course, we read the newspapers; Miss Gregory and I have been talking about it, trying to decide what it all means. Is it your thought that the serum will actually change our civilization? Or is that just the dream of the newspapers?"

"I do not believe that anyone knows just what it will do," was the scientist's serious reply. "We are too close to it. I feel that it will take twenty-five years at least before the final results can be analyzed. But there is no doubt that it will improve the health of the nation, lower the tax rate and, I hope, increase the happiness of the individual."

Mary Gregory sighed:

"We received your letter, and have given it serious thought. Of course we are going to help you give our children the serum. It is impossible for us to refuse; but we feel that we know more about these children than you do, and we feel that we should warn you not to be overconfident with the results. You explain how we look at it, Doctor Bonchields."

"It seems to us," said the Doctor, taking up the thread of the conversation, "that you should realize that mental deficiency is not a disease but a condition; not a unity, but a scrapbasket. It arises from many causes. Some cases are hereditary, but feeble-mindedness can occur as a symptom of a number of other diseases and surgical conditions. In many instances, the brain is so damaged that the intelligence is completely destroyed. We feel that there may be an improvement in the general health of the children following the injection of your serum, but there will not be any noticeable change in their deficiency. They will remain feeble-minded."

"You may be right," admitted the scientist. "You certainly know a great deal more about it than I do. Mental defect was something I could not experiment with in the lower forms of life. Some of the convicts were rather low, but there were not enough of them to make any definite conclusion possible. All we can do is to give the serum and wait thirty days. I know that the maximum results will be reached in that time. I feel sure your own physicians will be able to do the work. There has been so much notoriety that I hesitated asking you to secure additional help. Of course, there was another reason."

"You mean the boy?" asked Mary Gregory.

"Yes. You see I have been considerably worried about him. The entire work was done with him in mind. I have tried to keep him in the background as much as possible. Now that I can be a little selfish and devote some time to my personal problems, I do not want the matter a subject of world gossip. How is the boy?"

"As well as can be expected. You know how those Mongolian cases are, low vitality, poor resistance to infection, always getting scratches and colds."

"You have no idea of the cause of Mongolianism?"

"No. Nothing new. It just happens."

Biddle stood up, placed a suitcase on the desk and opened it:

"I brought the serum along with me. Some of my own make; I wanted to be sure of it. If you are ready, suppose you call in the staff, explain matters to them and start with the injections."

"May I watch?" asked Mary Gregory.

"Certainly. You should be very much interested."

"I am. Fifteen million dollars worth. You realize what this will do to the School if it is successful? I will have to find some other use for it.

Of course, some of the children will have to be cared for anyway; they have no families. But if these children are given normal minds by your serum, the Mary Gregory School for Unusual Children will be simply a historical memory."

"And I," added Dr. Bonchields, "will be a man without a job."

"I will take care of you," said Mary Gregory, "if you will let me do it. Are you going to give us the serum, Mr. Biddle?"

"If you want me to. I thought we might as well give it to you and the staff so they can observe my exact technique."

"Do you want to take care of your little boy yourself?"

"No. I have rather definite plans for him. I want you to give all your patients the serum. Then wait thirty days. If, at the end of that time, you feel that it is curative, if you are pleased with the results, then give the regular dose to my boy. I am going up to Canada to rest and think. In sixty days, I will be back for the boy. I am thinking of a trip to Europe with him. If he is well, he will enjoy that. How old is he now, Doctor?"

"Nearly twelve."

"Just right to be a dandy companion on a walking trip through the Black Forest. Let's get started. You know my plan. Just wait thirty days, and then, if the other little boys and girls are helped as much as I hope they will be, give him his serum."

"Why not give it now, Mr. Biddle?" asked the Doctor.

"Because he is my son. I have to be sure. All this work was done to restore him to normal mental health. If I give it to him and there are no results, life will not mean very much to me. I promised his mother before she died that I would try to help him. There must be no failure. I must be sure. I will be able to pass the sixty days very nicely. I have a lot to work over in my mind. I know you people, and I trust you to make a correct decision."

"Will you give us your address?" asked the Doctor.

"No. I am giving that to no one. But I will be back in exactly thirty days after you give the boy his injection, sixty days from today; and now, Miss Gregory, will you let me give you the medicine?"

Sixty days later, the scientist walked, unannounced, into Dr. Bonchield's office.

"Well, Doctor, how are the children?" he asked.

The specialist looked up:

"Oh! It is you, Mr. Biddle. The children? Why, they are all well. In fact, the children are very well."

"Did the serum work?"

"Something did. Our boys and girls are normal, physically and mentally. The lame are walking, the blind seeing, the dumb talking. The idiots are learning to read and write. You never saw a healthier, happier, more intelligent lot of young people."

"That's fine. Hurry and get the boy ready. I want to go right back to Quebec, and take the next boat for France."

"Your boy? Oh! I forgot. You see, we did not know where you were, so there was nothing to do; no way to let you know."

"Didn't the serum help him?"

"He never received it. We had arranged to give it on the thirtieth day according to your orders. The night before, he went into a coma and, in a few minutes, he was gone. I saw him as soon as I could, but it was too late."

"Do you mean he is dead?" asked the puzzled scientist.

"Yes. I am terribly sorry."

"And you did not give him the serum?"

"No. You see, he was dead before I could get to him."

"I wish you had given it to him anyway."

"But I didn't know—you surely do not mean that the drug brings the dead back to life—not that, Mr. Biddle? Surely, not that?"

"I don't know. Perhaps it would have done no good."

"I am sorry."

"That is all right. But I wish you would have given it to him anyway, even if he was dead, even though it would not have helped him. Perhaps in some way he would have known about it; known that I had not forgotten him, known that I wanted him to have his chance, like the rest of the children. Perhaps his mother can explain it to him."

"Will you stay awhile with us? See the children?"

"No," replied Biddle. "I'll be going, back to my place in Canada. You see, I have a lot of things to think about, now."

CHAPTER XVI

Life Is Different

THE BIDDLE SERUM BILL, passed by Congress in record time, provided that every man, woman, and child in the United States should receive, free of charge, one dose of the serum. Where possible to do so, preference should be given to the sick and aged, and the little children. After that, everyone should be cared for.

It was anticipated that there would be resistance from the antivivisectionists and certain religious organizations. This opposition was provided for in the bill. No one had to take the serum, but they could not refuse and continue their residence in the United States. It was believed that the greatest benefit could not be derived from the drug, if a residue of the population remained capable of contracting disease, becoming insane, or remaining social menaces.

There was, therefore, an exodus of conscientious objectors from the States. Most of these were good citizens, but poor logicians. In addition, a large number of the underworld made every effort to escape the effect of the purifying drug. They fared rather well once across the Mexican border, but those who tried the Canadian route fared badly. Once caught and identified, they were injected with the Biddle Serum and sent back to the States, better men, in spite of themselves. For Canada, in close spiritual sympathy with the United States, had not neglected to avail herself of this new medical gift.

The actual giving of the serum was done by the members of the medical profession. As rapidly as they were supplied with the serum, the one hundred and eighty thousand physicians and surgeons in the country started their campaign. Once it was made universally available, the demand for the drug increased daily. Long lines of rich and poor stood in front of the office of every physician. Not only the sick, but also the well; not only the miserable, but also those fairly happy who wished to stay happy. Children brought their aged parents; parents brought their little children. No longer the question, "would it work?" was asked, but the questions, "how soon?" and "for how long?"

To the tens and hundreds of thousands of hopeless cases in hospitals, asylums, and prisons, the future that opened was such a startling change that there was, of necessity, a rather difficult period of readjustment. Those who had been insane for years recovered perfect health and sanity only to find their families dead, scattered, or lost. Men discharged from prison after years of servitude found their wives remarried and their children almost strangers to them. But these were minor incidents; fortunately, these rejuvenates re-entered a friendly, kindly world, where the question was, "how can I help you?" rather than "how much can you pay for my services?"

For the people of the United States were growing richer and happier every day. They were free from the need of supporting the sick, the indigent, the crippled, abnormal, epileptic, insane, criminal, and psychopathic. There was neither drunkenness nor drug addiction. The courts closed for lack of work, the police force of every city was decimated. Clear-eyed, steady-handed, free from sickness, the laborer was able to perform more work and was willing to do it.

There had always been enough wealth in the United States. Now with the political leaders taking every opportunity to secure an equal distribution of the necessities of life to every one, poverty ceased to exist. It cost less to live. There was a gradual decrease in food consumption. Hunger became unknown. Work became joyous, amusements pleasurable, and sleep a pleasant pastime.

While large masses of industries ceased to exist, those who were thrown out of work had no difficulty in finding other fields of activity.

The working day shortened. The dollar was

more easily earned, and constantly increased in buying value. Everyone had something to do, received a living wage for doing it, and had lots of time for recreation.

Before the end of eighteen months, the President was able to announce that over ninety-nine percent of the populace had been injected. Then began a concerted drive to force the remaining one percent to fall into line and receive their serum. The work now was considerably slower, but at the end of the second year it was thought that everyone in the United States had been protected against disease.

The Biddle Serum Act provided for a Committee of Scientists who were to make constant observations on the efficacy of the new drug, and from time to time report to the President of the United States and his Cabinet concerning the changes resulting in the social, economic, and hygienic life of the people. It was provided in the act that the first report be made one year after the serum had been given to everyone. Thus the first report was made three years following the giving of the first serum following the passage of the Act.

Biddle was supposed to be a member of this committee, but Biddle had disappeared. No one had the remotest idea where he was. Certain questions would have been asked him had it been possible to do so. The thinkers of the nation were beginning to wonder. Other factors were forcing their way into the mental life of the nation, results of the serum that no one had foreseen clearly during the months when the nation had become free from disease. These problems had to be faced.

In the first place, the death rate had dropped to a vanishing point. Except in cases of destructive accident, people had ceased to die. The senile had rejuvenated to a healthy middle-age, the young appeared to grow no older, and the infants and adolescents simply continued to make the normal growth for their age. But no one died.

This in itself was not a cause for instant alarm. It was considered that finally the effect of the serum would wear out, and that death again would appear as a friendly enemy of the human race. Perhaps old age could be deferred by repeated doses of the serum, but eventually the human organism would wear out and man would die; perhaps of no special disease, but simply from a weariness of life.

But the thing that was startling and a little difficult to explain was the fact that the birth rate was as rapidly diminishing as the death rate. For a while after the giving of the serum, babies had been born, but as the months passed there were fewer of them and from the thirty-third to the thirty-sixth month of the experiment there was not a single birth reported in the entire United States. It was noticed that, physiologically, women were no longer slaves to the Moon. There were still lots of little children, growing up; beautiful little bronzed darlings, learning to walk and talk and do things; but there were no more babies.

What did it mean? Was the cessation of death to be compensated for by the cessation of new life? Had Biddle known this?

The third factor that was causing interest was the increasing efforts of the human race to entertain itself. The long hours of leisure had to be filled in some way. Healthy, vigorous, active, men refused to become idlers simply because they were not driven to effort by the spur of necessity. The dominance of production by machine power was beginning to pall. Mankind began to use their hands.

Social life become fuller and physically richer. With the increase of health and wealth and leisure, there came greater opportunities for marriage. It was no longer necessary to wait till a man was thirty or more for him to marry. Fewer women worked, and more devoted themselves to the cultivation of happiness. A life free of illness and the tedium of pregnancy and child care made marriage an entirely different factor in the life of the human race from what it had been in the pre-serum years. One philosopher said that all of its joys had been simplified and elaborated, and all of its sorrows and burdens minimized to the point of disappearance. It appeared that the human race was experiencing the co-relation and contacts of angels rather than the mere union of animals.

All this should have gone far to prolong the individual marriage, and cause divorce to disappear as a social process. To the astonishment of the students of human behavior, this was not the case. The percentage of divorce increased in direct proportion to the decrease in the death rate and the cessation of childbirth. Everybody was happy, everybody was married and were happy in their marriages, and nearly everyone divorced their mates and tried again to make a more favorable and happier union. It really did not make much difference to a woman who her husband was so long as she had one. All men were rather alike—all healthy, industrious, vigorous, and happily kind. All women were beautiful, intelligent, and true to their husbands of the month. Everybody acted in a gentlemanly and ladylike manner, but they just did not seem to be able to live together for any length of time.

And the reason was not hard to find. The physical relation constituted marriage, but the family had disappeared. Husband and wife remained as ever, but children had vanished. In married life, there was no cementing force.

CHAPTER XVII

HIRAM SMITH TAKES A TRIP

THE PURPLE FLASH, more than any other newspaper, had profited by the changing social conditions. From the first, under the insistant urging of its secret owner, Hiram Smith, the one-time Wolf of Wall Street, it had been the leading proponent of the necessity of the world rapidly adjusting to the new order of life.

As a tabloid, it had ceased to exist. The pabulum on which the tabloid publications fed, which made possible the interest, fleeting and infantile, of the adenoid moron, was now a thing of the past. Gone were the days of murder, scandal, and disclosures of gross immorality. These ceased to exist with all other diseases. Of all publishers, Smith was the first to see the handwriting on the wall, and the need for a radical change. His daily was now called the *Rosy Dawn*, a name strikingly symbolic and suggestive of the new era. It now was a paper for the intelligentsia, the editorials of which appealed only to the best interests of the race.

Smith saw, with ever-increasing interest and a growing concern, the changes in the emotional life of the country. Most people simply felt the increasing comfort and happiness, and cared little for the profound biological changes back of them. Smith was interested. He was not sure that all was well with the new cultural pattern of life.

He wanted to talk things over with Biddle. But Biddle was gone. Smith thought about it for one day, talked it over with his wife for another day, and then issued his order. It was a short command of three syllables:

FIND BIDDLE!!

As that order had back of it over a hundred million dollars, there could be no doubt that Hiram Smith was in earnest.

Six months and five millions were spent in the search, and there was nothing to show for it except failure. It was Sally Fanning who, with her womanly intuition, supplied the necessary clue. She reminded Smith that at one time Biddle had used the name of Harry Ackerman. Was it possible that he had reverted to the use of that name? So Smith issued another order:

FIND HARRY ACKERMAN!!

And that order brought results.

Hiram took the night plane to Quebec, and the first boat out of there for Chicoutimi. He had to go down the St. Lawrence river and up the Saguenay river. On the little steamer chugged, between high, precipitous cliffs of Laurentine granite, till at last, a thousand feet above them, to the left, they saw a Madonna holding in her arms the Christ Child. Made out of wood, painted white, and eighty feet high, it seemed little larger than a child from the river below.

"Go on to the next landing to the left," Smith told the Captain, "and let me off there."

"I do not think there is anyone living there now," protested the Captain. "Better go on to Chicoutimi."

"No. I know what I am doing."

So he got off at the next landing. For the next hour, the rich man toiled up the mountain path, arriving finally at the top. There he found a little stone house, with a little stone fence around it, and smoke pouring out of the chimney.

Smith knew that he had come to the end of the trail.

He knocked at the door; and, hearing no reply, opened it.

At a table, looking through a microscope, was Biddle.

"Hello, Biddle!" called Smith.

"Well! Well!" replied the astonished scientist. "How did you find me?"

"Cost me a lot of time and a lot of money, but it was time and money well spent. What are you doing here? Your place is back in the world, receiving the well-earned applause of the nation."

"I am not so sure about that. But won't you stay? Have you your baggage? I have not heard from the world for so long that I am interested; and then, besides that, I want the news from my friends. How are they—Mrs. Smith and the boy and Harry Wild and Sally and everybody?"

"You would be surprised. And you would not be asking that question, if you were back in the world. No one ever says, 'How are you feeling?' because the answer is too obvious. The nation is gloriously healthy and wealthy, and perhaps wise, though I am not so sure about that. The Missus is fine, we are still together, and the boy is almost a man, the finest lad you ever saw. Harry Wild and Sally are married, and they are still living together. I guess we hold the record for lengthy marriages. But I wanted to see you. I just had to see you."

"I am glad you are here. How is the *Purple Flash?*"

"Has the largest circulation of any paper in the world, a real money maker. I changed the name to the *Rosy Dawn,* and believe me, it is a real mental hygiene, cultural sheet. You would not know it, if you saw it."

"And you are still the Wolf of Wall Street?"

"In memory only. Wall Street has disappeared. When Congress passed the Stabilization Act, trading in stocks and bonds became a thing of the past.

It was just like trading pennies, nothing to it; it was not even good sport."

"So the financial world has changed?"

"Everything has changed. You would not know it for the same place. Come on back with me on the next steamer. You surely must be interested?"

"Yes, and no. I realize that I should be, but I am working on a new problem. You see, I have a lot of little animal friends in the next room. I guess I was always happier with unsolved problems than with solved ones. If the world is purged from disease, I feel that I should be satisfied to leave it be that way. So, I just came away and left it. I would have had too many interruptions, if I had remained."

"Of course, you had your own reasons for isolating yourself?"

"Certainly! Most hermits do. But tell me about things. What are they doing in little old New York?"

"You mean the men or the women?"

"Everybody."

"Well, they are all healthy and happy. Work about three hours a day four days a week, and the rest of the time amuse themselves in all kinds of new ways. That question of amusement would interest you. All the old-fashioned cottage industries are being revived, like weaving and metal working. Most women are doing their own sewing and housekeeping. Not much cooking; you see, people do not eat the way they did, just drink lots of water.

"Everybody is married and just as happy as they can be till they decide to get a divorce and try somebody else. It is all a perfectly lovely arrangement, and so far, there seems to be no jealousy. I have talked to lots of the divorcees, and they simply say they just want to live with somebody else, and so they do it for two or three months and then try it all over again."

"Seeking happiness?"

"No. Everybody is happy all the time. Just want a change."

"How is the death rate?"

"There isn't any. Nobody dies unless they have some kind of a terrible accident. You see, there is no disease. Tell me one thing, Biddle. How long are we going to live?"

"I do not know."

"Do you think it is going to be *life everlasting?*"

"I really do not know."

"I hope not. You see, there is not much excitement in life nowadays. For some reason, the thrill has gone out of it. It has too much precision and not enough poker. Everybody has enough to eat, enough to wear, enough to amuse themselves with, enough money to pay their simple expenses. There is nothing to worry about. In fact, some of my friends say that the young people who were just growing up when they received the serum cannot understand what we older ones mean when we say that we used to worry over the problems of life. They cannot understand what a life filled with sickness, debt, struggle, birth, and death means. Even with the adults, the memory is fast fading."

"I guess that is natural," said the inventor.

"Perhaps."

"What are the men doing with their spare time?"

"Oh! Various fads had their day. Jigsaw puzzles, and cross-word puzzles, and cross-country walking, and all that sort of thing. Lately, a good many of the men are whittling."

"What?"

"Just making things out of a piece of wood with a penknife. Did you ever see a man do that? Take a nice, soft, piece of white pine without any knots in it, and just make a lot of nice long shavings? If you want to, you can do it mechanically, without thinking. The men were making all kinds of little things: model rowboats, and napkin rings, and little wooden birds, and that sort of thing. Keeps the women busy at that."

"In what way?"

"You see, women always have been sort of clean creatures, but since they are free from disease, and family duties, and various cares, they had a lot of time on their hands; and it seemed that the healthier they became, the cleaner they wanted their homes and surroundings to be. So, every woman spends a few hours a day on the streets of New York making the town tidy. It would be real comical if it were not so serious. I bet that for every whittler there is on the sidewalks of New York there is a woman, and sometimes two, waiting with a dusting pan and brush, to sweep up the shavings when the man gets through. Sometimes they even hold a little bag so the shavings can drop right into the bag instead of on the street. Makes the man nervous, and he goes somewhere else; but wherever he goes, a woman is after him tidying up. I hear there is an exclusive club in the Nineties just for whittlers, and they brag that never a woman will enter to disturb them or their shavings."

"Well, so long as everybody is happy."

"Sure! What difference does it make? Let the chips fall where they may, I said in an editorial. What difference does it make so long as they are clean chips? But the women are certainly keeping after us men. I don't recall when they have ever kept us cleaner."

"How do the men feel about it?"

"Oh! Just about the way they always have. You see, the sexes are rather nice to each other; not like the old days when there was so much bickering. I suppose there is really very little to quarrel about, the way things are."

"Unpack your things," suggested Biddle, "and then we will take a walk. We will go down as far as the Madonna. You will be interested in that as a work of art."

Two hours later, they stood in the cold chill of the afternoon in the shadow of the giant Mother. Smith looked at the scientist.

"By the way," he suddenly asked. "How is your boy?"

"I think that he is fine."

"Did he get better? You know what I mean. You said you were working on the serum for his sake."

"Yes. I remember I said that."

"And is he well and happy?"

"Yes. I think so. I haven't seen him for some time. You see, he is with his mother."

Smith bent over, picked up a rock, and threw it over the cliff into the river, a thousand feet below. He looked at the inventor.

"You are white, man!" he exclaimed. "That's odd! You must have been staying in the house too much. But all the rest of us are brown, a golden brown, a healthy, beautiful, hazel, brown. The doctors said it was the effect of the serum. You are not that way; you are white."

Biddle smiled as he replied:

"You see, I never took the serum myself. With the wife and the boy away from me, somehow I thought I would be happier if I went without it."

"But some day you will get sick, like we used to, and die!"

"That is why I never took it. It is cold. We should go back."

CHAPTER XVIII

THE ROBOT BABIES

MARY GREGORY had nothing to do. Her School for Unusual Children was closed.

There were no more unusual children.

In fact, there were few children of any kind, and no babies.

Her restless mind, her ability as a philanthropist, and her millions, were all idle for lack of opportunity. She felt there should be something for her to do, some way in which she could benefit her nation. Deliberately seeking an opportunity for welfare, she went to New York City. There she called on Hiram Smith. Since her father's death, he had cared for the Gregory estate, and had made a good job of it. He had just come back from his trip to Canada doing a lot of hard and difficult thinking.

"I am glad to see you, Mary," he said. "I have a lot to do with the investing of your money, but it is not often you spend the time to come and see me. You look well!"

"I am well. I guess we are all well since we took the serum. I came to New York a week ago to see you, found you were out of town, and decided to visit some of my old friends till your return."

"How are they all? Happy, I suppose."

"Certainly. Everybody is happy; but I will say this: So many of them have developed the most peculiar way of spending their time. Of course, that seems to be the hardest thing to do nowadays—finding things to fill in the leisure."

"What are they doing, Mary?"

"Playing with toys, playhouses, and little sets of china, and taking care of pets. I never saw so many different kinds of animals and birds in my life, outside of a zoo. One of the girls even had a denatured skunk.

"And dolls! China, and rag, and bisque, black, white and yellow, big and little, pretty and ugly, fat dolls, dolls with spider legs, dolls with hair and without hair. Every woman is collecting dolls.

"Spending her time making dollie clothes, and giving tea parties for them. And that is not all. Some of them pretend that they are just little girls instead of big women. Found one of my friends playing on a toy piano. Waits till her husband goes to work, and then starts with one or two fingers playing:

> *Pony! Pony! Stepping high,*
> *I will ride you bye and bye.*

"And that woman can play by the hour from Mozart and Beethoven. It does not seem to affect the men the same way. One of my old college chums, however, took me down into the cellar of their home. They live in a house that actually has a cellar. She said that her husband developed the habit of spending a good deal of time down there, and at last she became so curious that she just had to go down and see what he was doing. The man had been whittling dolls out of wood, put black shoe buttons in for eyes, and made the mouth red with red ink, or it might have been his blood, she thought. He had bought pieces of silk downtown, had tried to make dresses for the dolls, and had made little beds for them to sleep in. She said that in the old days she just knows she would have cried, but, of course, nobody cries now because they are too happy. She never told him she knew what he was doing; only after that, when he went to work, she went down the cellar and played with his whittled dolls. She said that, in some way, it made her feel that she was closer to him. They were thinking of a divorce, but now, though they do not talk about the dolls in the cellar, they feel that they had better live on together for a few more months."

"So that is the way they are spending their time?"

"That is the way. I thought and thought about it, and finally I decided what to do. All this fuss over dolls, and pets, and childish pleasures, is just a substitution. They are not honest with themselves, for what they really want is something alive—real babies."

"It seems that they cannot have them," answered Smith.

"It seems that way, but perhaps they will have them sometime, and if they wait too long, they won't know how to care for them. If this condition of childless society keeps up, there will be millions of women who have never held a little baby in their arms and would not know what to do if they found one there. You see, a lot of the knowledge of infant care is transmitted by word of mouth and actual practice from the older generation of women to the younger. If we wait fifty years before a new lot of babies are born, they will suffer from lack of actual knowledge on the part of their mothers to care for them. Even the nurses won't know how. There won't be any nurses anyway, and not many doctors.

"So, I have an idea. I want you to take some of my millions and start a school for mothers. Get the best physicians and nurses you can hire to prepare lectures. Buy a broadcasting station that will reach every part of the country. Give regular lectures on the care of the child at different ages from birth to the age of six. I am sure that every woman will be glad to listen to the broadcasting of these talks, and practice the various lessons on her baby."

"But the woman will not have a baby, Mary!! That is what the whole trouble is. There aren't any babies."

"I want you to have some made!"

Hiram Smith threw up his hands in despair:

"How? Where? When? What do you mean?"

"Silly! I mean robot babies. Start your inventors to work. Fabricate babies out of rubber. Put machinery inside of them so they will take milk, and cry, and move their arms and legs. I just have the general idea, but any clever inventor will supply the details. Make babies that can be washed, and fed, and dressed, and put to sleep. Make different-sized babies so they can be exchanged when the time comes for them to grow older. Put tonsils in them to be taken out, and adenoids to make them snuffle, and intestines to give them colic. Start in and make twenty million of them as fast as you can. Sell them to the women who can pay, and give them away to the woman who cannot pay, and send the bill to my estate. Do you see my idea? Get the fathers interested in it. Have lectures for them. Have such talks as this: 'What to Do When Your Wife Is Sick and the Three Year Old Daughter Complains of the Earache.' I wish Biddle was available. There is a man who would understand what I mean."

"Biddle is up in Canada. I have just been visiting him."

"You have? Did you talk about the vanished birth rate?"

"I did."

"What did he say?"

"Not much. Something about having to pay a price for everything in life. That nothing was ever given away. I suppose he thought that the absence of death was paid for by the absence of birth, or something like that. He did not want to talk about children. Do you know about his having a boy? Told me the boy was doing well, and was with his mother."

"He said that?"

"Something like that. Do you understand it?"

"I do. That was just his way of saying they both were dead."

Hiram Smith started Mary Gregory's millions to work. He gave the new idea considerable space in the *Rosy Dawn*. The novelty spread like wildfire. Women discarded their pets and their fantastic dolls, and put in their application for a robot baby. Factories were opened, thousands of men put to work. That was an odd thing. Every invention making the robot babies possible, every minute of work done on them in the factories, was masculine. Men almost fought for the right to work in these factories.

Women were turned away in disdain. This work, said the men of the nation, was a purely masculine one.

Meantime, the series of lectures were being prepared. Here only the greatest experts were employed. Experiences were exchanged, old books read, elderly women consulted, and at last two hundred lectures were written covering every possible situation up to the age of six years. Then men and women were carefully tested for their ability to broadcast these lectures. At the end of a year, everything was ready for the start of a six-hour daily programme. By that time six million women had infant robots, and more were being fabricated at the rate of a hundred thousand a week.

And from station MAMA, the lectures went to the waiting women in America. The seven o'clock bedtime lecture was instantly popular. Listen to it:

"Good Evening, Mothers of America. This is Station MAMA broadcasting:

"Your speaker is Doctor Wilkins, the celebrated bedtime lecturer, brought to you through the courtesy of the Mary Gregory Maternity Radio College.

"Last evening, we spoke of the material necessary to give our little ones their evening bath. No doubt all students have this material assembled in the proper place. Have you tested the water with a thermometer? Never use your hands or elbows to do this. It is too dangerous. Now take the little one in your lap, and take off the dress. In doing this, be sure to support the neck with the left hand. Now the slip comes off. The band and the diaper next. I know that you have the clean night clothes in front of the fire getting warm. Never put on cold clothes after a bath. It is apt to chill the infant. Have the little one sit in the tub while you wash it with pure soap and a soft cloth. Now dry by patting. Remember that rubbing may irritate the sensitive skin. Now dress the baby for the night. Be sure to use a powder; and, if there is any nasal congestion, a bit of vaseline in each nostril, and a few drops of camphorated oil well rubbed on the chest. Now, are all the babies ready for sleep? Let's all be old-fashioned mothers for a while, and forget the newer teachings. Tonight we are going to rock the little one, and sing it a lullaby. It will not be a baby long. Some day it will be too big to rock. Let us give it a little love. That is what makes babies and plants grow. Now, all join with me in 'Sweet and Low, Sweet and Low, Wind of the Western Sea.' Soon the baby will be fast asleep. Place it carefully in its crib. See that the room is properly ventilated. And that is all till 9:00 P.M. tonight, when Mrs. Rollins will broadcast from this station on the care of the infant during the night.

"*This is Station MAMA, Doctor Wilkins speaking. This programme will be continued tomorrow evening. It is brought to you through the court-*

esy of the Mary Gregory Maternity Radio College."

Thus it was that women once again learned how to care for babies. But cleverly built as they were, they were, at their best, simply well-designed machines. They could be cared for, but they could not love. More than ever, the women of America realized that their lives were empty, and would remain empty till once again they were able to hold little children, real little children, pitiable, lovable, needful, helpless babies, in their arms.

Mary Gregory, she who had never known what it was to be a mother, recognized this more and more clearly. She told Smith so.

"You have to find out whether Biddle can and will do something to help us," she demanded. "He knows more about the serum than any other living man. He ought to know what it can do, and what it cannot do. If he will only tell us that in twenty-five, fifty, years from now, the American women can have children, we will be satisfied. It seems that we are all going to live a long time, and we can wait if there is hope during the waiting, and babies at the other end of the long years. You have to see him, and tell him how we feel. See if he cannot help us in some way. More women in America now know how to take intelligent care of babies than ever before in the history of the world. What good is that knowledge, if there are no babies? What good is living without babies? See him. If you cannot convince him of the need, let me take a number of representative women up to Canada, and state our case to him."

"I'll go," agreed Smith. "But I am afraid that he will not see this the way you see it."

"He will have to see it our way," exclaimed Mary Gregory.

CHAPTER XIX

THE WOMEN DECIDE

MARY GREGORY lead a company of women into Canada.

At the last moment, Hiram Smith refused to undertake the negotiations with Biddle, the inventor. He felt, somehow, that it was none of his business. He was not sure that he wanted to tell where the scientist had his house of refuge from the world. But after talking it over with his wife, he determined that he would throw the dice, and let Fate determine what was in store for the future of the human race. So, he told Mary Gregory where Biddle lived, and how to get there.

Biddle was accustomed to have the unexpected happen in his life, but he was genuinely surprised when twenty-one women suddenly came up to his stone home and knocked at the door. He did his best to be polite, and tried to find seats for all of his visitors. He made tea for them, and served it with some little cakes; but they had to take turns drinking the tea, because no lonely hermit ever had twenty-one teacups unless he had a mania for collecting them, and not many isolates had even twenty-one little cakes at one time.

At last, everyone had a little tea, and then the women asked Biddle to sit down and listen to the reason for their visit. Mary Gregory acted as the spokesman for the delegation.

"We represent the Federated Women's Clubs of North America," the rich woman explained. "These women stand for the best of womanhood in every walk of life. We feel that we know what the American woman thinks, how she feels, what she wants. Our requests to you come from fifty million mature women; any action we take will be satisfactory to all of our sisterhood. Now that you know who we are, may we ask you some questions?"

"You may ask them. I am not sure I can answer them."

"We understand that," said Miss Gregory. "We know that some questions may be hard, even impossible, for you to answer, but at least we know that you will tell the truth. First, how long will the serum last? Will it have to be renewed? Will future doses be as powerful? Will the individual reach maturity, and remain there indefinitely?"

"I am not sure. My opinion is that the first dose of serum will last a very long time. All that it did was to liberate power, which power is evidently capable of splitting the hydrogen atom to make more power. Consequently, it may act something like perpetual motion.

"If it acts the way I think, no one will ever have to take the second dose. But if they should take a second dose, it probably will act like the first dose. Of course, it may not. It seems that when a person once has the serum he will live for a long time, a full-grown, healthy, vigorous, adult. He could die by drowning, or by being cut in two by an accident; but unless something terrible happened to him, he would live a very long time."

"Why have the women of America become childless?"

"I am not sure. All I know is that all the animals I experimented on became sterile. Perhaps it is a provision of nature to increase the power of the serum. Perhaps there is something in the serum that acts. But I knew it to be true in the animals I experimented with, like mice. I hoped that it would not be true in the human race; that was one of the things we had to gamble on."

"Do you believe that some time, twenty-five years from now, or fifty years, that the conditions will change, and children will once again be born into the world?"

"Probably not. I have twelve mice who have had the serum for nearly five years. That is a long time for a mouse to live. They have never had any little ones."

"What is your thought in regard to the problem?"

"It looks as though it was a kind arrangement, the only way things could happen. Suppose, with the help of the serum, the average man and woman lives to be a thousand years old. Suppose that every three years each woman gave birth to a child. Gloriously healthy herself, fully realizing what the serum did for her, she would insist that her children receive the serum as soon after birth as possible. In no time at all, the world, large as it is, would be overcrowded with humanity. Now we have a population that can be cared for. It will never grow any larger, and only very slowly grow smaller."

"Do you realize what it means to the women of America to face those childless years, those barren centuries of existence?"

"Perhaps. As much as a lone man can realize a woman's feelings. But you women have everything else; health, happiness, ease, the love of your husbands, every possible comfort. You have a life that is incomparably easier than the old life ever could be. It looks as though you should be happy."

"Is there anything you can do to us that will enable us to have families?"

"Perhaps. There again I am not sure. But the principle of opposites is a very strong one in nature. We have light and darkness, strength and weakness, men and women, heat and cold. We used to have laughter and tears, happiness and sorrow, health and sickness, sweet and sour, pure living and sin. And we have serums and antiserums. After I discovered the Biddle Serum, I started to look for the antidote, or antiserum. I did not want to use it, but I wanted to see if there was such a thing."

"Did you find it?"

"I think so. At least, this is what I did. I found a mouse with cancer, and gave the serum. The cancer disappeared, and the mouse lived on; far past the usual length of life for a mouse. I became rather fond of her, and I guess she liked me a little. But she never had any babies. Two months ago, I gave her an injection of the antiserum. She produced a little family, raised them to independence, started to grow the cancer, and died. In that case, the antiserum did all that could be expected of it."

"Could you give the antiserum to the nation, like you gave the serum?"

"Yes, if it became the right thing to do."

"And it is your opinion that, if a woman received the antiserum, she would have children?"

"Yes. Of course, it would be necessary for her husband to have the antiserum also. Perhaps not. I am not sure, but I think so."

"Would you excuse us, if we talked this thing over privately?"

"Certainly. I will walk over to the Madonna.

You can find me there. It is only a few city blocks from here."

One hour later, the women walked over to where Biddle was standing in the shadow of the Madonna.

"We have decided," announced Mary Gregory. "The women of America ask you for the formula of the antiserum."

"For general distribution?"

"No. But we feel that every man and wife who really want to have a family should be allowed to make the decision. Those who wish to remain childless can do so."

"Are you sure you know what you are asking for?"

"We are."

"It cannot be," declared Biddle. "Never in the history of the human race have women been as free as they are now. They can come and go, free from the chains of a home and family. No longer slaves of the Moon, their love-life is liberated from anxiety. There is no longer sickness to fear, the death of loved ones to dread. You are happy, healthy, and able to compete in every way on equal terms with the male. Everything woman has striven for in the past you now have. Do you mean to say that you are going to give it up?—deliberately sacrifice all you have gained?"

"We want our babies!" cried the women.

"But in having them you lose your immortality. Having them, you no longer are eternal. You will become sick, diseased, crippled. Some of you will die in childbirth. Some of your children will die; others will live to become defectives, epileptics, cripples. Some of the ones who live to maturity will cause you shame; they will become insane, criminals, prostitutes. You will see children die in your arms. In the years to come, you will wish they had died while they were sweet babies. Sickness will come, suffering, sorrow. Your health will break, your husbands will leave you for fresher women. You will die with one hand on your breaking heart, and the other on the broken cross. That is what you are asking for. Do you mean to tell me that you, knowing what the old biological urge for offspring meant to womankind, want to change your glorious existence of today for that?"

"We must have our babies!" cried the women.

"You must remember what life was. A brief childhood of dolls, and then the chains that made you slaves to the Moon. A brief period as a pampered plaything to a man, and then a slow death, that you might bring a new life into the world. Sickness, invalidism, the breaking back that never lost its ache. Another child, and another, and with each child, a loss of beauty and strength. At last, freedom from the Moon, leaving you a sexless creature—miserable with flashes of heat and seconds of cold—to pass out at last, an old woman, nursed by children who dread you and grand-children who do not know that you play with them because you are in the second childhood of senility. Are you going to stand there and tell me that you want the old life back?

"I am going to give you one more chance. Here, in the shadow of the Madonna who knew what having a child meant to a woman, are you going to tell me that your sex will deliberately go back into that shadow when you can spend centuries in the sunlight of childless freedom?"

Mary Gregory stepped forward:

"Give us the formula, Sidney Biddle. We have decided. Nothing you can say will make us change our minds. You have not told us a thing we do not know. We know that we speak for our sisterhood. Give us the formula, Sidney Biddle. Give us back our babies."

Trembling, the scientist took out a notebook, and wrote slowly on a blank page. At last, he tore this page out, and handed it to the rich woman

"Here is what you are asking for. Any chemist can make it; any physician give it. Now may I ask you to leave me here? I want to be alone once more."

They all left except Mary Gregory.

"Why do you stay here in the shadow?" she asked.

"Because that Woman knows how I feel. She knows what it means to have a son die, and not be able to save him. Like her Son died, and mine."

"Why did you not take the serum, Sidney Biddle?"

"Because I did not want to live forever," he replied.

CHAPTER XX

OLD LIVES FOR NEW

BIDDLE lived alone for two more years, and then determined to go back to civilization. The first person he called on was Hiram Smith, the secret owner of the *Rosy Dawn*. The rich man was delighted to meet his friend again:

"You look a little older, a few more white hairs, but still very fit. I guess that arctic air agrees with you, Biddle."

"I guess so. Clean living and hard work are fine medicines. How are you? Not quite as brown as when I saw you last. Anything happen?"

"Slightly. That boy of ours decided to fall in love. Mighty nice girl, and we were all in favor of their marriage. The first thing we knew, after the wedding, they went and took a dose of your antiserum, so they could have a child. That just spoiled it all for the wife and me. We had been making plans to live at least for a thousand years, but that would mean that we would see our children and our grandchild grow old and die while we were still in the vigorous golden maturity of the Biddle Serum. So, what did we do but go and get some of the antiserum ourselves. Now when the grandchildren come to visit us, they will have the old-fashioned kind of grandparents, just nice, old, white-haired people who can try to relive their youth in their children's children."

"So, you sacrificed everything, not for the love of a child, but for the love of a grandchild?"

"That's it. You would think it was a sacrifice, if you had seen me with an attack of rheumatism this last winter."

Biddle laughed, a friendly, sympathetic, tearful laugh:

"Just an old fool, you always were, Smith, just an old fool. By the way. Where are my old friends Harry Wild and Sally Fanning?"

"They are married. He is back at the old news stand, and they have a little apartment close to where they both lived before you met them."

"Give me the address."

"Sure; but I do not think I would go and see them. You remember how they were the time you saw them on the lawn in front of my home? Well, when you remember them, just think of the way they were then."

"I will have to see them the way they are

now," replied Biddle. "I have to find out something."

He called at the little apartment late at night. Harry Wild answered his knock on the door:

"It's Ackerman! Sally, it's Ackerman, our old friend, and more than welcome. Come right in and sit down. Let me have your hat, Sir. This is an honor, to have you come and see us."

"It is, indeed," echoed Sally.

"And how are all the mice?" asked Biddle.

"You should see them," replied Sally. "Dozens of them, into everything, but I will say this: that the Baby is fond of them. Keeps quiet for an hour at a time when I am too busy to amuse her, just watching them play around the floor."

"So there is a baby?"

"Finest girl you ever saw," said the newsboy. "Looks just like her mother. Glad it was a girl. We would not have known what to do with a boy."

"We are telling her that so she won't think we were disappointed," explained Sally. "We are saying it now, before she knows the meaning of words, so we will be sure to say it when she learns to talk. We want her to be sure we loved her."

They insisted that he come and see the baby. They made him say that he had never seen a finer baby; and they fed him coffee and sandwiches, and made him promise he would come often to see them.

When he left, Harry went down to the front door with him.

As they stood in the doorway, Biddle looked at the little man curiously:

"You are lame, Harry," he said. "Have you hurt yourself?"

"No. But my old trouble came back. My bad leg is short again, and my back is slowly growing crooked."

"Well, well! That is too bad. But you keep on smiling?"

"Sure. I have everything to live for now. Fine wife, sweet baby, good business. Why shouldn't I be happy?"

"That is fine, Harry. Keep on smiling."

"I will, Mr. Biddle. By the way, do you know of a good remedy for asthma? Sally has had some real bad spells since the baby came, and I do wish someone knew what to do for her."

"I am sorry. I'll send her some stramonium leaves. Burn them and inhale the smoke. That will help her. Asthma is a difficult thing to cure. Well, good night, Harry, my boy. I am glad about the baby."

"Good night, Mr. Biddle, and thanks for looking us up. Send me your address. Next week, the old *Purple Flash* is going to come back on the stands, and I want to send you some of the first copies. I bet that the Wolf of Wall Street will make it a real tabloid. It ought to go big. The people are getting hungry for that kind of a paper."

It was all too much for Biddle.

He took the first train for Quebec and the first boat for his mountain home. He walked slowly up the mountain path. It was a hard climb. He was not as young as he had been. He found the house open and a fire burning in the fireplace, but no one was there.

He put down his bag and walked across the crest of the mountain to the Madonna. Under the shadow, a woman sat. As he came near, she walked over to meet him.

"Mary Gregory!" he sighed, "what are you doing here?"

"I wanted to come," she replied. "You need a woman. If you had a woman in the house with you, you might do something worth while, invent something that would be of real help to mankind."

"But I am an old man, Mary," he cried, "an old man growing older."

"I have taken the antiserum," she said. "Now I can grow old with you."

THE BONELESS HORROR

THE Emperor of Gobi sat proudly on his marble throne.

Below him, on the Steps of the First Magnitude, sat the Seven Wise Men, on whom the Emperor depended for the welfare of his realm, and the continued power of his dynasty.

And, on the other Steps of Magnitudes Two down to Seven, stood the nobles of the realm, all of them selected because of some brilliant achievement adding to the splendor of Gobi.

One after the other, the Seven Wise Men read from parchment scrolls, the record of their departments for the past month, and the Emperor praised them for all they had done. Especially did he give credit to the Royal Mathematician, the Royal Engineer, and the Royal Geographer; for these three men, separately and in unison, read of the plans they had prepared for the destruction of the Land of Mo, that great kingdom of the south, which dared to dispute with Gobi the supremacy of the world.

For the Emperor of Gobi had issued orders that

Mo not only must be conquered, but also actually destroyed; and for months the three Wise Men in charge of the Departments of Mathematics, Engineering, and Geography had studied over the problem, and now they had a plan. It was a good plan; and, at the end of it, Mo would be no more.

There was one flaw in the beauty of the plan, and that was the long time needed to accomplish it. Tunnels had to be dug under the sea, and under the great gulfs of water separating Mo from Gobi; and even though all of the slaves and all the machinery and great skill of Gobi—though all of these were put to work—still years would pass before the desired end would be accomplished.

So the face of the Emperor darkened, for he was now passing his fifty-ninth birthday; and he knew that ere thirty more years faded away, he and his Seven Wise Men and all who had helped him make Gobi great would be worm food and dust in their golden coffins, or else so old that their greatest worry would be the dragging of broken bodies through another day. He thought back over all the great men who had served the kingdom in past ages, and he saw that about them all only one fact remained certain; and that was that they lived a while and then died.

And thinking thus, his face grew hard and sad; and he chewed the end of his mustache in such a way as to make the Royal Barber tremble. Finally, he cried:

"All of your plans are folly and your thoughts foolish vain, for who of us will be here to see this ending of our enemy thirty years from now? And what comfort if a few of us live on, yet lack the mental power to glory in our triumph? Give us youth! Take away from us the weight of the years gone by, and there would be satisfaction in the perfecting of your plans. Give me youth! Take from my shoulders the weight of years, from my head the whitened hair, from my face the little wrinkles—fateful handwriting of Time, the Conqueror—and then you can destroy Mo. Which of you Seven Wise Men can make a man young?"

Silently, the Seven looked at each other, fiddling their fingers and toying nervously with their dragon rings, emblems of the immortality they believed in but lacked. The Emperor, too, had a ring like theirs, only his was carved from a single garnet, while theirs were just made of gold. The dragon swallowing his tail—the never ending, ever beginning symbol of fadeless youth—made the rings sacred to the Seven and to their Emperor.

From his throne, the ruler commanded that seven of his slaves be brought in. These he had his Chief Executioner kill in seven different ways—by the silken cord, and decapitation, and the bleeding from the wrists, the pouring of molten lead in the ear, the golden needle stuck slowly past the eyeball, the placing of a drop of poison on the tongue, and, finally, the frightful death by command, wherein the mighty Ruler need but command a man to die, and the man dies from fear of being disobedient.

And the seven dead bodies of the slaves lay stretched out on the floor of the palace; and the Emperor rose and whispered:

"I can give death, but I cannot make myself live on till I see the end of Mo. Hear me, you Seven Wise Men! Am I ruler, or am I not?"

The Seven bowed before him and assured him that he was indeed their Lord and King.

"Then attend to what I say. Meet me in three months, and at that time tell me how to prolong my life ten-fold so I can glory in the conquest of this country I hate so much. Do this, or I shall kill you Seven Wise Men, and other men will take your place and wear the dragon rings. The manner of your deaths will not be easy like the deaths of these seven slaves, but you shall be weeks in the ending of your lives. All that time you shall have due cause to reflect over your lack of intellect, in that you could not make me live on for long enough to glory in the fall of Mo. You are all wise men, and you have worked well for the Land of Gobi, but all of your wisdom will not suffice, unless you give this immortality to me."

They bowed their heads and withdrew from his presence, stepping aside so their silken robes should not touch the dead bodies of those who had died to teach them how they could go on lying.

Other slaves came and removed the carrion, and the Nobles left the great hall. At the last, only the Emperor sat there. He rang a gong. At that summons, came the High Priest, a man who knew all the wisdom of the Gods; and what he did not know, he would not admit. The Emperor permitted the Priest to sit near him.

"Tell me again, Norazus," the Emperor asked, "about the dragon whose ring I wear."

"This dragon lives far to the north of Gobi," the High Priest began. "He lives perpetually with his tail in his mouth, thus never reaching either an ending or a beginning, but going in a circle, which is thus an emblem of eternity, a symbol of immemorial, immortal life. Yet is he nothing like everlasting, for every seventh year he lays seven eggs in the sands of the desert; and, of these seven, he selects one which he swallows, hatching it out in the heat of his stomach. When it ripens, the new dragon eats the old one and emerges from his inner gut; but in his body is the soul of the old dragon, and in his head the wisdom of the ages. Thus is the life of the dragon renewed every seven years by means of a new body; but the skin of the old dragon lies dried and bloodless on the ever-shifting sands."

"A pretty tale, Norazus; but is it true?"

The two men looked at each other. Then the priest whispered:

"What if I showed you eggs of the dragon, some of the six he discards and leaves to turn to stone in the sand?"

"Eggs or stone, what boots it? How can you tell the dragon egg from the giant awk, or the dodo, or other birds my wise men prate of?"

"Some things must be taken on faith."

"What is that? A bubble for children. We are wise. I wear this dragon ring because it is the emblem of power. My father and his before him wore this ring, but we must seek elsewhere for life everlasting. The dragon may know how to renew himself, but we cannot use his power."

"Have you benefited from the daily blood of a new-born child?"

"Not much. In fact, I fear that it has harmed my appetite. The meals are not as good as they were before I took this tonic. Several times I have belched, making necessary the death of my cook. No, Norazus, let us wait till the Seven Wise Men report on their method of prolonging life. Whatever they advise, I will share it with you and with them. But we will never learn the secret of the Dragon or of the Salamander or of the Phœnix, who buildeth a fire for a new life through the burning of the old body. Not in such forms must we seek added years. Yet I must live to see the ending of Mo.

At that time, there were three great Empires in the world. Atlantis occupied all the land west of

Ireland, an island reaching far west till, from its farthermost shores, the coast of America showed as a purple haze on the horizon. From this country went emigrants to Egypt, Greece, and the other countries of the Barbarians bordering on the Great Sea.

The Empire of Mo filled in all the great waste that is now covered by the waves of the Pacific. To the west, it was separated from Asia by three hundred miles of water, but on its eastern borders it was almost in touch with Central America. It had colonies all through North and South America, but the largest of these were in Central America. Some of these colonies were commercial, others led toward the spreading of the service of the All-Good-God whom they worshipped diligently, and one, in the valley of the Colorado river, where Arizona now stands, was intended for a city of refuge if, at some future time (as the dismal priests believed), all of Mo should be destroyed.

The third great Empire was Gobi. This kingdom occupied all of Asia, at that time a lowland covered with fertile plains and dark forests. There were little rolling hills, but the Himalayas still slumbered unborn, in the womb of the earth.

Of these three countries, one, before its destruction, gave of its learning to Egypt, which in turn made the culture of Greece possible. Mo, most brilliant of all three as far as learning was concerned, died so quickly that nothing remained save a dim memory in the places where once her peoples had ruled in their might; while Gobi, shattered by a grim cataclysm, managed to live on in the desperate cold and barbarous country of Thibet. The three lands died together, but men lived on, forced by circumstance to forget all they ever knew, and learn it all over again. Gradually, man rose again in the scale of civilization, and by the time fourteen thousand years had passed, the human race had relearned perhaps half of what it knew before they had destroyed the three fairest empires the world had ever known.

At the end of three months, the great men of Gobi met again, but this time no plenteous splendor marked their gathering. Secretly, they met by night in the bowels of the earth, many feet under the Palace, in a room that only a few of each generation knew of and which none ever dared to name above a whisper. It was a room of black marble. Around the walls were nine dragons of red stone from whose eyes came a glow that lit the room. In the belly of each dragon was a seat. Thus there was a seat for the Emperor and one for each of the Seven Wise Men and one for the High Priest. On the floor sat a blond man of about thirty. His eyes were blue and his hair flaxen, and there was an unafraid look upon his face. On him there were neither bonds nor fetters.

The Chief of the Navy of Gobi began the tale of the stranger.

"O most illustrious Emperor, Representative of the Dragon in human form, Wearer of the Ring, when you commanded us to find for you the secret of longevity, if not even that of immortality, each of us went our varied ways to find the answer to your command. To me came the inspiration to search the sea between our land and Mo in the hope that among the prisoners I might capture would be a man of learning in the art and sciences of the cursed country of our enemies. In order to examine those we captured, I took in our fleet one of our learned men, and also men skilled in obtaining the truth from such persons, no matter how unwilling they are to disclose it. We cruised for some weeks and took several vessels which had sailed too far from Mo for their safety. Of the men we captured, we killed most, either as ignorant folk or else stubborn ones who died when the tormentors began to work on them. However, we were fortunate in obtaining one of their physicians, who, when he found out what we wanted, claimed the power to lengthen life. This man you see here. If his ability is equal to his boasts, he can satisfy our desires to prolong the life of your Highness."

The Emperor looked thoughtfully into the face of the young man.

After a long pause, he asked:

"Have any of you Seven Wise Men questioned him to find wherein his power to prolong life lies?"

"We have done so, Your Highness," replied the

Royal Physician, he who knew more about the healing arts than any other man in the realm. "I talked over the matter with him."

"And what opinion did you arrive at concerning his method?"

"It has all the elements of philosophical truth in it."

"But will it really work in the lengthening of life?"

"That cannot be said without a trial."

Again silence, filled with suspense, covered those in the mystic room, the sacred Hall of the Dragon.

And then the Emperor asked the young man:

"Are you a man from the land of Mo?"

"No, I come from far away Atlantis."

"How came you in a ship of Mo?"

"Years ago, as a child, I was taken prisoner from my home; and since then I have lived in Mo. They thought they saw in me astonishing aptness to be a physicker and a dealer in drugs and magical healings, so they taught me all they knew; and of all the young men in their college of medicine none knew more than I did. When I was taken by your ship, I was voyaging to a far land to heal a mighty man of his disease."

"So you have no tie of love for Mo?"

"Why should I, when they killed my family and took me from the home of my childhood."

"Would you stay with us?"

"One place is as good as another, since I cannot be a free man."

"But suppose I make you free? Give you a place at my right hand?"

"It would all depend on what was in your right hand," answered the young physician, and there was no fear in his eye as he said it. "For I have been in the presence of the King of Mo, and I have seen mighty ones sit at his right hand and die there from poisoned wine or the silken cord around the neck."

The Emperor frowned; for even so did great men die in Gobi.

Can you make me live beyond the age of common men?" he finally asked, and in his words was a great longing for years sufficient to see the ending of Mo.

"I can."

"How?"

The young man eased himself on the floor, and then spoke in answer:

"The life of the working bee is six weeks. They work that long, and then they die. Mo is full of flowers; and the bee is there, a sacred insect. For centuries, the Royal Bee-Keepers have studied the habits and manners and diseases of these bees in the Royal Hives. They know that the working bees live six weeks, but the queen bee lives for five, and sometimes six, years. All those years, she is lively and full of vigor, and does her work in the world of bees with a healthy constitution. Long years ago, this difference was seen in the relative age of the bees. The men who worked with the bees tried to lengthen the lives of the workers so that more honey could be produced, but no one was able to tell why one bee lived six weeks and another five years. Then I was told of the problem, and how the wise men had failed to solve it. I worked on the matter, and now I know why the queen lives so long. It is all a matter of the food she eats from the time she first crawls from the broken egg shell. This food, the 'queen jelly,' has in it the elements of immortality. I think, if she were protected from the younger queens, she would never die; but the time comes when she is killed, and perhaps that is best for the hive—but at least she lives a life that is nearly two hundred and fifty times as long as the life of the working bee, who eats what he can and when he can, and dies after six weeks of toil."

Thus the young man came to the end of his talking, and the Emperor replied:

"Would such food work on a man?"

"I think so."

"But how could it be made in quantities to keep a man alive? We have no bees in Gobi; and if there were, it would take large numbers of hives to make a meal for a man."

"When I studied this queen jelly, I made thereof an analysis, and found of it the various components and their amounts, and the formula for the making thereof. I can take the blood of a bull, the fat of geese, the oil of the turtle, and the flesh of certain fish; and, by a way that I know, I can make a food in abundance that will do even as the food of the hive. This food I have tried with creeping things and flying things and little mice. All thrive on the food, and their life appears to be greatly lengthened. This food I can make here in Gobi if I have a place to work and dishes of glass and of gold and all the parts of the formula brought to me. I will make the food, and this food you shall drink and eat, and nothing else. Some of the food I will flavor and serve solid, and some will seem like wine with the perfume of the vine and the poppy; and in every way, your thirst and your hunger shall be satisfied. This, only, shall you eat and drink and nothing else."

"You shall have what you need to work with!" swore the Emperor with a horrible oath; "and I shall eat and drink of the food, and so shall these Seven Wise Men, and so shall this High Priest, and so shall you. We ten will eat and drink of this food, and we shall see the ending of Mo and the destruction of our enemy. Because of this thing, you shall have great honor and shall sit at my right hand. All the people shall reverence you. I will give you land and places of beauty and women to delight your soul, and you shall be the child of my old age. The ten of us shall one day gather here in this sacred place and hear of the ending of Mo. Now, you Seven Wise Men, harken unto me, and do as I command! For even though your bellies are filled with this bee food, yet can your throats be cut as easily as ever. Give this physicker all he demands, satisfy his every desire, aid him in every way. Do this first; and, after that, use all your power for the hastening of the destruction of Mo. For life will be tiresome to me so long as they rule in splendor all over the South Seas and deny me the right to levy taxes and take tribute from them."

Thus the meeting came to an end; and all of the Seven went to worship their special Gods, for that a way had been found to prolong their Lord's life and thus permit them to live longer with their sons and their wives.

Heracles, the wise young physician from Mo, was given a place of his own with special rooms for him to work in and others for him to live and love in. All of the wealth and wisdom of Gobi went to aid him in his work. Assigned to help him were certain young men who labored for him as he commanded, but the final preparation of the food was done in secret. At the ending of the third month, the first supply of food was made and ready to feed the ten who were appointed to eat of it. In every way it was delicate, and delicious, and dainty, in its taste and smell, and in the pleasure it gave to the tongue and palate. The Emperor was pleased and sent a dozen dancing girls to Heracles as a present, and each girl bore on her body jewels that would have served as a king's ransom. Heracles put the jewels in a place he knew and the girls in his harem, and promptly forgot about both for he was engaged in a mighty work.

After that, the Emperor and the Seven Wise Men and the Priest ate all their meals together; for after he had found that the food was healthy and not in any way poison, the Emperor would at times excuse Heracles from attending at meat with the others, as he knew how hard he was working preparing food for all of them. Yet this absence from the Royal Table caused the Emperor sadness on account of the great love he bore for the young physician.

Meantime, the wealth and manpower of Gobi was working as it had never done before. To the North and West lay the Kingdom of Gobi, while to the South and East, for more miles than man could measure, was the beautiful land of Mo. Sixty million men and women of power lived in that land, besides untold slaves and common folk. Between the two lands rolled three hundred miles of ocean. Neither country could transport armies large enough to conquer the other. Thus each grew in greatness and wealth and hatred of the other. They knew of Atlantis, the third kingdom, but that land gave neither of them concern, for her ways were peaceful, and her ambitions more in the conquest of art than of other nations.

Gobi determined to destroy Mo.

Mo brooded over the ending of Gobi.

Each used all the skill and energy and determination they possessed toward the accomplishment of their purpose, and, while each had a partial idea of the plans of the other, they laughed at the impending danger because it seemed so fantastic.

The plan that Gobi was working out was simple and yet gigantic in its scope. It was nothing more nor less than to blow their enemy to pieces. Tradition and their ancient wise men whispered of large caverns under the land of Mo, huge reservoirs ten miles under the surface of the land; and these were filled with explosive and inflammable gases. It was believed the entire land of Mo rested on a thin crust of earth, and that beneath that crust were vast caves, large caverns, tremendous open spaces, filled only with threats and sullen murmurings from the hidden fires that lived silently so many miles below. Mo rested on top of a living Hell. Unconscious of their danger, the people laughed, and sang, and loved, while beneath them a scarlet doom awaited, with endless patience, the signal for its release.

This was the way the land of Mo was built, and on this fact the Seven Wise Men of Gobi built all hopes. Their plan was simple in its scope, though it would take years in its working. It was nothing more nor less than the digging of a tunnel under that three hundred miles of ocean, and then from that tunnel a dozen side tunnels, till all of the land of Mo was burrowed under, even as a mole works in a garden after worms. At the end, deep shafts were to be sunk till the fire of the Pit made it impossible to work any longer, and in these pits powder was to be put, not just pounds nor yet tons, but all of each of the the twenty-seven vast pits were to be filled with powder, and the lateral tunnels were also to be filled and even part of the tunnel under the sea.

This powder was not the kind made of saltpeter, but was of a power that was mighty and so great in its might that even the men of Gobi dreaded it. No greater punishment could be given a criminal than to be sentenced to work in the houses where it was made.

All the dirt from these tunnels had to be carried back to the mouth of the tunnel in the land of Gobi, and there it was piled in long rows. The mountains thus made are still to be seen in parts of Asia though few knew how they came there.

The finishing of this tunnel and the placing of the powder would take thirty years, but the actual exploding of the powder would be but the time of the taking of a deep breath. Even so, it would take a day for the final, distant charges to be exploded, so great was the distance to the far parts of the land.

Only a part of the destruction would be accomplished by the powder exploding. The flames from this would light the large caverns of lethal gases, and these would explode and blast holes into the very bottomless Pits of Despair. From these pits would come the fire of Hell, and what that fire would do to the hated land of Mo could hardly be guessed.

Part of this plan had reached Mo through its secret spy system; but it was so fantastic, so peculi-

THE BONELESS HORROR 209

arly impossible in its greatness, that little attention was paid to it. Besides, they knew that it would take years for Gobi to dig such tunnels under their land and under the far corners of their kingdom, and before that time had come they had a very pleasant surprise to hand to Gobi which would give the wise men of that land plenty to worry about besides spending an eternity of years digging tunnels under the sea.

For there were also wise men in Mo. Perhaps their wise men were possessed of more wisdom than the Seven Wise Men of Gobi, though at this time, fourteen thousand years after both lands died and lost their wisdom, it is hard to evaluate such a delicate matter as the intelligence of a nation. However, the end results confirmed the boast of Mo that they would win a victory over their enemies before those enemies could come to an end of their tunnel.

Now it is an interesting fact that the men of Gobi knew of the plans of Mo just as the men of Mo knew of the plans of Gobi. Each had a partial idea of how the enemy was going to attack, and each felt that the schemes were impracticable and foolish. It is not to be wondered at that the Seven Wise Men made a special report to the Emperor of Gobi, and in that report told him that Mo would try to destroy them; but that the method was an impossible one and opposed to all the known laws of nature. To be brief, Mo intended to have the laws of gravity set aside for a short period over the entire land of Gobi, with the result that the land, no longer held down by gravity or the weight of the atmosphere, would leap into the air and leave the entire kingdom miles above the ocean in an atmosphere of bitter cold where pleasure would cease and men be so occupied with fighting the winter that no time or energy would remain for the pursuit of pleasure or the softer recreations of life. The people of Gobi would have neither time nor energy for building tunnels to destroy Mo. If they remained in their former land, they would have to fight the cold. If they left it, they would have to fight the Barbarians. Meantime, the gentle folk of Mo would continue to live in pleasure and a warm place under the tropical sun.

Thus each country lived in what proved to be a fool's paradise.

Yet not all, for the Emperor of Gobi had built in the far east a special retreat and a place of refuge, and there he and his rich men and their wives went for six months every year, when the summer sun was the warmest in Mo. Many centuries before, it had been foretold that when Mo was destroyed it would be during the period of intense heat; and now for several decades the chosen few protected themselves against such a fate even though they laughingly told each other that it was impossible.

The plans of the wise men of Mo were not as fantastic as might be imagined. Even today, in our dense ignorance, there are East Indians who can suspend themselves in the air in absolute defiance of the laws of gravitation. If a man can do this now in our dark ages, why should not a field or a forest do the same in a time when men knew many things that so far we have failed to learn? At least, what really happened was this: Heracles had not come to Gobi by accident. His capture was simply a part of the plans of the conspirators of Mo. Had he not been captured on ship board, he would have come to Gobi anyway. His ability to make the life-prolonging bee jelly was just a happy coincidence, something accidental in its occurence; but at the same time such was the wisdom of this young man that had almost anything else been asked of him, he would have been able to give a satisfactory answer. He had come to Gobi to lift that unhappy country three miles into the air; his making of the bee food simply made it easier for him to carry out his plans. Now the trusted friend of the Emperor, in fact, the man who was making his royal food, he had full access to every part of the Kingdom of Gobi.

What Heracles did is easily told. How he got his results cannot even be guessed, but there is this to say: If any wise man of today duplicated his experiment, there would be no similar result, so it must be true that this man of Mo knew something that the scientists of today do not know. All that Heracles did was to set aside a room, and into that room no one came but himself. In that room, he built with his own hands a table on four legs, and the top of the table was near the floor. The legs were telescoped, so that when air was released into them from a tank where it was stored under pressure, the table slowly rose into the air till it came near the ceiling of the high room. On the top of this table, Heracles built out of sand and stone and little painted pieces of wood a replica or relief map of the Empire of Gobi. When the time came, he intended to raise the table; and even as the table rose into the air, so would the entire land of his enemies.

The plan was perfect; and yet, at the very end, a little thing destroyed the perfect consummation of it, and allowed things to end as they did.

To select this room, to secretly build the table, the tank, and the apparatus for compressing the air, and to make a perfect duplicate of the Kingdom of Gobi on top of the table, took time. Even in his moments of greatest fancied security, Heracles could not relax his caution one moment. Every piece of wood and metal had to be carried into the room under his flowing robes or at the dead of night. At times, a year passed without his being able to even enter the room, for often the Emperor insisted on trips of inspection to the far corners of the Kingdom, and on these trips he was careful to see to it that the Seven Wise Men, the Priest, and the Physician accompanied him.

Meantime, the years passed. The special food, the nourishment of queen bees—the only nutriment of Emperor and Wise Men—was working admirably in every way. The Emperor was not only retaining his original age, but also seemed to be growing younger. It was rumored that the High Priest, who had been nearly ninety at the beginning of the experiment, had become a father through the aid of one of the ladies of the Temple. There was no doubt about the rejuvenating value of the food. The Emperor at fifty-nine had ceased to visit his harem. Now, at eighty-nine, he had his trusted emissaries hunting for the fairest women in the world to help him pass away the time, which sometimes hung so heavy on his hands.

Thirty years had passed.

These years had not been idle. Thousands of men worked to destroy Mo, while one man patiently worked to destroy Gobi. Meantime, the Emperor of Mo spent more and more time in his special retreat under the mountains of Arizona. In a royal trireme, he would sail eastward till he came to the mouth of a large river, the one that is now called the Colorado. Up this he would sail to a harbor from which place the royal elephants would carry him and his escort to the mouth of a tunnel. Here he changed to litters carried on the shoulder of slaves, and for twenty-seven miles under the massive mountains they would walk on a pavement of red sandstone through a tunnel illumined by the torches of marble slaves who patiently stood in almost endless rows. The light from their torches never varied and was cold. Since then, the secret of a cold light has never been rediscovered.

At the end of the twenty-seven miles, there came an end to the tunnel, and there, in a natural crater, was built the splendid royal city. It was a small place, room for a hundred of the nobility and their servants at most, but in that little city was the wealth of the land of Mo. For seven hundred years, each Emperor had carried there his finest treasures, and left them there. Such was the place where the great men of Mo waited for the prophecy to come true. From here, every six months, they returned to Mo, glad that another year of safety had passed over them.

Yearly and half yearly, Heracles sent messages to the King's Councilors at the capital of Mo, reporting his progress and warning of the dangers that threatened the country; but little attention was given most of these warnings, while the certainty of the destruction of Gobi was fully believed and occasioned much joy.

Finally, at a meeting of the Wise Men of Gobi and the Emperor, the time for the finishing of the tunnels and the exploding of the powder was determined; and it was announced that in one year this would take place. This filled Heracles with boundless determination to finish his work and thus prevent the destruction of Mo by first hoisting Gobi into an eternity of cold and snow. Of the work he was doing, little remained unfinished. One or two more nights would see an ending of the preparation, and then Gobi would be destroyed.

But not at once.

Heracles was not content with simple destruction. The years of study, the sacrifice of a lifetime among strangers, had filled him with the determination for a deeper and more terrible vengeance than simply the freezing of his enemies. For thirty years, he had plotted this vengeance; for all those years, he had studied and planned and experimented and now he was prepared to begin a deed that would strike terror in all people. In after years, when it became known, it would place the name of Heracles, the Physician of Mo, among the names of the Great of the whole Earth.

During these thirty years, he had fed the Emperor and his Seven Wise Men and the High Priest. He had fed them and given them drink. Nothing passed their lips save what he had prepared for them. Years of wonderful health, boundless vitality, and splendid vigor, gave these men the greatest confidence in the honesty and integrity of the man who had fed them. Now Heracles, with their fate in his hands, prepared for them a future that was so different from what they had expected, that not even their wildest dreams could anticipate it.

In preparation for this fate, he held a long, secret converse with his friend, the Emperor, and warned him of the danger of the explosions they were going to make. Once the bowels of the earth were teased till they vomited fire, it was hard to tell where the trouble would end. Would it not be best to prepare the Hall of the Dragon with beds and food and all necessary luxuries, and retire there with his Wise Men before the electric spark was fired? Would it not be wise to have the wires run into the Hall of the Dragon so that the Emperor himself could have the joy of personally pressing the golden button and thus, all by himself, have the satisfaction of blowing the Hell of the Bottomless Pits into the faces of his enemies of Mo? The Emperor was delighted with the plan. He agreed to all that was suggested. He even went further and arranged for a month of entertainment in the Hall of the Dragon, consisting of feasting and amusements and loving of strange women and the delightful killing of slaves in strange and unusual ways. He gave orders that for all that month he and his Seven Wise Men and the Priest and a few of the Nobles should lie on golden couches on pads of goose feathers covered with fine velvets and silks. There, on the soft bosoms of their women, they would drink the wine and eat the bee food that their friend Heracles had prepared for them; and, when the time came, the golden button would be pressed and Mo destroyed, and when it was safe, they would go to the seashore and sail over the land of their enemies and see for themselves the deadly fate their energy and hatred had prepared for them.

Now all was to the liking of Heracles. During

THE BONELESS HORROR

the month of drunken debauch, he would work his final plans. Then, on the day before the pressing of the button, Gobi would move slowly into the air, and what cared Heracles how long the Emperor and his advisers lived, so long as they lived the life he prepared for them?

Thus, at the beginning of the debauch, Heracles changed the food. It tasted like, and had the fragrance of, the former food and wine, and it still contained large amounts of the bee jelly, but in addition there was opium added to lull their senses and allay their suspicion, and hyoscine to make their dreams more pleasantly erotic; and, finally, a secret compound made from the internal glands of actual men and women collected carefully during all these years from the bodies of slaves and criminals condemned to death.

This medicine, given in proper doses, melted the bones of those who took it, so that finally they became boneless bags of skin within which bags they lived and thought but could not move, but simply lay where they were placed till someone placed them in a different shape.

Men in their normal minds would know of the changes taking place in their bones; men walking or taking exercise would have fractures and strange changes in their shape due to the gradual weakening and bending of their long bones; but men who lay in a long debauch for a month dull with opium and pleasured with drug-dreams and fair women who were no dreams at all, would gradually weaken and become helpless without knowing what was happening to them.

This was the final revenge of Heracles. To turn these men into boneless horrors, men without skeletons, jelly fishes of humanity, helpless in their despairing terror—and they would not die! That was the crowning horror of it all—that they would live on forever, like the queen bee. In their system was food, concentrated and powerful, to keep them alive a thousand years, yet what would such a life mean to them?

And Heracles, in his joy, visioned these helpless men in the Hall of the Dragon hurled thousands of feet into the air. He saw them living in a palace, cold and cheerless, with the damp of doom at noonday turned into a freezing, living death of cold as soon as the weakened sun dropped behind the western mountains. There they would live, perhaps worshipped and cared for as Gods by a few shivering mountaineers, perhaps neglected and forgotten; but no matter what happened, they would never die. That was the beauty of it— the fact that they would keep on living. He was going to send them up, up, up, into the air, so high there would be no wolves to tear their boneless bodies and so cold that no flies would larvate in their helpless nostrils. Perhaps for a year or so he would visit them and talk over matters with them, or he might even induce the Emperor of Mo to come on an excursion and see for himself the fate that had come to those who plotted the destruction of Mo.

So, to the bee food, and the opium, and the hyoscine, was added the juice of the internal glands of thousands of criminals and slaves, and the entertainment began. The Emperor of Gobi was happy in that he had such a wise Physician and such a long life ahead of him, and such a fine ending to Mo, and such lovely women, and such a skillful High Executioner who could think of so many new and novel ways of killing men slowly. They laughed, and loved, and drank, and stupidly thrilled over the men who died in front of them for their entertainment, not once realizing that their bones were slowly being dissolved within them; for each day Heracles increased the dose of opium.

Across the Hall of the Dragon, Heracles had his seat of honor. He only, of all those in the hall, could come and go at will, for the Emperor had given command that of all who came into the hall at the onset of the month, none should leave it till the golden button was pressed—that is, none except the dead slaves and those who killed them. Heracles sat there day after day and saw his enemies weaken from the disease now known as *osteomalacia* but the servants and the queens and those concubines who were not beautiful enough to please the Emperor, yet were shapely enough to comfort the Emperor by serving as pillows for him and his Wise Men, all these servants, and concubines, and dancing girls, were spared the disease and simply lived on in a phantasmagoria of vice, thinking that the growing incapacity of the Emperor and the other great men was simply the reaction born of surfeit and drunkenness.

Then on the twenty-eighth day, when Heracles knew that all of his plans were ready, he lessened the dose of the opium and thus allowed the drugged men to come to their senses. Leaving food and wine in abundance, he left the Hall of the Dragon; and, cautioning the guards to let no one in or out, he retired to his palace, there to finish the destruction of the hated country.

When he had shut and barred and double-locked the room in his castle wherein stood the table with the map of Gobi on it, he had left everything in readiness for the debacle. The tank was full of compressed air. From it ran a tube divided finally in such a way that each of its four parts connected with the hollow of the telescopic legs. The joints of these legs had been carefully oiled with grease obtained by boiling the bodies of virgins. On the table was the finished map, perfect in every detail. A turn of the screw loosened the compressed air, the pressure of which would raise the map thirty feet into the air. As the map would rise, so would all of Gobi.

The secret of such scientific magic is now lost to mankind.

Heracles had left all in readiness when he went away.

Now he had come back.

He turned on the screw, and there was a hiss of air.

Nothing happened.

For a very little and unexpected and unheard-of event had taken place during the twenty-eight days the chamber had been tenantless. A little, hungry, mouse had wandered into the room, and for some reason had taken a fancy to the taste of the fibre tube through which the air passed. During many hours, that mouse had eaten of the tube in a great many places little holes hardly to be seen, yet large enough to prevent the tube from holding the air.

Heracles, for all his wisdom, had not been able to forsee this mouse. Now, with but two days at his command, the entire plan was ruined unless he could repair the tube. It was useless to try and make a new one. There was nothing else to do except go to work; and this he did, tirelessly, systematically, persistantly, repairing hole after hole. But even with all his ability, the tube remained weak and not fully worthy of trust. Finally, when the full pressure of air was turned into it, it still leaked, so that it was not sufficient to raise the table. Heracles spent more precious hours refilling the tank with compressed air, and then he did the only thing he could do. He took part of the map off the table to lighten the load. Thus all of the map representing what is now Southern China and Burma and the lower part of India were taken off the table and shared no part in the cataclysm that befell the rest of Gobi.

Eventually, all was ready, yet in this delay many precious hours had been wasted. Heracles stood there, swaying from tiredness, and nervous fatigue, and worry. Beneath his hand lay the screw that, turning, would destroy Gobi.

Yet he waited.

Suddenly, he heard a dull roar, and then another and another, like a distant thunder storm, and he sickened, for he knew that he had waited too long.

There being nothing else to do, he turned the screw and sent the full force of the air into the legs of the table. It worked, and up went the map of Gobi into the air; but one leg was weaker than the rest, so the table rose unevenly and there was some sliding and slithering of the earth forming the map.

Heracles and the palace he was in went up into the air slowly because all of the land under it was in upward motion. It was a slow movement and hard to realize in that part of Gobi, for all of the land for thousands of miles was going upward in perfect harmony. There was no way, in that part of the country, to detect the movement save by the gradual increase in the coldness of the air.

Heracles knew that his experiment had been a success.

Yet, from far away, there came the rolling thunder; and, with a sickening sense of failure, he knew that he had been a little late and that already Mo was sinking under the tormented waves of the Great Ocean.

Sighing, he put on the heavy furs he had prepared against this hour, and walked slowly through the deserted streets of the great city. Here and there a small house had fallen, but all of the royal palaces remained as they had been. For the most part, the people, accustomed to a semi-tropical climate, were seeking warmth in their houses. Thus the streets were deserted. On the great Physician went to the Royal Palace and on to the Hall of the Dragon. There he found the guard on duty but almost numb from cold. With pity in his heart, he bade them seek warmth if they could find it. Then he went into the inner Hall of the Dragon where he knew the Emperor of Gobi and his Seven Wise Men and his High Priest lay helpless. Perhaps with them would be a few of the queens, but of this he was in doubt.

While he had been working in almost a frenzy to repair the air tube, the Emperor and his advisers had slowly regained their normal senses. Almost dazed, it was hard for them to realize what had happened to them; but of one thing they were sure, and that was the useless state of their bodies, for a strange sense of helplessness overcame them, and all efforts to move resulted in a peculiar writhing and a sad changing of their shape, but there was no progression.

The Emperor was no fool. While unable to know what had really happened to him, he had no difficulty in determining who was at the bottom of it. Only one man in all Gobi could work such a wonder as dissolving of a man's bones in his body! He looked upward and saw that he was being supported on cushions held by his favorite fancy-woman; and, not daring to speak, he made signs with his eyes that he should be lifted up a little. She did so, but slowly, for the sudden bending of that which had been his backbone caused fearful pains to shoot through him which nearly killed him with the dreadful agony.

The woman wiped the sweat from his face, and he looked around him. There, on the divans, he saw the men who had been his counselors. They lay in odd shapes like leather bags full of thin sausage. On the face of all of them was a Hell of despair, because something had come over them, and they knew not what it was, save that they could not move and were growing cold and realized that they could not die.

One by one, the women took the gold, and the silver, and the precious gems, and fled from that accursed place. Only one remained; and she held the head of the Emperor and tried to ease him of his pain, for she was his favorite woman and was going to bear him a son.

The Emperor tried to remember what it was all about, and how he had come to this depth of trouble.

Then he recalled his bitter hate, and knew that Mo still remained undestroyed; and he breathed harshly, and his woman knew that he desired to talk. She put her pink shell near his mouth; and, with a great effort, he told her to press the golden button. This she did.

Thus Mo was destroyed by the dainty fingers of a slave woman who had no name and was simply there and faithful to the Emperor, whom all others had left, because she loved him, and was to bear him a son.

In the room it grew colder, and the woman gathered the rugs and the silken sheets, and wrapped each jelly fish of a man up as warm as she could; but the warmest things she put around the Emperor. There the nine lay, boneless and unable to die, while the breath from their nostrils congealed like steam in the frosty air.

Thus Heracles found them.

He sat down by the Emperor, and told the story of what he had done; how he had planned that his enemies should live on for centuries filled with the long life of the bee jelly and boneless because of the gland juice he had given. The Emperor heard it all, but was soundless and motionless. In his eyes was a look of hatred that only a great man can devise, and in his heart was a deep content for he knew from the rolling thunder that Mo was being destroyed.

Meantime, it grew colder.

The woman, shivering, feared for her unborn son.

* * * * *

Mo was being blown to pieces. The damage done by the thousands of tons of powder was only a small part of the harm done to that fair land. The buried gases, exploding, tore the deep rocks into a million fragments; and all over Mo, volcanoes burst into activity. Tidal waves overflowed the land; lava buried it. Sixty million people were drowned, burned, or suffocated with the poisonous fumes. A continent was destroyed, leaving scattered islands as small fragments—Borneo on one side and the Easter Islands on the other—Australia to the South was formed, arid, cheerless, a fit home for Bushmen. Some of the citizens of Mo survived on the mountain peaks hurled upward as in the Hawaiian group, but their culture, temples, wealth, and even their tradition, were hopelessly lost.

The Emperor of Mo, with his favorite wives and nobles, was feasting in their small city of refuge. The shock of the cataclysm reached them even in that far away rock-bound enclosure. They feasted on, each man and woman pretending to his neighbors at the banquet table that the sound was thunder.

The banquet passed on through the night, and the next day, a breathless messenger arrived with news that could be given only to the Emperor. This news was whispered in the royal ear as the great man sat at the head of the table. Shivering, he commanded a certain wine to be served and, in all seriousness, that a health be drunk to their beloved land of Mo. All of the great men and their lovely women drank of this wine and then sat down and died, while their servants fled in terror to press on into the desert where they died in various ways.

Fourteen thousand years later, three prospectors, typical desert rats of Arizona, prospected for gold near the Colorado river. One day, while working in a twenty-nine foot shaft, one of them drove his pick through the roof of what seemed to be an abandoned mine shaft. It was paved with square, beveled stones fastened together with cement. These stones had the appearance of great age. Descending into this shaft with torches, they followed it for twenty-eight miles and came to a buried city. Here they found many old buildings, one of which was a circular chamber with a large table of marble around which sat the dead, dried bodies of seventy-two persons, all over six feet tall, with blue eyes and white skins. Their flesh was white and firm, being preserved in some wonderful manner. On these dead bodies, was wonderful jewelry, but most of the clothing had fallen into dust. In another large room, were the dead bodies of over two hundred women who looked as though they were lovely in their day. This place, the desert rats thought, might have been a harem. Throughout the city there were peculiar trap doors and all kinds of interesting levers and mechanisms, the use of which was hard to determine.

Taking a lot of the jewelry with them, they sought civilization to secure help in the exploration of this city. When they returned, a freshet of the Colorado had covered the opening of the tunnel with sand, and they were unable to locate it.

Thus died the great land of Mo.

* * * * *

The fair country of Atlantis had no enemies. It lived only for pleasure and art. From Ireland to the shores of America it lay in the sunshine. Then one day, a continent across the globe was destroyed. A terrific shifting of balance of weight took place; large tidal waves rolled from one sea to the other; and suddenly, the continent of Atlantis was swallowed up by the waters of the Atlantic Ocean. Thus a kindly, lovable, people paid the price of the hatred between two nations they had never harmed. So perished the second of these great lands.

* * * * *

Where Gobi once ruled supreme now rule the Himalayas. These mountains, the greatest in the world, run nineteen hundred miles from east to west, and an average of ninety miles from north to south. They cover a total of one hundred and sixty thousand square miles. Of these mountains, the greatest peak, Mount Everest, reaches upward to the sky twenty-nine thousand one hundred and forty feet above the sea level. Immense sections of these mountains are inaccessible to modern man. Mount Everest remains unconquered.

Hidden in the tops of these mountains, unknown to man save by tradition, lies the ancient capital of the lost Empire of Gobi. Half-frozen Tatars, insect-ridden Lamas, barbarians of every description, remain as the sole descendants of what was once a great people. Even the memory of their former greatness has been lost in the changing struggles of fourteen thousand years. If they are asked how old these mountains are, they will reply that they have always been there. How could they know that once all this land was lowland, forest land, a pleasant country for rich folk to live in? How could they know of the physician from Mo and his magical table and map thereon?

Yet amid those mountains lies the ancient city and the Hall of the Dragon. There on their silken cushions, their beds of goosefeathers, lie the boneless Emperor and the boneless Seven Wise Men; and, though their bodies are chilled with the frost of centuries, should there come a pleasant day of springtime with blossoming almond trees and a warm, gentle shower, those frozen hearts would once again send pulsing life through those boneless sacks. Full of the jelly food of the queen bee, they can never die, at least not for a long, long, time.

On the floor in front of the Emperor lies the body of Heracles, dead of a dagger thrust by the nervous hand of the woman beloved by the Emperor. The body of the physician, frozen, decays not. Neither does the body of the beloved woman.

And frozen in her body lies the unborn Prince of Gobi, last of a royal line that dared all for their hatred of a bitter enemy.

Thus perished Gobi.

UNTO US A CHILD IS BORN

FORWORD

THE Earl of Birkenhead, in his recent book, *The World in 2030,* gives his idea of life of that time; and presents, in a most matter of fact way, his opinion of the changes which will take place in the very short space of a hundred years.

Even more remarkable than his conceptions is the fact that the words are the sober statements of a prominent scientist and sociologist. They are not uttered with the fantastic manner and pseudo-scientific language of some of our modern prophets, but rather in a dull, prosaic delivery.

The reader is forced, by the very manner in which the subject is presented, to feel that such changes in our social and economic life may take place. After all, they are not greatly different in the wonder element from the changes of the last one hundred years.

Yet, throughout the reading of this prophecy, the student of human relations is forced to feel, with a certain uneasiness, that the author has become so intent upon the marvelous that he has tended to overlook the fact that the people of 2030, in spite of every scientific gain, will still be human beings, and that, because of their being human beings, certain of their reactions will be very similar to those of their ancestors.

So, we can well ask ourselves just what these people of this new year of 2030 will be thinking, just how they will be reacting to the changes of a super-scientific era? Will the emotions be wiped out or will men and women still react to beauty, the love of life, the fear of death, and the clinging fingers of a little child?

THE STORY

JACOB HUBLER, seventh of that name and direct descendant of that Jacobus Hubelaire who had emigrated from Strassburg to Pennsylvania in 1740, had at last earned for himself a very satisfactory place in life. As Government Official, Class D, Division 7, No. 4829, Gross Number 25978432, he was now entitled to maintenance of the 5th type, which station made a man feel very comfortable.

He had earned that position by his inventions which made possible the artificial production of all food supplies in the individual home. Prior to his work in this dietary field, large laboratories in every city had produced synthetic food and meats, grown in large test tubes. The method was adequate in every way to the needs of the populace, but the manner of distribution was still antiquated. Hubler perfected a small, but complete production laboratory, not much larger than the electric refrigerators of the past century. His product, in its preparation, was entirely automatic and practically foolproof. It would generate, day by day and year by year, a complete and attractive food supply for a family of two. It not only created the food, but there was an auxiliary machine which prepared it for the table in any form desired by the consumer. All that was necessary was the selection of one of the twenty-five menus, and the pressing of the proper control button.

The inventions became very popular with the type of women who still took pride in their home life; and when he added a service unit which automatically served the meal, removed it, and washed the dishes, it was more than most women could resist. Thousands of women ceased to eat at the community restaurants, and accepted home meals as an ultra-refinement. Hubler's name became a household shibboleth. The woman who had three units in her home could serve three meals a day with no greater effort than the pressing of fifteen push buttons. It was his ability as an inventor that placed Hubler in Class D, Division 7. The promotion carried with it certain rewards. It entitled him to complete support for the rest of his life, and it gave him the right to prolong that life to the age of one hundred and fifty years, if he so desired. Most valuable of all, it gave him permission to marry.

Years before, the State, realizing the important value of recent discoveries, passed laws which made the nation, rather than the individual, the sole owner and beneficiary of all inventions especially those pertaining to the comfort of the individual, the welfare of the Commonwealth, and the prolongation of life. Thus, the age of usefulness was rapidly advanced to an average expectancy of one hundred and fifty years, but only those who, by their performances, showed that they were of real value to the nation, were allowed to live on.

Similarly, the right to marry and have one child was carefully guarded by the State. Strict laws of bio-genesis had been followed for three generations, and, as a result, the prisons and the hospitals for the abnormals had been made useless. These had been converted into nurseries and adolescent homes. Thus, a man and woman, under the most strict supervision, could marry and have one child, but only the most worthy were accorded that right.

However, if a man showed a real value to the nation, and it was determined that his child would also be of value, then he was allowed to marry, provided a suitable and scientifically proper woman could be found for his wife. No couple could have a second child till the first one had reached maturity and had been found to be normal in every way.

Hubler, at the age of sixty, was told that he could marry. He was rather thrilled at the news. During the last few years, permits had not been plentiful. With the prolongation of life and the increase of efficiency, it was found best not to have too many citizens. So for twenty years, permission to marry had been given only to the men and women of the highest type.

Thus, it was really an honor to marry. Hubler talked it all over with his first assistant, Ruth Fanning. She had worked at his elbow for twenty-five years and was nearly as old as he was. She, too, had ambitions.

"I think that it is wonderful, Mr. Hubler," she said. "You deserve the honor, if any man does. Your inventions have made women desire homes and want to spend some time in them, and what is the use of having a home without a husband and a child?"

"It is kind of you to say that, Miss Fanning," the inventor replied. "You realize that much of the work would never have been done without your help and suggestions. I am proud of the honor, but I am not at all certain that I will ever marry. Just having the right is not all. They have to find a complimentary female for me."

"Oh! You are too easily discouraged. You, no doubt, will fall into an unusual group, but there will be some women in that group; and I am sure that one of them will be glad to have you for a husband."

"I hope so," he said, rather pessimistically. As an inventor of service units for modern kitchens, he was bravery personified, but when it came to marriage—why, that was something different.

He only worked an hour a day, five days a week. Nevertheless, it was thought advisable to give him a month's vacation, during which time he was to take the various examinations and prepare for married life. On the second day of his liberty, he drove his car to the Central Marriage Testing Bureau, and, with more than a slight degree of hesitation, he entered the main office with all his credentials.

The Head of the Bureau explained the procedure to him:

"This may seem very complicated to you, but, in reality, it is simple. We examine you in every way, and correlate the results. We then change everything into a mathematical formula, and this works out your final classification. After that, all that is necessary is to find a woman with the same classification, have you meet one another, and if you desire to be husband and wife, we will allow you to marry. Of course, it takes time. Even the development of your personality—the taking of pictures and their proper study—takes several days."

"One question," asked Hubler. "After I am typed, do I have to marry the woman you select for me?"

"Not at all. We give you a list of the unmarried eligibles of your special type number. Any one of these you select will be satisfactory to us."

"And the old emotion, love, does it not enter into it? You see, I do not know. I am only asking for information; but in one of the old books I have, it speaks of men and women falling in love."

The scientist looked stern.

"That is the way it used to be. That kind of

love produced the feeble-minded, the epileptic, the dullard, and, occasionally, a genius. Under the modern method, the birth and maturity of an abnormal child is not possible. You want your child to be perfect, do you not?"

"Of course! What father would want anything else?"

"Then do not allow yourself to fall in love, as your forefathers did."

For the next week, Jacob Hubler was an interested participant in the typing of his personality and body. Since he was an inventor, every step of the process was explained to him. At last, all the results were ready for the co-ordination machine. This was the one which produced the final mathematical rating. Buttons were pressed, cogwheels whirred, automatic type clicked, and, at last, a paper came out of the lower slot. The Head of the Bureau took it and studied it very seriously, and finally said:

"Just as I thought, gentlemen; this is a new type, and I believe the one we have been anxiously looking for. It is positively new, and adds a novel group to our known dominant factors. Would you like to look at it, Mr. Hubler?"

The inventor took the white pasteboard and read:

TYPE, Q—GROUP, X—DIVISION, 35—***

"You notice that it is a three star card?" remarked the Head. "In the last fifty years, we have had the three star card occur only nine times, and no one has ever had as high a rating as 35."

"What does it mean?" asked the puzzled Hubler.

"It means that we can be certain that your child will be a philosopher, and at present the country needs one or two philosophers rather badly. Those we have are growing old and are not as inspirational as we should like them to be."

"Then I can marry and have one child?"

"No. That is the unfortunate part of it. You are a new type, and consequently there are no women of that to introduce you to."

"Then my right to marry is just a hollow mockery?"

"Yes. You are so strongly dominant that it would be absolutely wrong for you to marry into another type. Still, the matter is not at all hopeless. We are making examinations every day, and we may find your type at any time."

"How many variations are there?"

"Over seven millions."

"Then I might as well go back to work."

"No, go ahead with your month's vacation. We will make a special study of the female applicants from now on, and we may be able to find one for you. We may even shade the results a trifle and give you a break. Of course, that would be pure experiment and might result disastrously."

Thirteen days later, Jacob Hubler received orders to report at once to the Marriage Bureau. The Head of the Department was all excited. He said:

"A most unusual thing happened yesterday. We have been testing and typing a very extraordinary woman, and we suspected from the preliminary examinations that something novel would result. Her license to marry was over twenty years old, but she had never been tested. She explained that by saying that the man she wanted to marry did not have a permit, so she decided to wait for him. A month ago, he received his permit, so she decided to be typed. To our surprise, she developed the same type and group you did, the new one. The only difference is that she is a **** person, while you are a *** one. She is the only **** one we have ever had. Four stars show a wonderful mental maturity. The mating should produce the finest kind of a philosopher. We did not tell her about you. Thought it would be best to talk it over with you first. It is most unusual."

"It certainly is odd," replied the inventor. "What is her serial number?"

Government Official, Class D, Division 7, No. 4830, Gross Number, 259799987. Her name is Ruth Fanning. Ever hear of her?"

"Slightly." The inventor smiled. "That woman has been my first assistant for a number of years. I could have told you offhand, without any instrumentation, that she was a four star personality. But I never thought of marrying her."

"She is in the next room. Suppose you go in and talk matters over with her?"

Hubler was far more embarrassed than the woman who was waiting for him.

"This is a great surprise to me, Ruth," he stammered.

"It is not to me," was her calm reply. "I had an idea it would be like this."

"Are you willing to marry me?"

"Certainly! What did you think I had been waiting for all these years? I could not marry you till you had your permit and were typed, could I?"

"But how did you know we were of the same type?"

"Womanly intuition," was her smiling reply.

They told the head of the bureau that they were willing to mary. After working together, it seemed the proper and natural thing to do. He gave them the proper papers, they received the general treatment, and started life in a two-person apartment.

The Hublers returned to their work. Life was very much the same as it had been, perhaps a little more intimate, more in unison than before, but, in a large way, not much different. They were living in a two-person apartment instead of two one-person apartments, but standardization had reached the point which made all apartments very much the same, irrespective of the number of occupants. They continued to work their hour a day, five days a week, spending the other hours in the pursuit of happiness and culture. After having worked together for twenty-five years, it was hard to put into effect any new or very novel social pattern of behavior.

In the course of time, their child was born in a Government hospital. A serial number was tattooed on his back, and he was transferred to a Government nursery, for the care of the infant was felt to be one of the most important duties of the Commonwealth. What use to produce babies one hundred per cent perfect and then have everything spoiled by an untrained mother! Why entrust this most delicate period of existence to the unskilled human mother, when it could be given with perfect confidence to a perfect machine? Thus, for the first two years of the child's life, it was cared for by machinery which did everything necessary for the welfare of the young citizen, and did it in a perfect and standardized manner.

The Hublers never saw the child. It was believed that much unhappiness was caused by the surplus affection of the mother, so the law provided that in these vital years there be a complete separation of parent and child. However, reports of the growth of the child were sent by mail every month, and at the end of the first and second years, photographs were taken and sent to the Hublers. The proud parents placed these in a baby book. If they fretted over not being permitted to see their child, they did not confess it to each other; they realized the advantage of such a life to their son and were willing to make any sacrifices necessary for the future welfare of the baby.

At two years, the Hubler boy was walking, talking, and able to dress and undress himself. He had an intelligence quotient of three hundred, which meant a mental age of six years. At that time, he was taken out of the nursery kindergarten and placed in the grade school. There, all the teaching was done by machinery, standardized in every respect. Contact between the young pupils and older adults was rare. While there were periods of relaxation and play for the young students, life as a whole was rather serious.

The education was varied according to the predetermined future of the child. If a boy was to become a musician, why give him the preliminary training necessary for the development of a scientist? Thus, each child became a specialist early in life, and many valuable years of existence were saved which had been wasted a century before.

The Hubler boy advanced rapidly. At eight years, he was past the help of machine instructors. From then on, he received the personal guidance of the few remaining philosophers, for it was early found that his mind was suited for philosophy and not for very much else. At ten, he was a beautiful boy, but such a deep thinker about things which no one else had ever tried to think of before, that he was both a trial and an inspiration to his professors.

At the age of twelve, his maturity was recognized, and it was thought advisable to give him a name, make him a full citizen, and assign him to a government position. The parents were asked to select a name, and naturally, they selected Jacob Hubler, Junior. They were delighted when they were told that he had been made Assistant Professor of Philosophy in the National University, and given full citizenship. A free unit of society, he could now do as he wished with his time, the only restriction being in the hour a day five days a week rule for all government employees. The first thing he decided to do was to visit his parents.

So far, they had not seen him.

But they had prepared for the happy event by moving into a three-person apartment. It was very much like their two-person apartment only a little larger and with an extra bedroom.

Jacob and Ruth Hubler could hardly wait for their son's arrival. They had his baby book out on the table; they wanted to tell him of their marriage, show him the reports and his baby pictures. They wanted him to know what his birth had meant to them and how they had loved him all these years. They did not look a day older than they had looked thirteen years ago, but, somehow, they felt more important and quite advanced in years.

Their boy was coming home to them!

UNTO US A CHILD IS BORN

Their son! The culmination of nearly a century.

At last, he came—a young man with a beautiful body and a wonderful intelligence. He greeted them without emotion, talked to them without effort. Recognizing them as his parents, he spoke only of the debt the individual owed to the state. He was courteous and polite, but, in some way, he did not seem to be interested in the things they were interested in. Jacob, Senior, spoke of his new household inventions; Ruth told of her part in the work. He, the young philosopher, looked a trifle bored, and talked of *Erkenntnisstheorie* and the undue subjectivity of the temper. At last, he rose from his chair:

"I must go," he said in a tone of polite apology. "I have an important engagement with a philosopher in China. I must take the next Oriental air machine for Canton. He is an old man, and it is very important that I confer with him before he dies."

The mother put her hand on his shoulder and whispered timidly:

"Won't you spend the night with us, Jacob? I made your bed myself, and your room is all ready."

"I am sorry, but I have made this appointment and must go."

"Well, come again, and as often as you can," said the father rather cheerily. "Always glad to see you, my boy."

Jacob and Ruth went out on the balcony of their apartment. It was on the two hundredth story and overlooked Greater New York. They stood there, and, somehow, his arm stole around her waist, and her head dropped on his shoulder. He touched her cheek as he whispered:

"That is a fine boy. Sure is great to be a father."

She shivered in his arms.

"I am cold," she said. "The autumn is past, and there is the chill of winter in the air. If you will pardon me, I will go to bed."

For a long time, Jacob stood there on the balcony, alone.

Once he was back in the living room, he took from his pocket a Government communication. It was from the Child Permit Department.

"YOUR SON, JACOB HUBLER, JR., HAS FULFILLED IN EVERY WAY THE EXPECTATION OF HIS PRENATAL CHARTS. AS A PHILOSOPHER HE IS A SUCCESS. BUREAU OF STATISTICS ADVISE US THAT THEY NEED SEVERAL MORE PHILOSOPHERS. THIS LETTER IS YOUR OFFICIAL PERMIT TO HAVE ANOTHER SON. REPLY AT ONCE DESIRE OF YOUR WIFE AND SELF CONCERNING THIS."

He read it over several times. At first it seemed to be hard to understand. He had been so busy improving the standard of kitchen equipment that he had given but little time to other matters. Still holding the letter in his hand, he went over to the central table and opened the baby book. He looked at the first few pictures and then could not see very well because of the film over his eyes.

Closing the book, he went over to the wall wireless and tapped out a letter in reply, addressed to the Child Permit Department. One sentence was the answer, one sentence and the name; and the message read:

"WE WILL NOT HAVE ANY MORE CHILDREN."

JACOB HUBLER.

He walked as quietly as he could to his wife's bedroom door.

Her room was dark, and he could hear her sobbing in the darkness.

He went in and touched her hair.

Wanting to comfort her, he did not know what to say. The world was no longer
all before them.
—MILTON

NO MORE TOMORROWS

IN thinking over the great disaster of my life, I am always impressed with the fact that I came near success. There was only a hairbreadth between success and my ambitions. It is true that I failed, but I am not the first man who failed because of too great trust in a woman.

The idea would never have come to me had it not been for a peculiar combination of circumstances. First came the fact that I was, by years of labor, one of the greatest of psychological workers in the entire world; perhaps it would be better to state that I was not one of the greatest, but THE greatest. Then came the failure on Wall Street and the loss of my entire fortune. At that time, while I needed ready cash, the thought came to me, and I lost no time in capitalizing it.

Fortunately for me, the Internationale had agents in New York. I had heard of them, their activity, and their unlimited funds. Within three days, I had arranged for a conference.

There were three of them. To this day, I

know of them only by their numbers. "Twenty-one" seemed to be the leader. He was a small, one-eyed man with a head that seemed to be a constant burden to him on account of its unusual size. It needed to be large to hold all the store of knowledge he possessed. "Forty-seven" looked like an idiot. He had the largest nose I have ever seen on anyone; it seemed to start at the hair line and, sweeping down over the face in a generous curve, ended within a short distance of his chin. In talking, he used that nose as a trumpet, varying the tone and volume by partly closing one or both nostrils with the tips of his fingers. He was nauseating to look at, but adorable to listen to. "Thirty-four" was a blind man with one arm. I thought for a long time that he had lost it in the late war, but one night I found that he had a very short arm growing out of the shoulder.

"Twenty-one," "Forty-seven," "Thirty-four"— these were the men Russia had placed in America to undermine our social fabric and make us easy plucking when the day of final reckoning came. These were the three men I met in the back room of a slum restaurant the night that I sold everything I valued for the gold they had so much of.

They sat there on three sides of the table, "Twenty-one," as usual, supporting his hydrocephalic head in his hands, elbows on the table; "Forty-seven" humming a Mozart melody through his nasal trombone, and "Thirty-four," his face with hollow sockets twitching pitifully, tapping nervously on the table with the one hand that was able to reach it. No wonder I was nervous and slightly nauseated, for, though I had a wonderful idea, I was not at all sure of my ability to convince them of its worth.

"The human brain," I began, "is the organ which differentiates man from the lower forms of life. We, the human race, the *Genus Homo,* owe our supremacy to the great development of that brain. The mid-stem, the cerebellum, is similar in anatomy and function to that of the lower types, but when we consider the cerebrum, the two hemispheres, the various lobes with their twisted convolutions, their deep sutures, then we see what makes us more than animals and only a little less than Gods.

"Gentlemen, I ask you a question: 'What do we do with those lobes of the bilateral cerebrum?' We accumulate knowledge. Once we acquire a fact, that fact is never lost; at the worst, it is only accessible in our subconscious, awaiting the proper stimuli to cross the threshold and become the property of our conscious ego. So, we acquire knowledge.

"In other words, we remember what we have learned, and that mental quality is called memory. How far back does memory extend? Who knows? Freud, Adler, Jung, White, all of them, quarrel over the question. They cannot agree as to whether memory can be inherited or only acquired. I, as a psychologist, have my opinions, but why bother you with what I think!

"For there is something more important to consider tonight. I am thinking of the mental power of preparing for the future. Ah! That power indeed is possessed only by man. The squirrel buries a nut; but, forgetting where, allows it to grow into a tree. The mason-wasp may place food in an earthen cell; but she fails to see that the scientist, Fabre, has carefully cut the bottom out of the cell, destroying its usefulness.

"Man prepares for the future. He does it not only as an individual, but also as a nation, and almost as a race. Working in the todays of life, all his plans ambitions, and desires are located in his tomorrows. How have the great nations of history attained their fame? By carefully planning the future of their national life. Every rich man has become such by having a vision of the future, and then making a programme for his tomorrows. Am I right?"

They agreed with me. The truth was axiomatic. There was no need of argument. In fact, I gave them credit for seeing where my argument was leading me before I reached the middle of it. So I went on:

"In every nation there are, at best, a hundred men who have a sufficient mental force to plan for the future life of their commonwealths. They sit and dream; and then translate their dreams into economic and militaristic programmes which, they hope, will make their nation greater. These men are not concerned with the naval tonnage of today. What they want to know is the ratios that will exist between them and their rivals ten years, thirty years, from now. They live in the future. They can look only one way—forward. Historians backward turn their piercing gaze through the vanished centuries, but these dreamers think only of the history that will be made in the years to come.

"All the nations have their eyes set on Russia. They know that she is a sleeping giant, a terrific entity that so far has not learned to apply its power. The nations fear Russia, and the dreamers of all the nations are preparing for all the tomorrows, when the Great Bear will come down from the Ural Mountains.

"Your country faces a superhuman task in its plan to socialize the world. You also have your dreamers. I know that you have plans for the next ten, the next fifty, years. But the nations are playing a game of chess with you, and their intelligentsia is at least as brilliant as yours.

"Now here is my thought: Suppose something should happen to the one hundred great thinkers in a dozen of the supreme countries of this earth? Suppose that something should happen simultaneously to all of them? And what if this something prevented them from paying any more attention to the tomorrows of their nations? Can you visualize what would happen with England, France, Italy,

Japan, the United States, and a half dozen more, simply living in the todays of life? Legislation would collapse for lack of leadership. Finances would become despairing wrecks. The economic foundations of the world would be shaken. Armies would disappear, and navies would rust away in the harbors. Only Russia would plan, only your country would be able to progress; and, whenever you wished to, you could crush the rival nations as a steam roller crushes out the ruts in an earthen road. That is the idea I want to sell you."

"Magnificent!" shrieked "Twenty-one."

"Beautiful!" whistled "Forty-seven" through his trombone.

"But an impossible nightmare," sighed "Thirty-four," his pallid face twitching as he threw aside my plan as a fantastic dream.

"I am a psychologist," I continued, not in the least dismayed by their criticisms, (for I knew the real truth of the theory). "For years, I have studied the human brain, normal and abnormal. With scalpel, and every known instrument of precision, I dug into that greatest of all creations. And some time ago, I found out something that no one in the whole world knows. *I located the brain center which enables man to visualize the future and plan for it. I have found out the part of the brain where he keeps his tomorrows.*

"That in itself is an achievement of note. But," and here I lowered my voice to whisper, "what would you think if I told you that I have isolated a toxin, so specific, so powerful, that it can be given to a man in his food, just a few drops, and at once the ability of this *Tomorrow Center* is destroyed? It simply ceases to function. The man lives on as he has always done, but he has no more tomorrows."

"You say it can be given in food?" whinnied "Forty-seven."

"A drop or two in a grape, or in a glass of wine?" trembled "Twenty-one."

"I see it all! I can leap forward and in imagination visualize the results!" cried "Thirty-four." "It will make Russia ruler of the universe overnight."

"You are confident of your ability?" asked "Forty-seven."

"Absolutely!" and I was confident. More than that, I knew that these representatives of the greatest power in the world believed me, and would pay me well for the formula necessary to manufacture the drug. The manner of giving it, the ways that would have to be devised to finish the treatment; why, that was their business. So, I simply smiled at them as I repeated:

"Absolutely!"

They believed me. It was not even thought necessary to consult with the higher men in the Internationale. There would be no signatures, they said, and no incriminating document; but ten thousand dollars that very night and ten million upon the delivery of the first four ounces of the drug with the complete directions for making it.

We shook hands on it, and "Forty-seven," pulling from his pocket a roll of bills, counted out twenty $500 "yellow boys." At the sight of what he had left, I cursed myself. I could have had ten times ten thousand without protest, but I knew the other money soon would be mine. And Leonora would be mine. She had resisted the love of an unknown scientist, but when she knew that she could help in the spending of ten million dollars, what would she say? And there would be more than that. These men had told me that if the medicine worked, I could have anything I asked of Russia—anything I wanted, and they would be glad to give me my slightest desire because of the great gift I had handed them.

I wanted to tell Leonora about it that very night, but I had to go to the laboratory. Every moment was precious; with millions awaiting me, there could be no delay. Once in the workshop, I telephoned to her, whispering that I had real news and that I would see her soon. Was it foolish of me to end by saying that soon I would be able to give her all she had ever desired of life, everything she had ever dreamed of?

From the time I hung up the receiver, there was intense work. I worked and slept and ate and worked, and, as I watched the precious drops come out of the Berkfield filter into the sterilized beaker beneath, I knew that they were more than so many minims of devastating toxin. Far more! Each drop meant golden dollars, precious moments of happiness with Leonora.

At last, I was through. My agreement with the Russian representatives called for a first delivery of ten cubic centimeters of the drug. This was enough for experiments on ten men. If this experiment was satisfactory, I was to be given one million dollars, and was to start at once with the preparation of sufficient of the drug to paralyze the ambitions of great men all over the world. On the delivery of the final amount, there were to be nine million more handed me, and if it all worked as I said it would, perhaps ninety million more would be given me by the grateful mistress of the world.

I was to meet the men at twelve o'clock that night. At five, I had finished my task. The 10 c.c. was in a glass-stoppered bottle. I had it safe in my right hand vest pocket. In the left hand vest pocket was a similar bottle, filled with water. Held to the light, both bottles looked alike, one on one side and one on the other. I wanted to show them to Leonora. For that night, I was going to dine with her. Days of hard work and nights of tedious watching had separated us; now there was going to be an evening of pleasure and some pardonable boasting.

We ate in a semi-private alcove of a New York restaurant. I presume the food was good. All I can remember is how much like a wonder-woman the lady of my heart looked that night. She had always been inclined to tease me a little about my inability to succeed, but when I gave her the diamond pendant, she knew, she could not help but know, that I had struck my pace.

Then I told her all. Slowly, with microscopic exactness, I told her the entire story. I saw her shiver as I described the head of "Twenty-one," the nose of "Forty-seven," the blind face of the one-armed "Thirty-four." But when I spoke of the millions, she flushed and breathed deep, and I knew then that she was a woman with a price and I could at last buy her.

Very carefully, I explained what I intended to do. How, with the destruction of their tomorrows, the leaders of the universe would lie prostrate and helpless before the Great Bear. In words of one syllable, I described the centers of the brain, and told of my great discovery; and then I showed her the two bottles.

"Just like water, you see, my dear," I explained. "Think of it! A cook in our employ places a teaspoonful of this liquid in a cup of coffee, and a great man drinks that cupful. From that time he becomes useless to his country. He simply lives in his todays. Imagine a hundred of the leaders of England all being similarly affected in one day. Before substitutions could be made for them, the British Isles could be overrun."

"And they will do that to France, and Italy, and our United States?" asked the simple-minded beauty.

"Yes, to the whole world."

"And you will be great, rich, and powerful?"

"I will be everything you want me to be. Think of it! Able to give you anything you want."

"And it is all in that bottle?"

"Yes."

"Suppose we drink out of the one bottle. A toast to your success, and my happiness."

So I emptied the one bottle into our wine glasses, and we drank. And then I put the other bottle back into my vest pocket. It was past ten, and for a while, we just chatted. Then the woman started to laugh; at first a little chuckle, then low rippling peals like murmuring waterfalls. Of course, I wanted to know what she was amused at, and she did not hesitate to answer me.

"You have done something for me tonight, that I can never repay you for. And I have done something for you that you will never forget. All my life, I have worried about the tomorrows of my existence. I knew as a child that I would be beautiful, but I soon found that all beauty is ephemeral, and that perfection soon ripens to decay. No matter how earnestly I tried to avoid the unpleasant passages of life's poem, I knew that they were waiting for me just around the corners of tomorrow.

"In addition to that, I love this country of ours. Of course, I know its imperfections, its greed, racketeers, political scandals, marital failures, but it is a wonderful country, and I love it. I could not think of its being conquered by Russia, and when you showed me the bottles, I thought I saw my chance. You were looking at my pendant, the new plaything you had given me, and then I remembered your saying that the new medicine looked and tasted like water; so, while you were looking at the pendant on the woman you wanted to buy as you would a plaything, I shifted the bottles on the table, and—Oh! don't you see the humor in it all? You have the water in your pocket and we, each of us, have one half a bottle of the drug within us. I think it is working already, because for the first time in my life, I do not fear tomorrow; I have a peculiar sensation, a most startling, odd sensation, and that feeling seems to tell me that there will be no more tomorrows in my life."

"Nonsense!" I cried. "You just think you shifted the bottles. You wouldn't do a thing like that. You couldn't! You are just teasing me."

"Think so?" she jeered. "Then how about this? I'll marry you tomorrow."

And before I realized it, I had said it. I tried to choke it back. Even went so far as to raise my hand to cover my mouth. But it was too late. I said it, and I knew that it was true.

"But we shall have no tomorrows," I gasped, and hated myself for the admitting of it.

Well, it was done, and could not be undone. Eleven in the evening, and the three men to meet at twelve! But twelve would be the beginning of a tomorrow; so, I could never meet them. I had a little money, a few thousand left out of the advance. What could I tell them? The truth? Would they believe it? How could I show them that even in my horrible condition, I was proving to them that my invention was a success?

No doubt as to what would happen! They would kill me! That in itself would not be so bad, but how about Leonora? Even in spite of her treachery to me, I still loved her, was still insanely in love with her. Well, there was only one thing to do and that was to discover a cure. It seemed that somewhere, in the realm of medical skill, there should be something that would bring me back my tomorrows.

First, I thought of psycho-analysis. Then of hypnotism. Perhaps a long period of anæsthesia would enable me to turn the trick. All this came to my mind as I sat silently across the table from Leonora; and then, despairingly, I left her. She laughed at me as I left the alcove.

"Goodbye," she jeered. "I will see you tomorrow."

I went back to my rooms. Fortunately, the Russians did not know where they were. No one did. I worked in the laboratory, and I had told "Twenty-one" where that was, but none of my assistants knew where I slept. So, in those rooms, I felt safe. Arriving there, sleep overcame me. Waking, there came the thought that it all had been a horrible dream, a fantasy, born of indigestion, a corrosive nightmare. Hastily, the bottle in my pocket was analyzed, and then came the certainty—it was water. For me there were no more tomorrows. I was simply in a perpetual today.

Nine that morning found me in the office of a great psycho-analyst, a healer of souls, a prober of the subconscious. I told him my problem. He smiled at me kindly, assured me that my fears were groundless, and suggested a course of treatment.

"I can begin on your case tomorrow," he said, with a smile.

"That statement in itself is sufficient to show me that I can expect no help from you," I cried in despair. "How can you start treating me tomorrow, when that day will never come?"

So, I paid him his bill, and left the office.

I telephoned to the laboratory. Yes, there had been visitors there, just as I knew there would be, and they were hunting for me. Well, let them hunt! They never would come upon me unless I wanted them to.

A few hours later found me in the office of a celebrated hypnotist. That time, I was not taking any chances on a specialist's misunderstanding me.

"I want you to give me a tomorrow," I began. "I am not hunting for a dozen or a thousand tomorrows; just one. If I can find myself in the dawn of just one tomorrow, I will know that I am cured of my disease." And after a great deal of talking on my part, I showed him just exactly what he could do for me.

"I am sure I can help," he assured me. "My plan is this: We will wait till nearly midnight, and then I will hypnotise you. I will suggest to you that you revive your former personalities, go back into the age of the dawn man, the Roman, the Englishman, the settler of America, the Revolutionary patriot, and finally, I will bring you back to today; but your mind will be flowing so fast that it cannot stop, and when I awaken you, your existence will already have gone forward into the future. When that happens, you will be cured.

"That sounds good, and what time shall I be here?"

"About eleven tonight."

"Then I will stay right in your office."

It was there that he directed me to look at the revolving light. He whispered into my drowsy ear. And crashing backward into the dead past I went, just as he said I would; back to the dawn man and the saber-toothed tiger, back to the building of the first wall around Rome. I saw and took part in a sea battle between the fleets of Rome and Carthage, and even as my ship sank, I found myself with Columbus, sailing westward toward the fabled Indies. What was this new battle? Oh, yes! I was with Washington at Germantown, and later charged with Picket through the blood-stained wheat field of Gettysburg, and now I was in New York, in my laboratory, making devil's broth to sell to Russians, and then something snapped, and I awoke. There was the hypnotist gazing anxiously at me.

"How do you feel?" he said.

"How should I feel?" I almost shouted.

"How far did you get in the dream?"

"Only to the events of today."

"But you have been almost dead for hours. I never was so alarmed. For hours you have scarcely breathed."

"But is this tomorrow?"

"No. This is not tomorrow. That will not be here for eighteen hours. This is just today."

In spite of my anger, I started to sob. Just another failure; but, at the same time, another proof that my drug was doing all that it had claimed to do. I paid the man and slouched out of the office. Was I being followed on the street or was it just my jumpy nerves?

In a telephone pay-station, I listened to Leonora. She was having the time of her life.

"How can I thank you for what you did for your sweetheart? And where have you been? I have been having a most wonderful time, one thrill after another, and never a care or a worry. Now that I am sure there will be no more tomorrows, I am getting an awful kick out of the todays of life. Why not join me? Come on! I know a new night-club, and we will simply kick the hours away to the latest jazz."

But somehow, I could not look at it the way she wanted me to.

I lived on. That was the pitiful part of it. I ate and hid and tried to think; at times, I slept from sheer exhaustion. But always I found myself in the todays of life. At last, I sought the aid of a physician. He told me that I was living on my reserve strength.

"Unless you stop and rest, you are liable to collapse, and perhaps die. You must take better care of yourself," he advised.

"Just when do you think I shall die?" I whispered.

"Anytime. Perhaps during the next week, and it may be tomorrow."

"Then I shall live on forever," I told him. "Doctor, tell me honestly. Did you ever know of a case like mine? Have you ever treated a man who has lost his tomorrows?"

It was interesting to see the way the man looked at me. He almost must have thought that I was insane. At least, he started to phone to the police, and that was a signal for me to rush out of the office.

Police meant newspapers, and reporters, and notoriety. None of that for me.

But outside the office, right on the street, men closed around me, and forced me into a waiting taxi. Once in there, I could easily tell what had happened. A large head, a blind face, and another face, all nose, easily helped me to identify my traveling companions.

Later on, they took me into a bare room in a third floor back tenement. Just a table and four chairs.

"You tried to goldbrick us!" accused "Twenty-one."

"Took our gold and then endeavored to escape!" whinnied "Forty-seven," and he almost sang a tune with those eight words, as he breathed them through his nose.

But "Thirty-four" simply started to take off his coat. He took off his coat and his vest, and then his shirt. Fascinated, I looked at him undressing with his one capable arm. At last, I saw the mystery of the blind man. The unusualness of it made me gasp. "Twenty-one," who had been watching me closely, started to laugh as he explained it to me.

"Odd? Decidedly! Of course, he is blind, but that doesn't make any difference, because we bring his prey to him. His one long arm is weak, so much so that he uses it only for the nicer things in life, like eating and dressing. But look at that hand growing out of his right shoulder! That hand is unusual. It has been pronounced a real anomaly by some of our greatest anatomists. It is a hand without an arm, but it has muscles, the pectorals in front and the powerful back muscles posteriorly. Once that hand closes on a throat, it never lets go. During the Revolution, dear old "Thirty-four" just sat in a chair, and we brought him the nobility and he did the rest—with their throats. Odd? But not so much so when you know his history. Before he was born, his mother had to stand by while her husband was literally being torn to pieces by one of the Russian Nobility, who thought they were Gods. So, poor old "Thirty-four" was born with only one arm; but as you will soon find out, he has two hands, and one of them is very—yes, wonderfully, capable.

At that, I looked at the hand closely. It was beginning to open and close as if practicing for the sonata that it was soon to play. For a minute, I was sure that this was the end. In spite of myself, I trembled, and a cold chill swept over me. I knew that I had lost Leonora forever. Then the big-nosed "Forty-seven" blurted out triumphantly:

"We are going to wait till tomorrow, and then—you will die of air hunger."

At that I laughed. They looked at me in astonishment:

"Oh! This is too much," I gasped in my mirth. "Why, if you are going to wait till tomorrow, you will never be able to kill me. Don't you understand? The toxin was really a success. I tried it on myself! It worked. *YOU CANNOT KILL ME TOMORROW, FOR I HAVE NO TOMORROWS!*"

THE THING IN THE CELLAR

IT WAS a large cellar, entirely out of proportion to the house above it. The owner admitted that it was probably built for a distinctly different kind of structure from the one which rose above it. Probably the first house had been burned, and poverty had caused a diminution of the dwelling erected to take its place.

A winding stone stairway connected the cellar with the kitchen. Around the base of this series of steps, successive owners of the house had placed their firewood, winter vegetables, and junk. The junk had been pushed back till it rose, head high, in a barricade of uselessness. What was back of that barricade no one knew and no one cared. For some hundreds of years, no one had crossed it to penetrate to the black reaches of the cellar behind it.

At the top of the steps, separating the kitchen from the cellar, was a stout oaken door. This door was, in a way, as peculiar and out of relation to the rest of the house as the cellar. It was a strange kind of door to find in a modern house, and certainly a most unusual door to find in the inside of the house—thick, stoutly built, dexterously rabbeted together, with huge wrought-iron hinges, and a lock that looked as though it came from Castle Despair. Separating a house from the outside world, such a door would be excusable; swinging between kitchen and cellar, it seemed peculiarly inappropriate.

From the earliest months of his life, Tommy Tucker seemed unhappy in the kitchen. In the front parlor, in the formal dining-room, and especially on the second floor of the house, he acted like a normal, healthy child; but carry him to the kitchen, he at once began to cry. His parents, being plain people, ate in the kitchen, save when they had company. Being poor, Mrs. Tucker did most of her work, though occasionally she had a charwoman in to do the extra Saturday cleaning, and thus much of her time was spent in the kitchen. And Tommy stayed with her, at least as long as he was unable to walk. Much of the time he was decidedly unhappy.

When Tommy learned to creep, he lost no time in leaving the kitchen. No sooner was his mother's back turned, than the little fellow crawled as fast as he could for the doorway opening into the front of the house—the dining-room, and the front parlor. Once away from the kitchen, he seemed happy; at least, he ceased to cry. On being returned to the kitchen, his howls so thoroughly convinced the neighbors that he had colic, that more than one bowl of catnip and sage tea were brought to his assistance.

It was not until the boy learned to talk, that the Tuckers had any idea as to what made the boy cry so hard when he was in the kitchen. In other words, the baby had to suffer for many months till he obtained at least a little relief, and even when he told his parents what was the matter, they were absolutely unable to comprehend. This is not to be wondered at, because they were both hard-working, rather simple-minded persons.

What they finally learned from their little son was this: That if the cellar door was shut and securely fastened with the heavy iron lock, Tommy could, at least, eat a meal in peace; if the door was simply closed and not locked, he shivered with fear, but kept quiet; but if the door was open, if even the slightest streak of black showed that it was not tightly shut, then the little three-year-old would scream himself to the point of exhaustion, especially if his tired father would refuse him permission to leave the kitchen.

Playing in the kitchen, the child developed two interesting habits. Rags, scraps of paper, and splinters of wood were continually being shoved under the thick oak door to fill the space between the door and the sill. Whenever Mrs. Tucker opened the door, there was always some trash there, placed by her son. It annoyed her, and more than once the little fellow was thrashed for his conduct; but punishment acted in no way as a deterrent. The other habit was as singular. Once the door was closed and locked, he would rather boldly walk over to it and caress the old lock. Even when he was so small that he had to stand on tiptoe to touch it with the tips of his fingers, he would touch it with slow caressing strokes; later on, as he grew older, he used to kiss it.

His father, who only saw the boy at the end of the day, decided that there was no sense in such conduct, and, in his masculine way, tried to break the lad of his foolishness. There was, of necessity, no effort on the part of the hard-working man to understand the psychology back of his son's conduct. All that the man knew was that his little son was acting in a way that was decidedly queer.

Tommy loved his mother, and was willing to do anything he could to help her in the household chores; but one thing he would not do, and never did do, and that was to fetch and carry between the house and the cellar. If his mother opened the door, he would run, screaming, from the room, and he never returned voluntarily till he was assured that the door was closed.

He never explained just why he acted as he did. In fact, he refused to talk about it, at least to his parents, and that was just as well, because had he done so, they would simply have been more positive that there was something wrong with their only child. They tried, in their own ways, to break the child of his unusual habits; failing to change him at all, they decided to ignore his peculiarities.

That is, they ignored them till he became six years old and the time came for him to go to school. He was a sturdy little chap by that time, and more intelligent than the usual boys beginning in the primer class. Mr. Tucker was, at times, proud of him. The child's attitude toward the cellar door was the one thing most disturbing to the father's pride. Finally, nothing would do but that the Tucker family call on the neighborhood physician. It was an important event in the life of the Tuckers, so important that it demanded the wearing of Sunday clothes, and all that sort of thing.

"The matter is just this, Doctor Hawthorn," said Mr. Tucker, in a somewhat embarassed manner. "Our little Tommy is old enough to start to school, but he hehaves childishly in regard to our cellar; and the Missus and I thought you could tell us how to do about it. It must be his nerves."

"Ever since he was a baby," continued Mrs. Tucker, taking up the thread of conversation where her husband had paused, "Tommy has had a great fear of the cellar. Even now, big boy that he is, he does not love me enough to fetch and carry for me through that door and down those steps. It is not natural for a child to act like he does, and what with chinking the cracks with rags and kissing the lock, he drives me to the point where I fear he may become daft-like as he grows older."

The doctor, eager to satisfy new customers, and dimly remembering some lectures on the nervous system received when he was a medical student, asked some general questions, listened to the boy's heart, examined his lungs, and looked at his eyes and fingernails. At last he commented:

"Looks like a fine, healthy boy to me."

"Yes, all except the cellar door," replied the father.

"Has he ever been sick?"

"Naught but fits once or twice, when he cried himself blue in the face," answered the mother.

"Frightened?"

"Perhaps. It was always in the kitchen."

"Suppose you go out, and let me talk to Tommy by myself?"

And there sat the doctor, very much at his ease, and the little six-year-old boy, very uneasy.

"Tommy, what is there in the cellar you are afraid of?"

"I don't know."

"Have you ever seen it?"

"No, sir."

"Then how do you know there is something there?"

"Because."

"Because what?"

"Because there is."

That was as far as Tommy would go, and, at last, his seeming obstinacy annoyed the physician, even as it had for several years annoyed Mr. Tucker. He went to the door, and called the parents into the office.

"He thinks there is something down in the cellar," he stated.

The Tuckers simply looked at each other.

"That's foolish," commented Mr. Tucker.

" 'Tis just a plain cellar with junk, and firewood, and cider barrels in it," added Mrs. Tucker. "Since we moved into that house, I have not missed a day without going down those steps; and I know there is nothing there. But the lad has always screamed when the door was open. I recall now that since he was a child in arms, he has always screamed when the door was open."

"He thinks there is something there," said the doctor.

"That is why we brought him to you," replied the father. "It's the child's nerves. Perhaps 'as'f'tidy,' or something, will calm him."

"I'll tell you what to do," advised the doctor. "He thinks there is something there. Just as soon as he finds that he is wrong and that there is nothing there, he will forget about it. He has been humored too much. What you want to do is to open that cellar door, and make him stay by himself in the kitchen. Nail the door open so he can not close it. Leave him alone there for an hour, and then go and laugh at him and show him how silly it was for him to be afraid of an empty cellar. I will give you some nerve and blood tonic and that will help, but the big thing is to show him that there is nothing to be afraid of."

On the way back to the Tucker home, Tommy broke away from his parents. They caught him after an exciting chase, and kept him between them the rest of the way home. Once in the house, he disappeared, and was found in the guest room under the bed. The afternoon being already spoiled for Mr. Tucker, he determined to keep the child under observation for the rest of the day. Tommy ate no supper, in spite of the urgings of the unhappy mother. The dishes were washed, the evening paper read, the evening pipe smoked; and then, and only then, did Mr. Tucker take down his tool box and get out a hammer and some long nails.

"And I am going to nail the door open, Tommy, so you can not close it, as that was what the doctor said, Tommy; and you are to be a man and stay here in the kitchen alone for an hour, and we will leave the lamp a-burning, and then when you find there is naught to be afraid of, you will be well and a real man and not something for a man to be ashamed of being the father of."

But at the last, Mrs. Tucker kissed Tommy, and cried, and whispered to her husband not to do it, and to wait till the boy was larger; but nothing availed except to nail the thick door open so it could not be shut, and leave the boy there alone with the lamp burning and the dark open space of the doorway to look at with eyes that grew as hot and burning as the flame of the lamp.

That same day, Doctor Hawthorn took supper with a classmate of his, a man who specialized in psychiatry and who was particularly interested in children. Hawthorn told Johnson about his newest case, the little Tucker boy, and asked him for his opinion. Johnson frowned:

"Children are odd, Hawthorn. Perhaps they are like dogs. It may be their nervous system is more acute than in the adult. We know that our eyesight is limited, also our hearing and smell. I firmly believe that there are forms of life which exist in such a shape that we can neither see, hear, nor smell them. Fondly we delude ourselves into the fallacy of believing that they do not exist because we cannot prove their existance. This Tucker lad may have a nervous system that is peculiarly acute. He may dimly appreciate the existence of something in the cellar which is unappreciable to his parents. Evidently there is some basis to this fear of his. Now, I am not saying that there is anything in the cellar; but this boy, since he was a baby, has thought that something was there, and that is just as bad as though there actually were. What I would like to know is what makes him think so. Give me the address, and I will call tomorrow and have a talk with the little fellow."

"What do you think of my advice?"

"Sorry, old man, but I think it was perfectly rotten. If I were you, I would stop around there on my way home and prevent them from following it. The little fellow may be badly frightened. You see, he evidently thinks there is something there."

"But there isn't."

"Perhaps not. No doubt, he is wrong; but he thinks so."

It all worried Doctor Hawthorn so much that he decided to take his friend's advice. It was a chilly night, a foggy night, and the physician felt cold as he tramped along the London streets. At last, he came to the Tucker house. He remembered now that he had been there once before, long ago, when little Tommy Tucker came into the world. There was a light in the front window, and in no time at all Mr. Tucker came to the door.

"I have come to see Tommy," said the doctor.

"He is back in the kitchen," replied the father.

"He gave one cry, but since then he has been quiet," sobbed the wife.

"If I had let her have her way, she would have opened the door, but I said to her, 'Mother, now is the time to make a man out of our Tommy.' And I guess he knows by now that there was naught to be afraid of. Well, the hour is up. Suppose we go and get him, and put him to bed?"

"It has been a hard time for the little child," whispered the wife.

Carrying the candle, the man walked ahead of the woman and the doctor, and at last opened the kitchen door. The room was dark.

"Lamp has gone out," said the man. "Wait till I light it."

"Tommy! Tommy!" called Mrs. Tucker.

But the doctor ran to where a white form was stretched on the floor. Sharply, he called for more light. Trembling, he examined all that was left of little Tommy. Twitching, he looked into the open space down into the cellar. At last, he looked at Tucker and at Tucker's wife.

"Tommy—Tommy has been hurt—I guess he is dead!" he stammered.

The mother threw herself on the floor and picked up the torn, mutilated thing that had been, only a short while ago, her little Tommy.

The man took his hammer and drew the nails and closed the door and locked it, and then drove in a long spike to reinforce the lock. Then he took hold of the doctor's shoulders and shook him.

"What killed him, Doctor? What killed him?" he shouted into Hawthorn's ear.

The doctor looked at him bravely in spite of the fear in his throat.

"How do I know, Tucker?" he replied. "How

do I know? Didn't you tell me that there **was** nothing there? Nothing down there? In the cellar?

THE DEAD WOMAN

HE WAS found in the room with his wife, slightly confused, a trifle bewildered, but otherwise apparently normal. He made no effort to conceal his conduct, any more than he did to take the knife from his hand and the pieces from the trunk.

Fortunately, the inspector was an officer of more than usual intelligence; and there was no effort made to give the third degree, or even secure a written confession. Perhaps the police department felt it was too plain a case. At least, it was handled intelligently, and in a most scientific manner. The man was well fed and carefully bedded. The next morning, after being bathed and shaved, he was taken to see a psychiatrist.

The specialist in mental diseases had the man comfortably seated. Knowing he smoked, he offered a cigar, which was accepted. Then, in a quiet, pleasant atmosphere, he made one statement and asked one question.

"I am sure, Mr. Thompson, that you had an

excellent reason for acting as you did the other day. I wish you would tell me all about it."

The man looked at the psychiatrist.

"Will you believe me, if I tell you?"

"I will accept every part of your story with the idea that you are convinced you are telling me the truth."

"That is all I want," whispered Thompson. "If everyone I talked to in the past had done that, if they had even tried to check up on my story, perhaps this would not have happened. But they always thought that I was the sick one, and there was not one who was willing to accept my statement about the worms.

"I suppose that I was happily married. At least as much so as most men are. You know that there is a good deal of conflict between the sexes, and there were a few differences of opinion between Mrs. Thompson and myself. But not enough to cause serious difficulty. Will you remember that? We did not quarrel very much.

"About a year ago, my wife's health gave me considerable thought. She started to fail. If you are a married man, Doctor, you know there is always that anxiety about the wife's health. You become accustomed to living with a woman, having her do things for you, go to places with you; and you think about how life would be if she should sicken and die. Perhaps the fact that you are uneasy about the future makes you exaggerate the importance of her symptoms.

"At any rate, she became sick, got a nasty cough, and lost weight. I spoke to her about it, and even bought a bottle of beef, iron, and wine at the drug store, and made her take it. She did so to please me, but she never would admit that she was sick. Said it was fashionable to be thin, and that the cough was just nervousness.

"She would not go and see a doctor. When I spoke to her mother about it, the old lady just laughed at me and said, if I tried to make Lizzie any happier, she would soon get fat. In fact, none of our family or our friends seemed to feel that there was anything wrong with Mrs. Thompson, so I stopped talking about it. Of course, it was not easy on me; the way she coughed at night, and her staying awake so much. I work hard in the daytime, and it is hard to lose a lot of sleep. At last I was forced to ask her to let me sleep in the spare bedroom.

"Even that did not help much. I could hear her cough, and when she did fall asleep, I would have to tiptoe into her room and see if she was all right. Her coughing bothered me so much; but when she did not cough, it worried me more, because I thought something had happened to her.

"One night, the thing I was afraid of happened. She had a hard spell of coughing, and then she stopped. It was quiet in the house. I could hear the clock on the landing tick, and a mouse gnawing wood in the attic. I thought I could even hear my own heart beat, but there was not a sound of any kind from the other bedroom.

"When I went in there and turned on the light, I just knew it was all over. Of course, I was not sure. A bookkeeper is not supposed to be an expert on such matters, so I went and telephoned for our doctor. On the way to the phone, I wondered just what I should say; for he had always insisted that my wife was in grand health. So I simply told him that Mrs. Thompson was not looking well, and would he come over. Just like that I told him, and tried to keep my voice steady.

"It was about an hour before he came. I guess he had stopped to shave. He went into the bedroom, but I stopped at the doorway. He spent some time listening to her heart and feeling her pulse, and then he straightened up and asked me:

" 'She is fine. Just fast asleep. What did you think was wrong?'

"That surprised me so much that all I could do was to stammer something about not hearing her cough any more. He laughed at me, as he hit me on the shoulder.

" 'You worry too much about her, Mr. Thompson.'

"Right there, my difficulty started. There was a doctor who was supposed to know his business, and he said there was nothing wrong with my wife; and there I was, just a poor bookkeeper, and I just knew what was the matter. What was I to do? Tell him he was wrong? Send for another physician?

"It was growing light by that time, so I went down to the kitchen and started the coffee. Often I did that, and later fried some eggs and bacon. I then shaved, and made ready to go to the office. But before I went to the office, I sat down a while by my wife's bed—rather bothered, but I had to keep telling myself that the doctor knew better than I did.

"Before leaving the house, I telephoned to my mother-in-law. I just told her that Lizzie was not feeling well, and asked if she would come over and spend the day; and that she could get me at the office any time she called. Then I left the house. I felt better out in the sunshine; and after working a few hours over the books, I almost laughed at myself for being so foolish.

"No telephone calls came from the old lady; and when I arrived home at six, the house was lighted as usual. My wife and mother-in-law were waiting for me in the parlor. They told me supper was all ready. Naturally, I was surprised to see my wife out of bed, but tried to act naturally. At the supper table, I watched her just as carefully as I could without making the two of them suspicious of me. Mrs. Thompson ate about as she usually did, just pieced and minced her food; but I thought when she swallowed that the food went down with a jerk, and there was a peculiar stiffness when she moved. But her mother did not seem to think there was anything wrong, at least she did not make any comment. Even when I went with her to the front door to say good night to her, and we were alone there, she never said a word to show that she thought her daughter was in any way unusual or peculiar.

"I started to wash the dishes after that. Often I washed the dishes at night, while the wife sat in the front parlor watching the people go up and down past the house. After the kitchen was tidy, I lit a cigar and went into the parlor and started a little conversation; but Mrs. Thompson never talked back. In fact, I do not believe she ever talked to me after that, though I am positive that she talked to the others.

"When the cigar was smoked, I just said good night and went to bed. Later on, I could hear her moving around in her room; and then all was quiet, so she must have gone to bed. She did not cough anymore. I congratulated myself on that one thing, because the coughing had kept me awake a good deal. During the night, I lit a candle; and, shading it with my hand, tiptoed in to see her. She had her eyes open, but they were rolled back so all you could see was the whites; and she was not breathing. At least, I could not tell that she was breathing; and when I held a mirror in front of her mouth there was no vapor on it. My mother told me how to do that when I was a boy.

"The next day was just the same. My mother-in-law came and spent the day. I came home at night, and ate supper with them, and washed the dishes. The water was hot, and it was a pleasure to make them clean. Perhaps I took longer than usual at it, because I did not fancy the idea of going into the front parlor where the wife was sitting looking out of the window.

"But I went in this night without the usual cigar. I wanted to use my nose. It seemed there was a peculiar odor in the house, like flowers that had been put in a vase of water and then forgotten for many days. Perhaps you know the odor, Doctor, a heavy one, like lilies of the valley in a small, closed, room. It was especially strong in the parlor, where Mrs. Thompson was sitting; and it seemed to come from her. I had to light the cigar after a while, and by and by I said good night and went to bed. She never spoke to me; in fact, she did not seem to pay any attention to me.

"About two that morning, I took the candle and went in to look at her. Her eyelids were open, and her eyeballs rolled up, just like they had been the night before; but now her jaw was dropped and her cheeks sunken in. I just could not do anything but telephone for a doctor; and this time, I picked a total stranger, just picked his name out of the telephone book haphazardly.

"What good did it do? None at all. He came, he examined Mrs. Thompson very carefully, and he simply said that he did not see anything wrong with her; then down in the front hall he turned on me and asked me just why I had sent for him, and what I thought was the matter with her? Of course, I just could not tell him the truth, with his being a doctor, and I being just a bookkeeper. If he thought Mrs. Thompson was well, what was there for me to say?

"My mother-in-law went to the mountains the next day for the summer, and that left us alone. Breakfast as usual, and to the office, and not a word all day from the house. When I came back at night, the house was lit and supper was on the table. The wife was sitting at her end as usual. She had the food served on plates. She ate, but her movements were slower; and when she swallowed, you could see the food go down by jerks. Her eyes were sunken into the sockets and seemed shiny; and—well, like the eyes of a dead fish on the stalls.

"There were flowers on the table, but the smell was something different. It was sweeter, and when I took a deep breath, it was just hard for me to go on eating the pork chops and potatoes. You see, it was summer time and warm; and in spite of the screens, there was a fly or two in the house. When I saw one walking around on her lip and she not making any effort to brush it off, I just couldn't keep on eating—had to go and start washing the dishes. Perhaps you can understand how I felt, Doctor. Things looked rather odd by now.

"The next day, I phoned to the office that I would not be there, and I sent for a taxi and took

Mrs. Thompson to a first-class specialist. He must have been good, because he charged me twenty-five dollars just for the office call. I went in first, and told him just exactly what I was afraid of. I did not try to mince my words. Then we had the wife in. He examined her, even her blood; and all the satisfaction I got was that she seemed a trifle anæmic, but that I had better take a nerve tonic and a vacation, or I would be sick.

"Things looked rather twisted after that. Either I was right and everybody else was wrong; or they were right, and I was just about as wrong mentally as a man could be. But I had to believe my senses. A man just has to believe what he sees and hears and feels; and when I thought over that office visit, with the wife smiling, and the doctor sticking her finger for the blood to examine it, it just seemed impossible. Anæmic! Why that was a simple word to describe her condition.

"That night, the flies were worse than usual. I went to the corner store to buy a fly spray. I used it in her bedroom, but they kept coming in—the big blue ones, you know. It seemed as though they just had to come in. I could not keep them off her face; so at last, in desperation, I covered her head up with a towel and went to sleep. I *had* to work. The interest on the mortgage was due, and the man wanted something on the principal. It was a good house, and all I had in the world to show for twenty years of hard work keeping books.

"The next day was just like all the days had been, except that I made more mistakes with the books, and my boss spoke to me about it. When I arrived home that night, supper was not ready, though Mrs. Thompson was in the parlor and the lights were on. The heavy odor was worse than usual, and there were a lot of flies. You could hear them buzz and strike against the electric lights. I got my own supper, but I couldn't eat much, thinking of her in the parlor and the flies settling on her open mouth and pinched nose.

"She just sat there that night in the parlor till I went to her and took her arm to lead her up the stairs. She was cold, and on each cheek there was a heavy purple blotch forming. Once she was in her room, she seemed to move around; so I left her alone. When I went into her room later on, she was in bed and rather peaceful. It had been a hard week for me, so I sat down near her bed and tried to think; but the more I thought, the worse things seemed. The night was hot, and the flies kept buzzing; just thinking of the past and how we used to go to the movies together and laugh and sometimes come near crying, and how we used to bluff about the fact that perhaps it was just as well we didn't have a child so long as we had each other, knowing all the time that she was eating her heart out for longing to be a mother and blaming me for her loneliness.

The thinking was too much for me, so I thought I might as well smoke another cigar and go to bed and try to keep better books the next day and hold my job—and then I saw the little worm crawl out.

"Right then I knew that something had to be done. It didn't make any difference what the doctors or her mother said, something had to be done, and I must do it.

"I telephoned for an undertaker.

"Met him downstairs.

" 'It will be a private funeral,' I told him, 'and no publicity, and I think after you are through, you will have no trouble obtaining a physician's certificate.'

"He went upstairs. In about five minutes, he came downstairs. He said:

" 'I must have gone into the wrong room.'

" 'The second story front bedroom.'

" 'But the woman there is not dead.'

"I paid him for his trouble, and shut the door in his face. Was I helpless? Doctor, you have to believe me. I was at the end of my rope. I had tried every way I knew, and there just was not anything left to do. No one believed me. No one agreed with me. It seemed more and more as though they thought I was insane.

"It was impossible to keep her in the house any longer. My health was giving way: Working all day at figures that were going wrong all the time, and coming back night after night and cooking my supper and sleeping in a room next to the thing that had been my wife. What with the smell of lilies of the valley and the buzz of flies, and the constant dread in my mind of how things would be the next day and the next week, and the mortgage due, I had to do something.

"And it seemed to me that she wanted me to. It seemed that she recognized that things were not right, that she was entitled to a different kind of an ending. I knew what I would want done with me, if things were reversed.

"So I brought the trunk up from the cellar. We had used that trunk on our wedding trip and every summer since on our vacations, and I thought that she would be more at peace in that trunk than in a new one. But when I had the trunk by her bed, I saw at once that it was too small unless I used a knife.

"That seemed the proper thing to do, and I was sure it would not hurt her. For days she had been past hurting. I told her I was sorry, but it just had to be done; and if people had just believed me, things could have been arranged in a much nicer way.

"Then I started.

"Things were confused after that.

"I seem to remember a scream and blood spurting; and the next thing, there were a lot of people, and I was arrested.

"And the peculiar part of it all, Sir. Perhaps

you do not know it, but I am accused of murdering my wife. Now I have told you all about it, Doctor, and I just want to ask one question. If you had been in my place, day after day, and night after night, what would you have done? What would any man have done who loved his wife?"

HEREDITY

DR. THEODORE OVERFIELD was impressed.

The size of the estate, the virgin timber, the large stone house, and, above all, the high iron fence, which surrounded the place, indicated wealth and careful planning. The house was old, the trees were very old, but the fence was new. Its sharp, glistening pickets ranged upward, looking like bayonets on parade.

When he had accepted the invitation to make a professional visit to that home, he had counted on nothing more than a case of neurasthenia, perhaps an alcoholic psychosis or feminine hysteria. As he drove through the gateway and heard the iron shutters clank behind him, he was not so sure of its being a commonplace situation or an ordinary patient. A few deer ran, frightened, from the roadside. They were pretty things. At least, they were one reason for the fence.

At the house, a surly, silent, servant opened the door and ushered him into a room that seemed to be the library. It not only held books in abundance, but it seemed that the books were used. Not many sets, but many odd volumes were there—evidently first editions. At one end of the room was a winged Mercury; at the other end, a snow white Venus. Between them, on one side, was the fireplace with several inviting chairs.

"A week here with pay will not be half bad," mused the Doctor. But his pleasant thought was interrupted by the entrance of a small, middle-aged man, with young eyes, but with hair that would soon be white. He introduced himeslf.

"I am Peterson, the man who wrote to you. I presume that you are Dr. Overfield?"

The two men shook hands and sat down by the the fireplace.

It was early September, and the days were chill in the mountains.

"I understand that you are a psychiatrist, Dr. Overfield," the white-haired man began. "At least, I was told that you might be helpful to me in the solving of my problem."

"I do not know what your trouble is," answered the Doctor, "but I have not made any appointments for the next week; so that time and my ability are at your disposal. You did not mention in your letters just what the trouble was. Do you care to tell me now?"

"Not now. Perhaps after dinner. You may be able to see for yourself. I am going to take you to your bedroom, and you may come down at six and meet the rest of the family."

The room that Overfield was taken to seemed comfortable in every way. Peterson left the room, hesitated, and came back.

"Just a word of advice, Doctor. When you are alone in here, be sure to keep the door locked."

"Shall I lock it when I leave?"

"No. That will not be necessary. No one will steal anything."

The Doctor shut the door, locked it according to advice, and went to the windows. They overlooked the woods. In the distance he could see a few deer. Nearer, white rabbits were playing on the lawn. It was a pretty view, but the windows were barred!

"A prison?" he asked himself. "Bars on the windows! Advice to keep the door locked! What can he be afraid of? Evidently, not of thieves. Perhaps he has a phobia. I wonder whether all the rooms are barred? This seems interesting. And then that fence? It would be a brave man who would try to go over that, even with a ladder. He did not impress me as being a neurasthenic, but, at the same time, he wanted to delay the interrogation. Evidently, he feels that it would be easier if I found out some things for myself."

The Doctor was tired from the long drive, so he took off his shoes and collar, and started to go to sleep. The silence was complete. The slightest sound was magnified into a startling intensity. Minutes passed. He thought that he heard a doorknob turn and was sure that it was his door, but no one knocked and there was no sound of footsteps. Later, thinking about everything, he went to sleep. It was growing dark when he awoke and looked at his watch. It was ten minutes to six. Just time enough to dash into his dinner clothes. He did not know whether people dressed for dinner at that place, but there was no harm in doing so.

Downstairs, Peterson was waiting for him. Mrs. Peterson was also there. She must have known that the Doctor would dress for dinner; and, not wanting to embarrass him, also had dressed formally for the occasion. But her husband wore the same suit that he had on all day. He had even neglected to comb his hair.

At the table, the white-haired man kept silent. The wife was a sparkling conversationalist, and the Doctor enjoyed her talk as much as he did the meal. Mrs. Peterson had been to places and had seen many things, and she had a way of telling about them that was even more vivid than the average travelogue. She appeared to be interested in everything.

"Here is a woman of culture," thought Overfield. "This woman knows a little bit about everything and is able to tell it at the right time."

He might have added that she was beautiful. Subconsciously, he felt that; and even more deeply wondered why such a woman should have married a fossil like Peterson. Nice enough man, all right, but certainly no fit mate for such a woman.

The woman was small, delicately formed, yet radiant with health and vitality. Someone was sick in the family, but it evidently was not she. Dr. Overfield studied the husband. Perhaps there was his patient? Silent, moody, suspicious, locked doors and barred windows! It might be a case of paranoia, and the wife was forcing the conversation and trying to be gay simply as a defence reaction.

Was she really happy? At times, a cloud seemed to come over her face, to be chased away at once by a smile or even a merry laugh. At least, she was not altogether happy. How could one be with a husband like that!

The surly, silent, servant waited on the table. He seemed to anticipate every need of his mistress. His service was beyond the shadow of reproach; but in some way, for some reason, the Doctor disliked him from the beginning. He tried to analyse that dislike, but failed. Later on he found the reason. His mind was working fast, trying to solve the problem of his being there, the invitation to spend a week. Suddenly, he awoke to the fact that there was a vacant chair. The table had been set for four, and just then the door opened and in walked a young lad followed by a burly man in black.

"This is my son, Alexander, Dr. Overfield. Shake hands with the gentleman, Alexander."

Closely followed by the man in black, the youth

walked around the table, took the Doctor's hand, and then sat down at the empty place. An ice was served. The man in black stood in back of the chair and carefully supervised every movement the boy made. Conversation was now blocked. The dessert was eaten in silence. Finished, Peterson spoke.

"You can take Alexander to his room, Yorry."

"Very well, Mr. Peterson."

Again there were but three at the table, but the conversation was not resumed. Cigarettes were smoked in silence. Then Mrs. Peterson excused herself.

"I am designing a new dress, and I have gotten to a very interesting place. I cannot decide on snaps or buttons; and if there are to be buttons, there must be an originality about them that will make their use logical. So, I shall have to ask you gentlemen to excuse me. I hope that you will spend a comfortable week with us, Dr. Overfield."

"I am sure of that, Mrs. Peterson," replied the Doctor, rising as she left the table. The white-haired man did not rise. He simply kept looking into the wall ahead of him, looking into it without seeing the picture on it—without seeing anything that there was to see! At last, he crushed the fire out of his cigarette and rose.

"Let us go into the library. I want to talk."

Once there, he tried to make the Doctor comfortable.

"Take off your coat and collar if you wish, and

put your feet up on the stool. We shall be alone tonight, and there is no need of formality."

"I judge you are not very happy, Mr. Peterson?" the Doctor began. It was just an opening wedge to the mental catharsis that he hoped would follow. In fact, it was a favorite introduction of his to the examination of a patient. It gave the sick person confidence in the Doctor, a feeling that he understood something about him, personally. And many people came to his office because they were not happy.

"Not very," was the reply. "I am going to tell you something about it, but part I want you to see for yourself. It starts back at the time when I began in business. I had been called Philip by my parents, Philip Peterson. When in school, I studied about Philip of Macedonia, and there were parts of his life that I rather admired. He was a road breaker, if you know what I mean. He took a lot of countries and consolidated them. He reorganized the army. Speaking in modern slang, he was a 'go-getter.' Of course, he had his weaknesses—such as wine and women—but in the main, he was rather fine.

"There was a difference between being King of Macedonia and becoming president of a leather company, but I thought that the same principles might be used and would probably lead to success. At any rate, I studied the life of Philip and tried to profit by it. At last, I became a rich man.

"Then I married. As you saw, my wife is a gifted, cultured woman. We had a son. At his birth, I named him Alexander. I wanted to follow in the course of the Macedonian. I ruled the leather business in America, and I hoped that he would rule it in the entire world. You saw the boy tonight at supper."

"Yes, I saw him."

"And your diagnosis?"

"Not exactly true to form, but resembles the type of mental deficiency known as *mongolian idiocy* more than anything else."

"That is what I have been told. We kept him at home for two years, and then I placed him in one of the best private schools in America. When he reached the age of ten, they refused to keep him any longer, no matter what I paid them. So I fixed this place up, sold out my interests, and came here to live. He is my son, and I feel that I should care for him."

"It is rather peculiar that they do not want him in a private school. With your wealth..."

"Something happened. They felt that they could not take the responsibility for his care."

"How does he act? What does his mother think about it?"

"Do you know much about mothers in general?"

"A little."

"Then you can understand. His mother thinks that he is perfect. At times, she refuses to believe that he is feeble-minded. She uses the word 'retarded' and thinks that he will outgrow the condition and some day become normal."

"She is mistaken."

"I am afraid so. But I cannot convince her. When the matter is argued, she becomes angry; and she is very unpleasant when she is that way. We moved here. You saw our servants. The butler serves in several capacities. He has been in the family for many years and is to be trusted. He is deaf-mute."

"I understand," the Doctor exclaimed. "That accounts for his surly, silent, personality. All mutes are queer."

"I presume that is true. He keeps house for us. You see, other servants are hard to keep. They come, but they won't stay after they learn about Alexander."

"Do they object to his mentality?"

"No, it is the way he acts that worries them. I have given you the facts. They will not stay here. The man, Yorry, is an ex-pugilist. He is without nerves and without fear. He is very good to the boy; but, at the same time, he makes him obey. Since he has been here, it is possible to bring the lad to the table, and that makes Mother very happy. But, of course, he cannot be on duty all the time. When he has his hours off, he lets Alexander run in the park."

"The boy must like it out there. I saw the deer and the rabbits."

"Yes, it gives him exercise. He likes to chase them."

"Don't you think he ought to have some playmates?"

"I used to think so. I even went so far as to adopt another boy. He died. After that, I could not repeat the experiment."

"But any child might die," the Doctor replied. "Why not bring another boy in, even for a few hours a day, for him to talk to and play with?"

"No, never again! But you stay here and watch the boy. Examine him and see if you can give me advice."

"I am afraid that there is not much to be done for him beyond training him, and correcting any bad habits that he may have."

The white-haired man looked puzzled as he replied:

"That is the trouble. Some years ago, I consulted a specialist. I told him all about it, and he said that he thought the child had better be allowed a certain freedom of action. He said something about desires and libido and thought that the only chance for improvement was in letting him have his own way. That is one reason why we are here with the deer and the rabbits."

"You mean that the boy likes to play with them?"

"Not exactly. But you study him. I have told Yorry that he is to answer all your questions. He knows the boy better than I do; and God forgive me for saying it, but I know him too well. Of course, it is hard for me to talk about it. I would rather have you get the details from Yorry. It is growing late and perhaps you had better go to bed. Be sure to lock the door."

"I'll do that," the Doctor said, "but you told me that nothing would be stolen."

"No. Nothing will be stolen."

The Doctor went to his room, thoroughly puzzled. He knew the variety of mental deficiency known as *mongolian idiocy*. He had helped examine and care for several hundred of such cases. Young Alexander was one, yet, he was different. There was something about him that did not quite harmonize with that diagnosis. His habits? Perhaps that was it. Was his father afraid of him? Was that why he had a strong man to train him? Was that why the bars were on the windows? But why the rabbits and the little deer?

Almost before he was asleep he was roused by a knock at the door. Going to it, he called without opening the door.

"What is it?"

"This is Yorry," was the response. "Are you all right?"

"Yes."

"Let me in."

The Doctor opened the door, allowed the man to enter, and locked it behind him.

"What is the trouble?"

"Alexander is out of his room. We do not mind it in the daytime, but at night it is bad. Look over at the window!"

There was a white thing at one of the windows, holding on to the bars and shaking them in an effort to break them. Yorry shook his head.

"That lad, that lad! This is no place for him, but what are the poor people to do? Well, if you are safe, I will go out and try to get him. You lock the door behind me."

"Are you afraid of him?"

"Not for myself, but for others. I do not know fear. Mr. Peterson said you wanted to examine the boy. What time tomorrow?"

"At ten. Right here will do."

"I'll have him here. Good night, and be sure to lock the door."

The Doctor was tired, so he went to sleep with all the questions unsolved. The next morning breakfast was served to him in his room by the deaf-mute. At ten, Yorry came in with Alexander. The boy seemed frightened, but obeyed the commands of his attendant.

In most respects, the examination showed the physical defects of the mongolian idiot. There were a few minor differences. Though the boy was small for his age, the musculature was good, and the teeth were perfect. Not a cavity was present. The upper canines were unusual.

"He has very fine teeth, Yorry," the Doctor commented.

"He has, Sir, and he uses them," replied the man.

"You mean in eating his food?"

"Yes. Just that."

"They are the teeth of a meat-eater."

"That is what he is."

"I wish that you would tell me about it, honestly. Why did they turn him out of that private school?"

"It was his habits."

"What kind of habits?"

"Suppose you see for yourself. The three of us will go out in the woods. It is safe as long as you are with me, but you must not go by yourself."

The Doctor laughed.

"I am accustomed to abnormals."

"Perhaps, but I do not want anything to happen to you. Come with me, Alexander."

The boy went with them, and seemed to be perfectly docile.

Once in the woods, Yorry helped the boy undress. Naked, the lad started to run through the forest.

"He cannot get out?" the Doctor asked.

"No, nor for that matter, neither can the deer

and the little rabbits. We will not try to follow him. When he finishes, he will come back."

An hour passed, and then two hours. At last, Alexander came creeping through the grass on all fours. Yorry took a wet towel from his pocket, wiped the blood from the boy's face and hands, and then started to dress him.

"So that is what he does?" asked the Doctor.

"Yes, and sometimes more than that."

"And that is why they did not want him in the school?"

"I suppose so. His father told me that when he was young, he started in with flies and bugs and toads."

The Doctor thought fast.

"There was a little child brought here to be his playmate. The boy died. Do know anything about that?"

"No. I do not know anything about that. I do not want to know anything about it. It probably happened before I came here."

Overfield knew that the man was not telling the truth. But even in his lie, he was handing out useful information. The Doctor decided to have another talk with the boy's father. There was no use trying to help unless all the facts were given to him.

At the noonday meal, the conversation was not as sparkling as it had been the evening before. Peterson seemed moody. Mrs. Peterson was polite, but decidedly restrained. It seemed that most of the conversation was forced. After the meal was over, there was one part of the conversation that seemed to stand out in the mind of the specialist. Peterson remarked that one of his teeth was troubling him, and that he would have to see a dentist. His wife replied, "I have perfect teeth. I have never been to a dentist."

In the library, while he was waiting for Peterson to come, Dr. Overfield recalled that statement.

"I have examined your son, Mr. Peterson," began the specialist, "and I have seen him in the woods. Yorry told me about some things and lied to me about others. Up to the present time, no one seems willing to tell me the entire truth. I have one question that I must have answered. How did the boy die? The one you had for a playmate?"

"I am not sure. And when I say that, I am perfectly honest. We found him dead in his room one morning. A glass had been broken in the bedroom window. A lot of broken glass was around him. There was a deep cut in one side of his throat. The Coroner thought that he had walked in his sleep, struck the window pane, and that a piece of glass had severed the jugular vein. He certified that as the cause of the death."

"What do you think, Mr. Peterson?"

"I have stopped thinking."

"Was it before that, or afterwards, that you had the bars placed in the windows?"

"After that. Can you help the boy?"

"I am afraid not. The advice that the other man gave you years ago was bad. It has kept the boy in fine physical condition, but there are other things to be considered besides physical health. If he were my son, I would remove the deer and the rabbits, those that are still alive. And I would try and train him in different habits."

"I will think that over. I paid you for your opinion, and I value it. Now, one more question: Is this habit of the boy's an hereditary one? Do you think, that in the past, some ancestor of his did something like that?"

It was a puzzling question. Perhaps Dr. Overfield was right in answering it with another question.

"Any insanity in the family?"

"None that I ever heard of."

"Good! How about your wife's family?"

"Her heredity is as good as mine, perhaps better."

"Then all that we can say is that *mongolianism* can come in any family; and, as far as the boy's habit is concerned, suppose we call it an atavism? At one time, all our ancestors ate raw meat. The Mongolian type of mental deficiency comes to us from the cradle of the human race. The boy may have brought it with him as he leaped forward two million years, brought raw meat-eating with his slanting eyebrows."

"I wish I were sure," commented the father. "I

would give anything to be sure that I was not to blame for the boy's condition."

"Or your wife?" the Doctor asked.

"Oh! There is no question about her," was the half smiling reply. "She is one of the nicest women God ever made."

"Perhaps there is something in her subconscious, something that does not show on the surface?"

The husband shook his head.

"No. She is just good through and through."

This ended the conversation. The Doctor promised to spend the rest of the week, though he felt that there was little use in his doing so. He joined the retired leather man and his wife at dinner. Mrs. Peterson was more beautiful than ever, in a white evening dress, trimmed with gold sequins. Peterson looked tired; but his wife was brilliant in every way, in addition to her costume. She talked as though she would never tire, and everything that she said was worth listening to. She had just aided in the organization of a milk fund for undernourished children. Charity, it seemed, was one of her hobbies. Peterson talked about heredity, but little attention was paid to him or his thoughts. He soon stopped talking.

Through it all there was something that Dr. Overfield could not understand. When he said good night to the white-haired man, he told him as much.

"I do not understand it either," commented Peterson, "but perhaps, before I die, I shall understand. I cannot help feeling that there is something in heredity, but I cannot prove it."

Dr. Overfield locked the door of his bedroom, and retired at once. He was sleepy, and, at the same time, nervous. He thought that a long night's rest would help. But he did not sleep long. A pounding on the door brought him to consciousness.

"Who is there?" he asked.

"It's me, Yorry. Open the door!"

"What is the trouble?"

"It is the boy, Alexander. He has slipped away from me again, and I cannot find him."

"Perhaps he has gone to the woods?"

"No. All the outside doors are locked. He must be in the house."

"Have you hunted?"

"Everywhere. The butler is safe in his room. I have been all over the house except in the Master's room."

"Why not go there? Wait till I get some clothes on. Just a minute. He keeps the doors locked, doesn't he? He told me to keep my door locked. You are sure he has his door locked?"

"It was locked earlier in the evening. I tested it. I do that every night with all the bedrooms."

"Anyone with duplicate keys?"

"No one except Mrs. Peterson. I think she must have a set; but she sleeps in her room, and her door was locked. At least it was, earlier in the evening."

"I think we ought to go to their rooms. The

boy has to be somewhere. Perhaps he is with one of his parents."

"If he is with his mother, it is all right. They understand each other. She can do anything with him."

They rushed upstairs. The door to Mrs. Peterson's room was open, the room empty, and the bed untouched. That was something not to be expected. The door to the next room, Peterson's room, was closed—but not locked. Opening it, Yorry turned on the electric lights.

Before he did so, from the dark room came an odd, low, snarling, noise. Then the lights were on, and there was the Peterson family on the floor. Peterson was in the middle. He had his shirt torn off, and he was very quiet. On the right side, tearing at the muscles of the arm, was Alexander, his face and hands smeared with blood. On the other side, at the neck, the Peterson woman was fastened, drinking blood from the jugular vein. Her face and dress were stained with blood, and as she looked up, her face was that of an irritated, but otherwise contented dæmon. She seemed disturbed over the interruption, but too preoccupied to understand it. She kept on drinking, but the boy snarled his anger. Overfield pulled Yorry through the doorway, turned out the lights, and slammed the door in back of them.

Then he dragged the dazed man down the steps to the first floor.

"Where is the telephone?" he yelled.

Yorry finally showed him. The Doctor jerked off the receiver.

"Hullo! Hullo! Central. Give me the Coroner. No, I don't know the number. Why should I know the number? Get him for me. Hullo! Is this the Coroner? Can you hear me? This is a doctor talking, Dr. Overfield. Come to Philip Peterson's house at once. There has been a murder committed here. Yes. The man is dead. What killed him? Heredity. You can't understand? Why should you? Now, listen to me. He had his throat cut, perhaps with a piece of broken glass, perhaps not. Can you understand that? Do you remember the little boy? Come up, and I will wait for you here."

The Doctor hung up the receiver. Yorry was looking at him.

"The master was always worried about the boy," Yorry said.

"He can stop worrying now," answered the Doctor.

THE FACE IN THE MIRROR

JAMES FORDYCE was slowly, but surely, improving.

For some weeks past, he had remained quiet, and his physician was encouraged over his condition. He even went so far as to report to the Fordyce family that, if the improvement continued, their son might be completely restored.

He even wondered if, perhaps, he might not have been wrong in his original diagnosis, and that Fordyce was recovering from some toxic condition of short duration, instead of the serious mental disease that usually continued for life.

Fordyce was, therefore, transferred to a sunny room in a front ward with a comfortable bed. There was also a rocking-chair and a bureau with a mirror on it. James Fordyce sat in the rocking-chair, and read daily papers. He seemed content with the quiet life of a separate room.

The second week he was in this front ward room, he escaped. To him, it seemed a very easy thing to do. All the doors were unlocked. He dressed and walked down the halls leisurely, without rousing the sleeping night attendants and nurses.

Once away from the building, in the quiet, forested surroundings, he increased his speed slightly; not from fear of being followed, but because he was eager to arrive at his destination. There was no doubt in his mind as to exactly where he wanted to go. And he was as certain why he wanted to go to this particular place, and who would be waiting there for him.

Emerging from the evergreens surrounding the hospital, he came to the main highway. It was deserted that spring night, but Fordyce was not surprised at the absence of all traffic, even pedestrian. He saw no reason why he should not be absolutely alone. For an hour he walked in the brilliant moonlight. A solitary star gleamed near the full moon, and, as he walked, he told himself a little story about that star. In the telling, he realized that he had a story which, if given to the world, would be so new that all men would marvel at the originality of the creation.

Soon, surprisingly soon, he came to a road leading off the highway at right angles. It was a narrow, dirt road, with tall fir trees on either side, as it climbed straight up a fairly steep mountain. This road was not a thoroughfare, for, after a long space, he rounded the first turn in the moonlight-speckled way, and approached a high stone wall which came to the roadside and was joined together by a heavy, wooden gate with the sign—

PRIVATE ROAD
No Admission

painted on it. The words were painted large, and were clearly legible in the moonlight.

Fordyce laughed.

"Since I own the land and built the road and wall, framed the gate and painted the sign, it certainly cannot apply to me," he whispered to himself. Opening the gate, he passed through; turned, closed and locked it behind him.

"For," he said, "since I am now on my own land, I would have no one come after me, not even him."

The moonlight made the road a streak of dull silver, as it wound up the mountain between the dense forest of tall fir trees. Somehow, the grade did not seem steep to the man, as he climbed steadily upward, and he rejoiced in the solitude. He wanted to be alone, certain that, only in complete isolation from the world, could he attain to the desired perfection of life. He eagerly looked forward to long years, wherein he might complete the development of his individuality.

At last, he came to the top of the mountain. It must have been a very high mountain, because the moon was so near the earth that he could almost touch it; and the star, he knew, actually rested on the dome-like roof of the little circular building which occupied the exact center of a clearing from which the mountain sides dropped sharply. This building with the dome-shaped roof looked like an observatory, and the brilliant star rested exactly on the center of the roof, like a lode star, directing him to his place of emancipation.

"That star has many peculiar features," Fordyce remarked to himself. "It is a monstrous star and yet it does not crush the building. It shines, therefore it must have heat, but it does not burn the roof; and since it does not roll off, it must have adhesive qualities in its five sharp points. But I am not concerned especially with the star nor with the moon, which seems so near and cold and portentous in its steely gleaming.

"There is something of vast importance waiting to be done in the house. The door will be open; I will go in and do it. No one has lived here since I left so many years ago. I built the gate and painted the sign, so I know no one would dare enter against my prohibitions.

"The house must need minor alterations. Everything must be made spotlessly clean, cobwebs removed, and any dead fly taken out and properly buried. Pictures must be dusted and straightened if they hang askew. Books must be rearranged in proper order, and some will have to be burned, for I will have nothing in the house that is not clean. All the house must be renovated for my homecoming. Thus, after months of life alone in a quiet, clean, house, I will gain the peace that is so necessary for the salvation of my soul."

He walked through the unlocked door into a room so large that, in the dim light, it seemed to be the only room in the house; but he knew that dark corridors ran from it into still darker rooms.

"And of those rooms," he said, "I can only dream; for though I built them, I have never revisited them since. Neither do I wish to enter them, for the things I have seen there, when sleeping, are not pleasant things; and it is the better for me to live in this one large room, where I can find peace and understanding."

A small table with straight-backed chairs on either side occupied the center of this large, but sparsely furnished, room. On the table was a small standing mirror, and on either side of this mirror was a burning candle. Fordyce, suddenly realizing that he was tired, sat down on one of the chairs, closed his eyes, and rested his head on arms folded in front of the mirror.

Perhaps he slept, but of this he neither knew nor cared. There was no one to disturb him, but he knew he must open his eyes. Startled, he sat upright, staring straight before him.

A man sat in the chair across the table, and Fordyce could see him very clearly through the mirror. In fact, he could only see him when looking through the mirror, for when he looked above the glass or on the sides or under it, no part of the man was visible. It seemed as if the man was simply a picture in an old fashioned frame instead of an actual, living man with a face that could be seen only through a looking-glass.

Fordyce knew him well. From the very first second that he saw him, James Fordyce recognized him. And he also knew why he was there, what he would say, and the way it would all end. Fordyce frowned. This was not at all the way he had planned it. But the man on the other side of the glass laughed, leering. As Fordyce saw him laughing, he realized that he was the cause of the other's merriment.

Tauntingly, the man spoke:

"I have been waiting a long time for you. Were you afraid to come? There was no reason for fear; we have so much in common. I am as like you as though we were identical twins. If we could but fuse our souls, then how happy both of us would be. But whenever I make a suggestion of any kind, you meet it with positive refusal. Even when I suggest that you do the things I know you want to do, you refuse merely because I suggested them to you. That is so foolish! You deny yourself—and me—so much pleasure."

"You misconstrue everything," replied Fordyce angrily. "You have been a curse rather than a blessing to me. I could have accomplished much, become really great, had it not been for you. There was a poem I wanted to write, and every time I scratched a sentence, you suggested that it was not worded properly; and I had to cross it out and start all over again. And I've never written more than these first lines:

> *Too late the roses are falling,*
> *Over you and me...*

"I do not want you here," Fordyce continued. "I never wanted you, and I do not need you. Besides, this house is only large enough for one man. I built it, and I own it, so I command you to leave at once! Do you understand? Leave at once!! Give me the privacy I seek. I have many great things to do. The most important one is the understanding of my soul, and I can attain my objectives only when by myself."

The man behind the mirror continued to smile, mockingly.

"You say the house is too small for two men to live in? Don't you know there are other rooms besides this one, rooms at the end of those dark corridors? I spend much of my time there."

"I know about those rooms," cried Fordyce, consternation in his voice, his face white and sweating with fear and rage. "I know those rooms, and I also know you lived in one of them, and from that place you came to me in my dreams. For years you have come to me; and the creatures in the dreams you manufactured in your dank, slimy cell of a room must have been created by monsters of a bygone age and fed on the broth of Hell.

"I could stand life so long as you came to me only in my dreams for there was always the awakening and the cold, revitalizing freshness of morning; but lately you have visited me in the daytime. It is true I never saw you, but I heard your voice from inside the walls of the room, from behind the door; and one day you entered my brain and talked to me from there. And I will not have that.

"There must be an end to this persecution! You must go out of my life—out of my house, and especially must you go out of my soul; for in all these I have room for but one man. I will not share my soul with anyone, especially a man who has so foul a mind as you. Are you going freely or must I force you?"

The man behind the mirror became serious.

"I am not going willingly and you cannot force me. I am too vital a part of you to even think of leaving you. Perhaps that soul you talk of so glibly is not really your soul, but mine. Perhaps it is our joint possession? And if I have anything to do with it, I want it to be a clean, decent soul. Constantly you soil it with your adventurings in Borneo or Gobi. Perhaps you do not think I know about them? I was with you all the time and kept whispering to you that it would be best for you to behave more decorously."

"That is not true," Fordyce shrieked, his face convulsed with anger. "Alone I am pure, clean, a fine man. But you always come to me with your tempting dreams, made in that horrid place where you live; and those dreams seem so real, that were it not for my powerful resistance, I would perhaps live the dream-life in the sunlight of the daytime.

"Leave me alone! When I start doing something, cease your repeated urgings that I not do it! How can I ever do the things that have to be done if you are constantly blocking me? How can I ever finish the poem?"

"The poem is finished," laughed the mirror-man. "That is all there ever was to that poem; and when there is no more to a poem, it is finished. Likewise, your isolation is finished because, from now on, I am remaining very close to you. In fact, I am going to live in this room with you, and you are going to do the things I want you to do. Day after day, you will sit here with me, playing with the dreams I bring you and laughing when you hear the different voices in which I speak to you.

"If you cease struggling, there will be no more trouble for James Fordyce because his soul will be the soul of me and my soul will be that of James Fordyce, and you will never worry any more."

"I have considered yielding to you," whispered Fordyce. "For many reasons, such a life would be attractive. Some of the men in the house I left tonight have submitted to your allure, and in their sleep they are always smiling, no doubt because of their dreams; but in the daytime they sit in a corner, on the floor, and wish neither to eat or keep clean; no, nor even to breathe because they are so happy talking to you, and men like you.

"I have thought of ending life that way, no more struggles, no more conflicts, no more splitting of the personality; just a pleasant life of wandering with the Hell-men, and sharing with them the abominable pleasures they have devised in their houses by the Lake of Fire."

Fordyce sat musing, his face drawn with the inner struggle. He roused himself and continued:

"Yes, I have thought of it, but tonight I finally renounced such a life, and once I arrive at a decision, that decision cannot be changed. That is why I came here; to escape from you and your domination."

"But there is no escape from me. I am a part of you! I showed you that by talking to you from your brain. How can you escape from me when I am with you always, even unto the end of the world?"

"That is true. But you speak of the end of the world. What comes next? I suppose you know. You always know more than I do. You always say I am wrong and you are right, when I know that it is not so. But we were talking about your leaving this house and never returning. Again I ask: Will you go willingly, or must I make you?"

The mirror-man shook his head, in negation.

"I am never going, and you cannot make me, for I am you and you are me. How can I leave this house unless you go with me? This is a very comfortable room, and I enjoy your society, so here I will remain, talking to you; and if there is argument, that is your own fault, for I never argue—just talk."

Fordyce licked his parched lips with a dry tongue. He had arrived at a decision, and knew that he must move quickly, before that other man could block his movements. Leaping from his chair, he plunged head first through the mirror, grappled with the mirror-man, and, with a piece of the broken glass, he made certain that the other man would talk no more.

He smiled as he did this; the victory was his. There would be no more arguments; no more thwarting of desires. Now he could live quietly, alone in his house; and do the many important things he had to do—such as the better understanding of his soul.

First he must finish the poem. He was sleepy, but he could still clearly remember the beginning:

Too late the roses are falling,
Over you and me...

It seemed an excellent beginning for a poem, and he was sure he could complete it in the morning. He would also write that story of the star on the domed roof of the house, but now he was too tired.

His eyes closed, his head drooped forward as he fell into a deep, painless rest; and in that sleep, no dreams tormented him.

The next morning, when the nurse came to rouse James Fordyce, he was on the floor. On the bureau, the mirror was broken, and Fordyce held a jagged sliver of the glass in his rigid hand. He had, indeed, won the victory; now he could finish the poem.

THE CEREBRAL LIBRARY

WANTED. Five hundred college graduates, male, to perform secretarial work of a pleasing nature. Salary adequate to their position. Five year contract. Address No. 23 A, New York Times.

WANTED. Three librarians, well versed in world literature. Five year contract. Address No. 23 A, New York Times.

* * * * *

THESE two advertisements attracted a great deal of attention. The market of supply, as far as college graduates were concerned, was over-stocked; and there was any number of young men who were willing to do almost any kind of work for any kind of a salary, let alone a salary described as adequate. The letters poured into the 23 A box, and every effort was made to ascertain the identity of the advertiser so that personal application could be made; but all in vain.

Each of the thousands of applicants received a lengthy questionnaire. Each recipient filled out his paper, and sent it to a numbered letter box in the

New York Post Office. Those who were fortunate had a personal interview with a sharp business man who admitted that he was simply engaged to select 503 men, capable of doing a certain work and willing to do it for a five-year period.

At last, the five hundred and three men were selected. They were given tickets and expense money for a trip to an isolated town in Maine. They were told that the full scope of their work would be explained to them there, and that then, if there were any unwilling to sign the final contract, they would be permitted to leave.

In small groups of twenty or less, the collegiates left New York. Their absence was hardly missed. None of them had been able, so far, to do anything else but graduate from an A.B. course in some university. They were mainly plodders; good men, but not brilliant.

The town in Maine was simply a town in Maine. Including its two hotels, boarding houses, and private homes, it could, by crowding, take care of the unusual flood of visitors. The Methodist Church had been rented for a one-day meeting. It was understood that the meeting would take place when everyone had arrived.

At last, the five hundred and three men were in the church. The young men were, to say the least, slightly excited. Up to the present time, they had formed no idea at all of what they were supposed to do. A five year contract with an adequate salary was attractive, but, on the other hand, the work might be so unattractive that it could not be considered.

The three men selected for the position of librarians were seated on one side, up front, in the Amen corners. The others filled the church. The doors were locked. And then the speaker stepped out in front of the pulpit. He was a well known publicity man from Boston, by the name of Gates. He explained that he had simply been engaged to present a certain proposition to them, and that he had nothing to do with the proposed work after they had signed their five-year contract.

His client, he explained, was a man interested in literary research. He was working on a new plan of universal knowledge which would require the reading of hundreds and thousands of books of all descriptions and in at least three foreign languages, though most of the books would be in the English language. All that the five hundred young men would be asked to do would be to spend a certain number of hours each day in reading. There would be no note-taking and no examinations. They should simply read the books given them. The three librarians would, under instructions, run the library, issue books, and keep a careful record of the books read by each man. If a reader had a hobby, such as mathematics or biology, that hobby was to be given consideration in his reading assignment. Adequate facilities were to be given for exercise, and the salaries would be ten thousand a year for five years; but during those five years, the readers would be out of communication with the world. If they wanted to, they could consider that they were in a glorified prison, or in an excellent hotel on a desert island. At the end of five years, they would each have fifty thousand dollars and an extensive addition to their education. The librarians would each receive twenty thousand a year, or a hundred thousand at the end of five years.

Quickly, a hundred questions arose for answer. Mr. Gates answered them to the best of his ability. Some secrets, he explained, could not be divulged. In fact, there were some things about the whole affair that he himself was absolutely ignorant of. The Farmers' Bank in Philadelphia had informed him that the man in back of the plan was worth at least twenty-five million dollars, and no one need have any doubt in regard to receiving his salary. He did not know where the library was, where the reading would be done; but he did know that everything possible would be done for the comfort of the readers. Of course, it would mean isolation, but at that salary, isolation was preferable to contact and the ever present chance of poverty and actual starvation.

All that the applicants had to do was to sign a contract. They would then be given instructions as to their destination.

One and all rushed forward to sign on the dotted

line. They were all serious young men, and the work looked atractive to them, even with the threatened isolation. As they signed, each man was given a ticket to Boston and an envelope to be opened on arriving there.

Their journey to Boston was a far more cheerful one than the one to the isolated town in Maine. This condition was at least one of living. They had graduated, and now they had made good. They were white collar men, but they had an assured income that would put them on easy street in five years.

In Boston, each man opened his envelope. It contained a ticket to another city or town, expense money for the trip, and another sealed envelope to be opened on arriving there. And each ticket was to A DIFFERENT DESTINATION. Theirs not to question why; but each man was secretly sure that at the end of his trip he would find the new library and his five-year job.

The sealed envelope told another story. Another ticket, another amount of cash for traveling expenses, another destination. This time *the destinations for all were the same.* The guiding hand had deliberately tossed five hundred and three men to five hundred and three parts of the United States and Canada and had then tossed them back again to one place. There was no doubt of his purpose. Secrecy!

For some months, the realtors of Stroudsburg had been thrilled by the news that Pennsylvania

Manor, on the crest of the Poconos, was at last sold. For some years it had been a source of worry. Built on an elaborate scale to provide a pleasure resort for six hundred guests, it had failed to pay the necessary interest on the investment, and had been kept closed. Its wonderful ballroom, golf course, and four thousand acres of land had been useless and worthless. Now it was sold, and no doubt the resort business would pick up. There were a thousand rumors, ten thousand pieces of idle gossip. Everybody guessed, and no one knew the truth.

A high wire fence was run around the four thousand acres, and then the bare statement was given to the press that the Manor was to be used as a retreat for the intellectual, a place where education would take the part of religion and where, shut off from the rest of the world, consolation could be sought in higher intellectual development.

This information was all a very great disappointment to the people of Stroudsburg. They wanted the Manor filled with six hundred pleasure-seekers who had only one idea, and that should be to spend money. The thought of turning the place into a monastery, with higher education as the only aim and the world shut out with iron gates and a steel fence, was not at all what the business men of the community wanted. Still, there it was, and they had to make the best of it.

There were some changes made in the main building of the Manor. The most startling was the conversion of the ballroom and the rooms adjoining it into a library. Books were brought to the Manor by the truckload, books by the thousand, almost hundreds of thousands. The placing of the shelves, the arrangement of the books, the card cataloguing, were all done rapidly and efficiently by a trained company of librarians. When the work was done, the workmen left a perfect library. It was by no means the largest library in the United States, but few could compare with it in the scope of informa- which it covered.

The kitchen was opened; and servants, well-trained and efficient, were installed. The golf course and tennis courts were put in perfect order. A lounge was fitted for a moving picture hall. There was everything for comfort, but there was no post office.

One by one the young men arrived at Pennsylvania Manor. They were assigned to comfortable bedrooms. Verbal instructions of a very simple nature were given them. Additional data was obtained from them concerning the courses they had majored in while at college and their preferences in reading material. The three librarians, arriving, expressed delight at the perfect order of their workshop and at once arranged their part of the five-year program. Assignments were made to each man in such a variety that the entire range of human knowledge would be covered by their reading. Each man was to read three hundred books a year. That meant fifteen hundred books per man, or a total of 750,000 books for the five years.

That number of books, three quarters of a million, was by no means the largest in the world. The Library of the British Museum contained two million, was by no means the largest collection in the world. The Library of the British Museum contained two million books and over five million separate pieces of printed matter, while the Imperial Library in Petrograd contained nearly two million books. Even the New York Public Library held one million, eight hundred thousand books and hundreds of thousands of pamphlets.

But it was a remarkable collection of books, considering the fact that it was most hastily gathered together for an unknown purpose. It had been purchased mainly from second-hand book stores, which, with a thrill that comes once in a lifetime, emptied their treasuries into the Pennsylvania Manor.

Quiet days followed. The activity was constantly present, but almost noiseless. Following breakfast, the readers went in different groups to various sections of the library and handed in the read volume of the day before, in order to receive a new book for the new day's reading. Some read in the morning and evening and exercised in the afternoon, while others devoted the morning hours to exercise. The time during which the book was read was optional with the individual, the only requirement being that the book must be diligently and slowly read during the course of the twenty-four hours.

The young men had been carefully selected. They were all of the methodical, studious type, who took life seriously, and who would have felt insulted had anyone dared keep a watch on them. Each day five hundred books were read, each day five hundred were returned, and five hundred more issued in their places.

The library was being regularly and systematically used. The librarians were busy; the readers were busy. It was by no means the largest library in the world, but it was a well used one.

The work done by these men was monotonous in its nature, but diversified in its scope. The daily book was a new book, and it meant one less book to have to read before the new freedom could be won at the end of five years. One year passed, and then two. Pennsylvania Manor ceased to be a novelty to the casual summer visitor. It no longer was a curiosity; it almost ceased to exist as far as Monroe County was concerned. The summer sun burned the Pocono Mountains; the winter winds swept them clear of snow only to bring more snow; season followed season, but the readers read on.

For some years, the activities at Pennsylvania Manor had attracted the attention of the Chief of the Secret Service of the United States, headquarters Washington, D.C. He was a man who believed in the prevention of crime rather than in the detection of crime, and nothing pleased him more than to look forward into the future, see that a crime was premeditated, and then prevent the completion of the conspiracy by prompt action.

Among his various boxes of card indexes, was one which he called his question box. Here, each on a separate card, were listed the details of extraordinary occurrences and happenings in the national life which he could not explain. He claimed that behind each of these lay a crime against society, and he spent long hours in two forms of study with these cards, going over them slowly, one at a time, trying to prepare for the future, first, by their story, and second, by comparing the details of unsolved felonies by going backward to the story told in the cards.

He was at this kind of work when a caller was announced. He looked at the card:

Taine of San Francisco.

"I wonder who he is and what he wants? Some crank, judging by his card," he said.

"What do you want?" he asked. "This is my busy day, and I cannot give you much time."

"You sent for me. I thought you would know by my visiting card."

"Hmm! That doesn't tell me anything."

"It should. You wired the Chief of the San Francisco Secret Service for the loan of his best man; and here I am."

"So, the best they have out there is Taine?"

"It looks that way."

"I never heard of you."

"That may be true. But some of my best work has not been broadcast. I married the Chief's daughter. He likes me. Of course, she does too, but she is busy now, so the old man sent me. Want me?"

The Chief looked at the little man standing on the carpet in front of him. A trifle more than five feet tall, rather stockily built, with baby features and buxom cheeks, blue eyes and blond hair. It was a face hard to describe and harder to remember. There was no force of character there, and but little intellectual gleam in the eyes.

The Chief wanted to say something, but did not know how. At last he blurted out:

"Not the killer type, are you?"

"Is that what you wanted? And so sent to our city for it?"

"Just a joke," apologized the Washington man, "and I suppose not in the best of taste. Sit down and have a smoke."

"Thanks, I never smoke. I find that the nicotine injures the delicate enamel of the teeth, and when that is gone, all soon follows."

The Chief went to his files and came back with a folder of papers. He pulled one card out of his question box.

"Read this stuff over, and tell me what you think about it."

Taine started to read. An hour passed, and then

two. The Chief went ahead with his work, while the San Francisco man assorted and read the newspaper clippings.

At last, the Chief could not stand it any longer.

"What do you think about it?" he asked.

"About all those books, and the fence, and those young men?

"There must be someone back of it with lots of money and fond of books," said Mr. Taine.

"Quite original! You really think things like that?"

"I think worse things than that sometimes."

"How would you like to go up there for a year or two, and find out what it is all about?"

"Will it take that long?"

"How do I know? You might have to stay a lifetime. I honestly believe that there is something wrong going on up there, but all the information we receive makes it look perfectly harmless. At the same time, it will not do any harm for you to go up in some disguise, and give me a report on it."

"I have the very idea. The proper disguise for a case like that would be something literary, something like the Encyclopædia Brittanica. Well, I guess I had better go. If I have any trouble, I will let you know. Otherwise, I will report when the case is ended."

He was out of the office before the Chief had time even to reply.

The Chief took it out in thinking:

"Either he is a fool, or I am!"

Taine had a harder time than he expected in crashing the gate of the Pennsylvania Manor. He had expected that it would be easy to obtain employment in some way, but his polite questionings at the main entrance concerning work simply met with equally polite refusals. He watched that main gate for three days, but the only persons to go in were a few truck drivers, and they came out as soon as they unloaded their trucks. Taine finally was almost convinced that the only way he could go in was to enter disguised as a package of books.

But luck was with him. A little Italian came out on the fourth day, holding his jaw. He was bound for a dental office in Stroudsburg. Taine asked for a ride to town in the same automobile with the Italian, and was granted his request. The extraction of a tooth and the chance of a trip to New York with a hundred dollar bill in his pocket was too much for the little foreigner to resist. The exchange of clothing and credentials was an easy matter. Taine asked a hundred questions in Italian as he made up his face, not much, but all that was necessary.

The Italian took the first train for New York. Taine met the automobile from the Manor and returned in it to the gate, but this time he passed through. His papers were satisfactory. He was the new bus boy for six tables in the dining room of the Pennsylvania Manor.

He held that position for six weks, and then developed a severe attack of appendicitis. Humanity demanded his release from the bondage which held all the men within the fence. He was sent to Scranton for the operation. In the hospital, he disappeared. Twenty-four hours later, he was in conference with the Chief in Washington.

"I have spent six weeks inside the Manor," he said, "and I have perfected myself in the work of a bus boy. I do not think that I should care to spend a lifetime at that kind of work, but for a variation it is a very pleasant pastime. When the time came, I left. And some other bus boy is 'bus-boying' for me now, or, at least, I suppose so."

The Chief looked at him with a rather perplexed gaze, as he asked him in somewhat of a harsh tone:

"What did you find out?"

"There are five hundred young men there, Chief, and each one reads a book a day. It seems that they have a motto—'A book a day keeps ignorance away.' There are three men who simply act as librarians and keep tabs on the books that each reader reads each day. They are just reading books. Of course, they eat, and sleep, and golf, but their great business in life is reading books. Think of it! It is not much of a library, mostly second-hand books, but think of five hundred books being read day after day! I mean a different five hundred each day."

"Are you sure of that?"

"Absolutely. I tell you why I am so sure. As fast as a book is read it is burned. They have kept the Pennsylvania Manor warm for over four years now with the books they have destroyed, and you should see that library! Four-fifths of the shelves empty; in fact, they are taking many of them down, and putting up new partitions."

"That is damn queer! Man must be a fool!"

"Must be. Tell you what I think. He is burning the books, because he has no more use for them. That is what a book is for, you know, to read. Of course, I always keep my books or give them away for Christmas presents, but his way is the best."

"Who is back of it?"

"No one knows; at least, no one will tell. Here is another point—the men were engaged on a five-year contract, but they are going to start turning them loose sooner, at the end of the fiftieth month, if they have finished reading the fifteen hundred books called for in the contract. They are going to start next March, and let readers go at the rate of five a day. That means that some time next July the place will be empty, and all the books burned."

"Are they going to be paid?"

"They think they are. Fifty thousand to each man, payable in New York City."

"That is going to run into money."

"It certainly is; so much that I doubt if the poor readers will collect. But they have been having a good time and their education has certainly been on the up-and-up."

The Chief looked puzzled, as he said:

"Something back of this."

"I am sure of it, and I am sure of another thing."

"What?"

"That I am going to find out what it is. This is the most interesting case I have been on, and I am going to stay with it till I solve it. I guess I had better leave you now. Busy man and all that."

This was Taine's ultimatum.

"What are your plans?"

"Haven't any. Just going to drift till I get into the main current, and then I will be swept onward into the Great Unknown."

He walked out without another word. The Chief gave him credit for being at least unusual, probably a crank bordering on the insane.

Wing Loo may not have been the greatest surgeon of all times, yet he thought he was, and that is about the same thing. He was not on his way to America for the money which had been offered him, but because of the opportunity which he had to share in one of the greatest experiments of all ages. He might have performed it in China. However, he was a surgeon and not an electro-scientist, and the man who was to furnish the larger part of the machinery lived in the United States. So to the land of the barbarian, Wing Loo went. He did not know the full details of the experiment, but what he had learned through correspondence convinced him that he was in for a pleasant time.

On the voyage to San Francisco, an able-bodied seaman fell and fractured his skull. Wing Loo, hearing of the accident, offered his assistance and operated in a gale. It was a dangerous operation, performed under the greatest difficulties, so attracting the attention of a newspaper reporter on board ship, that he radioed an account of it to a San Francisco paper. In that article he called the Chinaman that he was on his way to America to give a series of "the greatest living brain surgeon," and intimated lectures before the various national surgical organizations.

The article was published while Wing Loo was on the high seas. He promptly repudiated much of it when he had his attention called to it in San Francisco. His negation was laid to modesty.

Without loss of any time, he took the Trans-Continental to New York. There he changed to European dress, went to Hoboken, took the D., L. & W. to Stroudsburg, and an auto from there to the Pennsylvania Manor. He had dinner there with the three librarians, looked over the card indexes, and by dark was in Philadelphia.

Darkness anywhere is unpleasant, in Philadelphia, it is more so. It was drizzling in Chinatown and dirty on Eighth Street. Without the loss of a single moment, Wing Loo went into the Hoop Sing tea store, went into the main room, and back through a door where a man was waiting for him.

"Are you Wing Loo?" asked the man.

"I am, if you are Charles Jefferson."

"I am Jefferson. Sit down. I have not had supper; let us eat. I have ordered the best there is, and I hope that it will suffice. Shall I talk?"

"I wait for your words as a bride awaits the footfall of her loved one."

"I hope that she does not have to wait long. Life is so short under the best of circumstances. I have millions, but I cannot prolong my life. That has been my thought. The shortness of life and the inability to accomplish what I desire in my alloted days."

"Some day a man can be so treated that he will never die."

"You think so?" asked Jefferson. "I have been told that you can keep tissues alive for years. Is it true?"

"It is. I have a kidney in glass. It has been working for twenty years. I believe it will keep on."

"You can do it with other parts of the body?"

"I can."

"So I was informed. I want you to help me with an experiment. If it is successful, we—you and I—will go down in history as the greatest scientists known."

"That would be wonderful!"

"It would. Now here is what I want you to

do—" and Charles Jefferson, the greatest specialist in electricity in the world, and also the queerest scientist of his age, outlined his plan for the world-revolutionizing experiment. He ended with:

"I will be responsible for everything except the operations and the keeping of the tissues alive. That will be your province. I will finance the glassware and any supplies you need, and when the experiment is finished and you have done your part, I will give you one million dollars."

"You spoke of adding to the money the Empress' black pearls?"

"I will add them."

"And only five hundred operations—! Five a day?"

"Yes, but you must keep them alive."

"That will be my greatest desire. I understand that the whole plan fails if one of them dies. When can I start?"

"Very soon. I have a place prepared in New York. The young men will come there for their money. As they are paid, they will pass from one room to another. You will be ready for them. The specimens can be brought to the Manor, five or six at a time, according to the size of the glassware you will need. If you give me the specifications, I will have my shelves built and all the pumping machinery installed. I do not want to begin the real experiment till your work is finished. Have I made myself clear?"

"Very. The clouds covering my doubt have been removed by the sunshine of your intelligence. What I do not know I can guess, and always I have faith in your wisdom. When will the feet of the young men hasten toward their reward?"

"The first five will arrive on the first of March. After that they will come at the rate of five a day."

"And each man will be paid fifty thousand dollars?"

"Yes, but the same money can be used over and over."

"Naturally. I can readily see that the young men will not have any desire to use their gold. Really clever, Mr. Jefferson."

"It has cost me enough, and they have had several very wonderful years—and to be permitted to take part in this experiment——"

"That," murmured the Oriental surgeon, "is the greatest reward."

On the first of March, five of the young readers left the Pennsylvania Manor, and five more followed on the second day. And so, day after day, the young men left, confident that life was very much worth while, and all eager for new and more active fields of mental activity. They collected the money, and then passed through the door.

* * * * *

On the seventh of July, the Chief of the National

Secret Service received a message in code. Deciphered, it read like this:

"BE AT THE MAIN GATE PENNSYLVANIA MANOR AT MIDNIGHT JULY NINTH. COME ALONE AND UNARMED. TAINE."

"I thought the boy was a fool, but he has flushed the game," exclaimed the Chief. "Though there is a chance that this may be a decoy. Taine may be a prisoner, and they may want to take me next. In a way, it is a fool telegram, sent by a fool. Guess I better go. But there is no use of going without protection."

The night of the ninth, he dismissed the taxi a quarter of a mile from the main gate of the Manor, and walked the rest of the way. There was a full moon, and it was really a very beautiful night. Even the unpoetical Chief felt the influence of the evening. At the gate he paused, and thought what a fool he was to stay in the full moonlight, but he had no reason to be afraid. Taine was there, just on the other side of the gate. They shook hands through the bars.

"Hullo, Chief! Good of you to come. Would not have blamed you if you had not, but it is going to pay you. You will be surprised, Chief. Have to see it to believe it. Let me unlock the gate."

"What is it, Taine?" asked the anxious Chief.

"Now, don't allow yourself to get nervous. If anyone gets that way, I will be the one. I just love to get all shaky and trembly now and then, teeth chatter and hair up on end and all that. Come on in. Even July is cold up here in the mountains."

He led the way into the library. A little table was in the middle of the large room, and two little splint bottom chairs stood on either side of the table. The rest of the room, except just over the table, was filled with black shadows. The Chief exclaimed:

"This is a whale of a room, Taine!"

"It ought to be. First it was a ballroom, then it housed one of the largest libraries in the world, and now it is the laboratory for one of the greatest scientific experiments ever pulled off in the history of the human race."

Taine took out an electric flashlight and swept it around the large room.

"See those glass jars?" he asked. "What do you suppose is in them? Well, you would not guess, but I guess we will find out tomorrow. I am going to put you to bed behind that screen. You will be safe there. Keep quiet. At nine tomorrow, the experiment will begin, and you can watch it; but don't get excited and come out too soon. That is why I asked you not to bring a gun. If you shoot, you might hurt somebody, and what I want is a full statement from the man, made in your presence."

"What man?"

"The man we want to arrest."

"And you are going to leave me here?"

"I am; and I do not want you to move till nine.

Then you can very quietly look through the crack and see what is going on. But don't shoot. No matter what happens, don't shoot."

"But you asked me not to come armed?"

"I know, but I do not think you followed my advice. You keep your gun, but don't use it. Watch me."

"Why don't you tell me more about it, Taine?"

"You would not believe me, Chief. Besides, I have to go through this on my own."

And that was all the satisfaction the San Francisco man would give. He fixed the Chief on a comfortable cot, and left him there behind the screen.

It was hard for him to do, but he kept his promise to Taine and did not look out through the crack in the screen till nine the next morning. And what he saw gave him occasion for many anxious thoughts.

In the center of the library was a large table of white marble, with thousands of little black points sticking out of it. Directly in front of the table, a middle-aged man sat, facing directly toward the screen sheltering the Chief. The detective could see his face distinctly, but he could not identify him. On one side of him, also facing the screen, sat a Chinese in flowing Oriental costume. At one end of the table was a mahogany box. At the other end was something covered up with a white sheet.

"And now," said the one man, "the time has come for the final experiment. I have asked you to be here, Wing Loo, because it is your right. Without your wonderful help, I could not have gone ahead. My knowledge of electricity would have been useless without your knowledge of brain surgery.

"This entire experiment was started by a statement of an eminent psychologist which said that nothing is ever lost in the realm of knowledge, that everything once appreciated by a human brain is retained by that brain till the organism is destroyed. That declaration made me think.

"For years I have worried over two things: The shortness of human life and my inability to learn all there was to be known. Think of it! One person, working as fast as he can, would yet be unable, in the scope of a lifetime, to learn all there is to know. I learned a little about electricity, but realized that I was pitifully ignorant about ten thousand other forms of knowledge. And I could only live just so long—and then I had to die.

"Then an idea came to me. From that came other ideas, like little bubbles springing from a central one; but I realized the hopelessness of the idea till I heard of you, Wing Loo, and of your wonderful surgery."

"I am glad that your servant could participate in your greatness."

"Yes, your surgery and ability to keep parts of the body alive were the necessary additions to my plan, and here is what I did. I engaged five hundred readers. They were each to read fifteen hundred books. Their books were to be carefully selected. One was to read biology and another chemistry and so on throughout all the various parts of human endeavor to solve the mysteries of life. And the books that each read were to be carefully indexed, both by subject and by reader. Each man had a number, though he did not know it, and each read every day a book. The three librarians kept up with their work.

"I brought the books here by the hundreds of thousands, and as they were read I had them burned. They were no longer necessary in my experiment because they had become engraved on the convolutions of the brains of the five hundred readers.

"All the time I was working on the electrodynamic part of the experiment. I had to have fine wire run from each of five hundred glass vessels. These five hundred wires finally came together and then separated again and became attached to the selective black posts you see in front of you. I have other apparatus, intensifiers, and radios, all ending finally in that little radio you see at the other side of the table.

"Now, suppose I want to know all there is to know about toadstools? I want in a few minutes and without any delay to hear a thousand word synopsis of the knowledge of the world on toadstools. I spell out the word on this little typewriter in the middle of the table. Then I go up and down among the thousands of little black points you see there, each of which has a name, and I press those I am interested in, as Food, Toxicology, Botany, Geography, General Interest, and a few others.

"Now I am all ready. I have asked my machine for what I want. I swing this lever and that starts the delivery of the information which I am asking for. I sit here in my chair, and listen to a thousand word essay on the toadstool. If I want to, I can take a subject like Anthropology and listen to it for several days. I can take one poem, such as Dante's *Inferno*, and have it recited to me. In fact, I can get anything I ask for, and all I have to do is to know sufficiently about it to ask the question, and press the necessary points. *All the information in that entire library is mine; all I have to do is to operate this machine. I do not have to read a single book,* yet, I have the knowledge gained by five hundred men, working nearly five years each."

"How wonderful that I could help you in all this!"

"Your surgery made it possible. You took the brains from the five hundred readers and three librarians, and, through your skill, you have made it possible for those brains to remain alive and functioning for many years. You placed them in the five hundred glass jars and arranged for the pumping of the fluid to keep them alive. The men are dead, but their acquired wisdom lives on; and I am the beneficiary. I am now the most learned man in the world.

"And I did all this—we did all this, without interference. No one has any idea of what we were doing."

"You are wrong," replied the Chinaman. "There was a man by the name of Taine. He suspected something, but he did not know what. He came here once too often. Early this morning, I caught him. His brain will give me great pleasure. It is not often that I dissect the brain of a perfect fool. Here he is, a little doped, but very much alive."

And at this point, he pulled off the sheet and there sat Taine, pitifully small, dazed, drugged, and tied to the chair with a rope. The American started to laugh.

"That is the best part of the experiment, Wing Loo. At least, it is the most ludicrous part. You are right. Better add him to the collection. Now suppose we start with the testing of the experiment?"

"There is one thing you forgot. How about my million and the Empress' black pearls?"

"I have them here. One hundred of them. Take them now if you wish to. Please do not delay me. See, I spell out *education*. Now I touch the following black points, *Australia, Statistics, Finance,*

History. And now I swing the lever and the information comes through the radio."

He rapidly went through the various steps. In a clear tone came the words:

"Now is the time for all good men and true to come to the aid of their party."

"That is very interesting! And is that the combined wisdom of five hundred and three brains?"

"It's that damn detective!" yelled the infuriated scientist. "I am going to kill him! You can do as you wish with his brains."

"No you are not!" shouted a voice. "Hands up! I have the drop on both of you. Sit down, and don't make any false moves, and keep those hands up."

The Chief of the Secret Service came across the space between the screen and the table. There was no doubt that he meant business.

"Thought you were going to kill one of the force, did you?" he sneered. "May be a fool, but he is a detective just the same, and we stick by each other. I will untie you, Taine, just as soon as I put the bracelets on these murderers. Hell! Five hundred and three good men gone! These fellows must be crazy."

He put the handcuffs on the scientist first, and then turned to the Chinaman.

"You are next, Wing Loo. Put your hands out, and don't try any monkey business."

"Don't you know me, Chief?" sighed the Oriental.

"Yes. I know you for a killer."

"Why, Chief! After all I did for you. Giving you a nice cot to sleep in, and letting you arrest the greatest scientist of the age, Charles Jefferson; and then you want to put the cuffs on me."

"Who the devil are you, anyway?" thundered the irate, yet puzzled, detective.

"I am Taine of San Francisco."

"Then who is that there, roped to the chair?"

"That is Wing Loo. I suppose he is the greatest brain surgeon in the world, but he has had so much luminal for the last three months that his mind is not working right. He has been all in a dream for many days. Had to keep him that way to control him."

"So he is the man who killed all those people?"

"No. He is the man who was going to. He never killed one of them."

Charles Jefferson had been following the conversation eagerly. He could stand no more.

"You are a liar!" he yelled. "How about those five hundred and three brains in those glass jars? How about the five hundred dead readers?"

"Those brains over there in the jars are just wax brains," answered Taine. "I was sure that you would not know the difference. You really are a child, in spite of all your learning. You and the Chinaman did not kill a single person, and I am not sure that you have broken a single law; though, of course, you did not give the readers what you promised."

"Just wax brains?" moaned Jefferson. "Oh! My beautiful experiment and my lost years!"

"Don't you worry. You can go to a library and read some books of your own."

"I cannot wait, Taine," pleaded the Chief. "Please tell me what you did and how."

"It won't take long. I was out in San Francisco with my family. Yes, there is a family now. Wife has a baby, a little girl, and we are all very happy over it. One day, I read in the paper about the great Chinese surgeon, Wing Loo, and his coming to America; but none knew what for. I had a hunch that I would like to find out. A man like that does not travel around just for fun. It was easier when I found he was traveling alone. I met him, drugged him with luminal, and the rest was easy. He had letters, giving the directions for an appointment with Jefferson. At that time, I did not know who Jefferson was, but I thought we ought to keep the appointment. So, I changed into a doctor, and brought Wing Loo with me as a very dangerous epileptic who had to be kept in twilight sleep all the time. I put him in a private New York hospital; and I took his clothes, and met Jefferson in Philadelphia.

"After that, I stayed in New York, and as the young readers came after their pay, I gave them a song and dance—told them they had been working for an insane man, but that if we could collect anything for them, we would. In the meantime, they should be thankful that he had not killed them. I told them all to keep still if they wanted ever to collect the money due them, and for a good many, I found jobs. In the meantime, I ordered five hundred and three brains made out of wax, purchased some glass jars and some fake pumping apparatus, and brought it up here. Jefferson paid all my expenses, including two good shows a week, though he did not know it. The tickets were in the wax brains, only he could not see them. He was not interested much in the brains, even let me attach the wire ends to the middle of the cerebrums. I do not think, to give the devil his due, that he was very enthusiastic over the idea of murder, but he just had to do it to finish his experiment. I pitied him in a way, so I put a portable phonograph in the radio so he could have his first cerebral message.

"When everything was ready, I sent for you, Chief. I told Jefferson that we could go ahead at nine the morning of the tenth of July. Then I made a special trip to New York, and rescued the Chinese from the hospital. He has had a rough time of it, Chief. He has lost in weight, and it has been hard on him. If I were you, I would put him on a ship, and let him go back to China. He is a good man, only over-enthusiastic. I brought him up here and dressed him in my clothes, and painted his face a little so he would look like me. I thought you would like a real confession, and I knew it would make Jefferson mad to think that a detective had been on his trail. So, there are your two babies, and you can do anything you like with them. As far as I am concerned, I am through with the mystery of *The Cerebral Library*. You can clean up the trash. I am on my way back to wife and baby."

"But how about your pay, man?" asked the almost dazed Chief.

"I have these black pearls. They are worth a king's ransom. I earned them honestly, and I know that Jefferson will not mind my taking them; and you can send me a check, if you want to. I don't have much use for the money; but—well, I am married, and Mildred understands what to do with it. Good-bye. Take care of my friends.

"I am sure that I am leaving them both in very good hands."

A PIECE OF LINOLEUM

IT WAS a plain case of suicide.

The Coroner absolutely refused to consider any other verdict.

And Mrs. Harker had the profound sympathy of her neighbors.

"I cannot explain it at all," she whispered to two of her friends. "Just why John had to do a thing like that, when we were so happy, is beyond me.

"It would have been different if I had not been a kind, loving wife to him. I was more than a wife: I was a helpmate. Take this house, for example. Do you suppose for one moment that it would belong to us, and every cent paid on the mortgage, if John Harker had been left to do it? Not in a hundred years. The first few weeks we were married, and I had found he was stopping at the station to buy flowers for the house on his way home, I knew what my duty was as a loving wife, and I lost no time doing it. From that time on, I handled the pay check. Of course, I gave him some spending money every week, and saw to it that he had his evening paper after supper, but I would not let him buy the paper on his way home, because he always mussed it so on the train, and it was never fit to put on the shelves afterward. But when I gave it to him after supper and spoke to him now and then about wrinkling it, it hardly got mussed at all.

"If we had had children, I would not have been able to take such good care of the house and furniture, but before we were married, the doctor told me I was delicate and better off without the responsibilities of maternity. He was so sweet about it when he said I could look on my future husband as my baby. Of course, it was hard for John to understand, so many men do not have the feminine viewpoint, but he finally submitted to the inevitable, though he always failed to understand why I decorated his bedroom in pink.

"Being alone all day gave me lots of time for sewing, and in a few years I was making all my own clothes and most of John's. He used to ask me to buy his shirts, told me I was too busy to spend time on them, but I told him I just loved to do things like that for him, and that he was all the baby I had; so, bye and bye, he stopped talking about it.

"I studied his health. Even sent to Washington for special books on invalid feeding, and if, in the twenty years of our sweet married life, John ever ate a spoonful of anything that was not pure and wholesome and fit for a man of his weight and digestive peculiarities, he must have bought it at a restaurant —he never ate it at his own table.

"I was always careful about his health. Every morning it was always the same thing. I'd remind him of his umbrella, be sure he had on his rubbers, and the right weight of underwear. If it was clear in the morning and damp at night, I would meet his car with a raincoat and overshoes. Nothing was too much trouble for me.

"And I kept a clean house for him. That is not so easy to do with a man in it. What he did not know, I taught him patiently, just as you would a little child. It took over two years to train him to come in the back door, take off his shoes in the woodshed, and put on his carpet-slippers before he came into the house. But patience and love and repetition finally helped him to form the habit.

We had lovely carpets, beautiful things that would last three generations if properly cared for; and when I found out how careless he was, I put squares of linoleum around where he was in the habit of sitting. When his friends came in and he would forget himself and ask them to smoke, I would always run and put a piece of linoleum under them so the ashes would not get on the floor. I was delicate and nervous after I was thirty. The dear doctor thought it was the change of life working on me, so I suggested that John save me by washing the supper dishes every night; but, do you know, he was so careless that I had to put several pieces of linoleum where he was working or he would get drops of soapy water on the beautiful waxed floor?

"I let him have his recreation. Once a year, I insisted on his attending a meeting of his lodge of Lofty Pine Trees, even though he would smell of cigar smoke when he came back; but I was patient with him and never threw it up to him how hard I had to work to get the smell out of his best suit. At last, I used lavender and heliotrope alternately; and finally, when he wore his suit to church, you could not smell anything but the perfume. It seems that the lodge appreciated what kind of a loving wife John Harker had, because the floral piece they sent to the funeral was perfectly lovely. Perhaps you ladies noticed it? I placed it in a conspicuous place at the head of the coffin. It was a large pillow made of little daisies with the words *At Peace* worked out in violets.

But of course you want to know just how it happened. You realize that in my delicate health we always had separate bedrooms. But as the dear doctor said, every husband has his rights; and so I never once shut the door between the rooms at night. I will say this: that John was a gentleman and never once took advantage of my kindness. You see, I told him right after we were married just what the doctor had said, about any sudden shock being likely to kill me; and, of course, realizing how delicate I was, he did not want my death on his conscience. I had his room decorated in pink; and on the wall facing the bed, just where he could see it the last thing at night and the first thing in the morning, I had an enlarged picture of us on our first trip to Atlantic City, me on a chair and he in back, standing, holding an umbrella over me to protect my complexion from the sun. You know how sacred such experiences are during the first weeks of matrimony. He had a nice, single bed, and I kept it and the room scrupulously clean. There was a piece of linoleum by the side of the bed, and on it I had a china spittoon handpainted with tearoses. I gave it to him before we were married. Of course, he was not vulgar enough to chew or smoke, though goodness knows he might have formed such habits had he been married to any other kind of woman; but he was fond of chewing gum, so every night I let him have one stick, and the instructions were for him to put the wad into the spittoon just before he went to sleep. When I was well, I used to turn the light out for him; but the nights of my martyrdom from headaches, I made him put himself to bed.

"The dear doctor says that just as soon as I change the headaches will stop—and I hope they do. No man knows just what a terrible thing it is to be a woman, especially if he is not married.

"This night, I went over his weekly allowance with him, and explained how, by drinking 'chicko' instead of coffee, I had saved three dollars and had spent all of it for a new piece of art linoleum for his bed. It had the loveliest design on it—a Cupid shooting an arrow at a trembling deer, symbolic of married life, I told him; and explained that it was a female deer, and that was why it was trembling. He did not say much, but later on, his light went out and he said 'Good-night.' I knew right away there was something wrong, because I had always taught him to say 'Good-night, Dear,' with the loving emphasis on the last word. Later on, I heard a drip, drip, drip, and I knew right away that either a faucet was leaking or that it was raining a little. I called, 'John, did you turn off the spigot tight in the bathroom?' and he just laughed, and told me everything was all right and to go to sleep and not worry.

"The drip, drip, drip, kept on, but fainter; so I went to sleep. When I went to his room to wake him, so he could go down and get breakfast—for that was the way we divided the work, and it gave me a half hour more of necessary rest every day—I found the poor man had cut his wrist with a safety razor blade and was dead. What I had heard dripping during the night was his life's blood.

The dear doctor explained it all to me. He said that he was psychotic; that no man, who had a loving, tender, wife like John Harker had, would do a thing like that if he was not insane. That must be the explanation. One thing I am sure of: During all the twenty years of our sweet married life, he never learned to appreciate my efforts to give him a nice, clean home. Even at the end, he was careless. If he had only moved down in bed eight inches, he could have bled on the linoleum, instead of on the lovely ingrain carpet."

THE THIRTY AND ONE

CECIL, OverLord of Walling, in the Dark Forest, mused by the fire. The blind Singer of Songs had sung the sagas of ancient times, had waited long for praise and then, disquieted, had left the banquet hall guided by his dog. The Juggler had merrily tossed his golden balls into the air till they seemed a glistening cascade, but still the OverLord had mused, unseeing. The wise Homunculus had crouched at his feet uttering words of wisdom and telling tales of Gobi and the buried city of Ankor. But nothing could rouse the OverLord from his meditations.

At last, he stood up and struck the silver bell with a hammer of gold. Serving men answered the call.

"Send me the Lady Angelica and the Lord Gustro," he commanded, and then once again sat down with chin in hand, waiting.

At last, the two came in answer to his summons. The Lady was his only daughter, as fair and as wise a Lady as there was in all Walling. Lord Gustro, some day, would be her husband, and help her rule in the Dark Forest. Meantime, he perfected himself in the use of the broadsword, lute, the hunting with the falcon, and the study of books. He was six feet tall, twenty years old, and had in him the makings of a man.

The three sat around the fire, two waiting to hear the one talk, the one waiting till he knew just how to say what had to be said. At last, Cecil began to talk:

"You no doubt know what is on my mind. For years I have tried to give happiness and peace and prosperity, to the simple folk of our land of Walling. We were well situated in a valley surrounded by lofty, impassable forests. Only one mountain pass connected us with the great, cruel, and almost unknown world around us. Into that world, we sent in springtime, summer, and fall, our caravans of mules laden with grain, olives, wine, and uncut stones. From that world, we brought salt, weapons, bales of woolen and silken goods, for our needs. No one tried to molest us, for we had nothing much that they coveted. Perhaps safety made us grow soft, sleepy, and unprepared for danger.

"But it has come. We might have known there were things in that outer world we knew not of and therefore could not even dream of. But this spring, our first caravan winding over the mountains found, at the boundaries of the Dark Forest, a Castle blocking their way. Their mules were not birds and could not fly over; they were not moles and could not burrow under. And the lads with the mules were not warriors and could not break their way through. So they came back, unmolested, 'tis true, but with their goods unsold and unbartered.

"Now, I do not think that Castle was built by magic. I have personally looked at it, and it seems nothing but stone and mortar. And it is not held by an army of fighting men, for all we can hear is that one man holds it. But what a man! Half again as tall as our finest lad, and skilled in the use of weapons. I tried him out. One at a time, I sent to him John of the flying ax, and Herman who had no equal with the double-edged sword, and Rubin who could split a willow wand at two hundred paces with his steel-tipped arrow. These three men lie, worm food, in the ravine below the castle. And meantime, our country is strangulated as far as trade is concerned. We have cattle in the meadow, and wood in the forest, and grain in the bin, but we have no salt, no clothes to cover us from the cold, no finery for our women, or weapons for our men. And we never will have these as long as this castle and this man block our caravans."

"We can capture the Castle and kill the giant!" cried Lord Gustro, with the impetuosity of youth.

"How?" asked the OverLord. "Did I not tell you that the path is narrow? You know that. On one side, the mountains tower lofty as the flight of the bird and smooth as a woman's skin. On the other side, is the Valley of the Dæmons, and no one has ever fallen into it and come back alive. The only path is just wide enough for one man or one man-led mule, and that path now leads through the castle. If we could send an army, 'twould be different. But only one man at a time can we send, and there is no man equal to successful combat with this giant."

The Lady Alngelica smiled as she whispered, "We may conquer him through chicanery. For example, I have seen this hall filled with fighting men and fair ladies almost put into an endless sleep by gazing at the golden balls flying through the air and back into the clever hands of the Juggler. And the Blind Singer of Songs can make anyone forget all except the music of his tales. And our Homunculus is very wise."

The OverLord shook his head. "Not thus will the question be answered. This madman wants one thing, and that one thing means everything in the lastward, as far as our land and people are concerned. Perhaps you have guessed. I will give you the demand ere you ask the question. Our Lady's hand in marriage, and thus, when I die, he becomes the OverLord of Walling."

Lady Angelica looked over at Lord Gustro. He looked at the OverLord's daughter. At last, he said:

"Better to eat our grain and eat our olives and drink our wine. Better that our men wear bearskins and our women cover themselves with the skins of deer. It would be best for them to wear shoes of wood than pantufles of unicorn skin brought from Araby. It were a sweeter fate for them to perfume their bodies with crushed violets and may-flowers from our forest than to smell sweet with perfumes from the trees of the unknown Island of the East. This price is too heavy. Let us live as our fathers and fathers' fathers lived, even climb trees like the monkey folk, than trust to such an OverLord. Besides, I love the Lady Angelica."

The Lady smiled her thanks. "I still am thinking of the use of intelligence overcoming brawn. Have we no wisdom left in Walling, besides the fair, faint, dreams of weak woman?"

"I will send for the Homunculus," her father answered. "He may know the answer to that question."

The little man came in. He was a man not born of woman, but grown for seven years in a glass bottle, during all of which time he read books held before him by wise men, and was nourished with drops of wine and tiny balls of Asphodel paste. He listened to the problem gravely, though at times he seemed asleep. At last, he said one word.

"Synthesis."

Cecil reached over and, picking him up, placed him on one knee.

"Have pity on us, Wise Man. We are but simple folk and know but simple words. What is the meaning of this sage word?"

"I know not," was the peculiar answer. " 'Tis

but a word that came to me out of the past. It has a sweet sound and methinks may have a meaning. Let me think. I recall now! It was when I was in the glass bottle that a wise man came and held before my eyes an illuminated parchment. On it was written in words of gold, this word and its meaning.

"Synthesis. All things are one and one thing is all."

"Which makes it all the harder for me," sighed the OverLord of Walling.

The Lady Angelica left her seat and came over to her father. She sank upon the bearskin at his feet and took the little hand of the dwarf in hers.

"Tell me, my dear Homunculus, what wise man 'twas who thus gave you the message on the illuminated parchment?"

"It was a very wise man and a very old man who lives by himself in a cave by the babbling brook, and yearly the simple folk take him bread and meat and wine, but for years no one has seen him. And perhaps he lives and perhaps he is dead, for all I know is that the food disappears. But perhaps the birds think that it is for them now that he lies sightless and thoughtless on his stone bed these many years."

"This is something we will find out for ourselves. Lord Gustro, order some horses, and the four of us will go to this man's cave. Three horses for us, my Lord, and an ambling pad for our little friend so naught of harm will befall him."

The four came to the cave, and the four entered

it. A light burned at the far end, and there was the wise man, very old and with nought but his eyes telling of the intelligence that never ages. On the table before him in a tangled confusion, were glasses and earthenware, and crucibles, and one each of astrolabe, alembic, and hourglass through which silver sands ran, and this was fixed with cunning machinery so that every day it tilted around and once more let the sand tell the passing of the twenty-and-four hours. There were books covered with mildewed leather and locked with iron padlocks and spider webs. Hung from the wet ceiling was a representation of the sun with the planets revolving eternally around that fair orb, but the pitted moon alternated with light and shadows.

And the wise man read from a book written in letters made by those long dead, and now and then he ate a crust of bread or sipped wine from a ram's horn, but never did he stop reading. When they touched him on the shoulder to attract his attention, he shook them off, murmuring, "By the Seven Sacred Caterpillars! Let me finish this page, for what a pity were I to die without knowing what this man wrote some thousand years ago in Ankor."

But at last he finished the page and sat blinking at them with his wise eyes sunk deep into a mummy face while his body shook with the decrepitude of age. And Cecil asked him:

"What is the meaning of the word, 'synthesis'?"

" 'Tis a dream of mine which only now I find the waking meaning of."

"Tell the dream," the OverLord commanded.

" 'Tis but a dream. Suppose there were thirty wise men learned in all wisdom obtained from the reading of ancient books on alchemy and magic and histories and philosophy. These men knew of animals and jewels such as margarites and chrysoberyls, and of all plants such as dittany which cures wounds, and mandragora which compelleth sleep (though why men should want to sleep, when there is so much to read and profit by the reading, I do not know). But these men are old and some day will die. So, I would take these thirty old men and one young man and have them drink a wine that I have distilled these many years, and by synthesis there would be only one body—that of the young man—but in that man's brain would be all the subtle and ancient wisdom of the thirty savants, and thus we would do century after century so no wisdom would be lost to the world."

The Lady Angelica leaned over his shoulder. "And have you made this wine?" she asked.

"Yes, and now I am working on its opposite, for why place thirty bodies into one unless you know the art of once again separating this one body into the original thirty. But that is hard. For any fool can pour the wine from thirty bottles into a single jar, but who is wise enough to separate them and restore them to their original bottles?"

"Have you tried this wine of synthetic magic?" asked the OverLord.

"Partly. I took a crow and a canary-bird and had them drink of it, and now, in yonder wicker cage, a yellow crow sits and nightly fills my cave with song as though it came from the lutes and citherns of faerie-land."

"Now, that is my thought," cried the Lady Angelica. "We will take the best and bravest fighters of our land, and the sweetest singer of songs, and the best juggler of golden balls, thirty of them, and I, myself, will drink of this wine of synthesis. Thus the thirty will pass into my body, and I will go and visit the Giant. In his hall, I will drink of the other wine, and there will be thirty to fight against the one. They will overcome him and slay him. Then I will drink again of the vital wine, and in my body I will carry the thirty conquerors back to Walling. Once there, I will again drink, and the thirty men will leave my body, being liberated by the wonder-wine. Some may be dead and others wounded, but I will be safe and our enemy killed. Have you enough of it—of both kinds?

The old man looked puzzled.

"I have a flagon of the wine of synthesis. Of the other, to change the synthesized back into their original bodies, only enough for one experiment, and mayhap a few drops more."

"Try those drops on that yellow bird," commanded Cecil.

The old man poured from a bottle of pure gold, graven with a worm that eternally renewed his youth by swallowing his tail, a few drops of a colorless liquid, and offered it to the yellow bird in the wicker cage. This the bird drank greedily, and of a sudden there were two birds, a black crow and a yellow canary, and ere the canary could pipe a song the crow pounced on it and killed it.

"It works," croaked the old man. "It works."

"Can you make more of the second elixir?" asked Lord Gustro.

"What I do once I can do twice," proudly said the ancient.

"Then start and make more, and while you are doing it, we will take the golden bottle and the flagon and see what can be done to save the simple folk of our dark forests, though this is an adventure that I think little of, for 'tis fraught with danger for a woman I love." Thus spake the OverLord.

And with the elixirs in a safe place, they rode away from the cave of the old man. But Lord Gustro took the OverLord aside and said:

"I ask a favor. Allow me to be one of these thirty men."

Cecil shook his head. "No. And once again and forever, NO! In the doing of this, I stand to lose the apple of my eye, and if she comes not back to me, I shall die of grief, and then you, and you alone, will be left to care for my simple folk. If a man has but two arrows and shoots one into the air, then he were wise to keep the other in his quiver against the day of need."

The Lady Angelica laughed as she suspected the reason of their whispering.

"I will come back," she said laughingly, "for the old man was very wise. Did you not see how the yellow bird divided into two, and the crow killed the canary?"

But the Homunculus, held in Lord Cecil's arms, started to cry.

"What wouldst thou?" asked the kindly Over-Lord.

"I would be back in my bottle again," sobbed the little one. And he sobbed till he went to sleep, soothed by the rocking canter of the war horse.

Two evenings later, a concourse of brave men met in the banquet hall. There were great, silent, men, skilled in the use of mace, byrnies, and baldricks, who could slay with sword, spear, and double-bitted battle-ax. The Juggler was there, and a Singer of Songs, and a Reader of Books, very young but very wise. And a man was there with sparkling eyes who could by his glance put men to death-sleep and waken them with a snap of the thumb and finger. And to these were added the OverLord and Lord Gustro and the trembling Homunculus, and on her throne sat the Lady Angelica, very beautiful and very happy because of the great adventure she had a part to play in. In her hand was a golden goblet, and in the hands of the thirty men, crystal glasses, and the thirty and one drinking vessels were filled with the wine of synthesis, for half of the flagon was poured out. But the flagon, half-filled, and the golden drug viand, the Lady Angelica hid beneath her shimmering robe. Outside, a lady's horse, decked with diamond-studded harness, neighed uneasy in the moonlight.

Lord Cecil explained the adventure, and all the thirty men sat very still and solemn, for never had they heard the like before, for they none feared a simple death, but this dissolution was a thing that made even the bravest wonder what the end would be. Yet, when the time came and the command was given, they one and all drained their vessels, and even as the Lady drank her wine, they drank to the last drop.

Then there was silence broken only by the shrill cry of a hoot owl, complaining to the moon concerning the doings of the night folk in the Dark Forest. The little Homunculus hid his face in the shoulder of the OverLord, but Cecil and Lord Gustro looked straight ahead of them over the banquet table to see what was to be seen.

The thirty men seemed to shiver and then grow smaller in a mist that covered them, and finally only empty places were left at the banquet table, and empty glasses. Only the two men and the Lady Angelica and the shivering Homunculus were left. The Lady laughed.

"It worked," she cried. "I look the same, but I feel different, for in me are the potential bodies of the thirty brave men who will overcome the Giant and bring peace to the land. And now I will give you the kiss of hail and farewell, and will venture forth on my waiting horse." Kissing her father on the mouth and her lover on the cheek and the little one on the top of his curly-haired head, she ran bravely out of the room. Through the stillness they could hear her horse's hooves, silver-shod, pounding on the stones of the courtyard.

"I am afraid," shivered the little one. "I have all wisdom, but I am afraid as to this adventure and its ending."

Lord Cecil comforted him. "You are afraid because you are so very wise. Lord Gustro and I would like to fear, but we are too foolish to do so. Can I do anything to comfort you, little friend of mine?"

"I wish I were back in my bottle," sobbed the Homunculus, "but that cannot be because the bottle was broken when I was taken from it, for the mouth of it was very narrow, and a bottle once broken cannot be made whole again."

All that night, Lord Cecil rocked him to sleep, singing to him lullabies, while Lord Gustro sat wakeful before the fire biting his finger nails, and wondering what the ending would be.

Late that night, the Lady Angelica arrived at the gate of the Giant's Castle, and blew her wreathed horn. The Giant dropped the iron-studded gate, and curiously peered at the lady on the horse.

"I am the Lady Angelica," said the Lady, "and I have come to be your bride if only you will give free passage to our caravans so we can commerce with the great world outside. When my father dies, you will be OverLord of   land, and perchance I will come to love you for you are a fine figure of a man, and I have heard much of you."

The Giant towered over the head of her horse. He placed his hand around her waist and plucked her from the horse and carried her to his banquet hall and sat her down at one end of the table. Laughing in a somewhat silly manner, he walked around the room and lit pine torches and tall candles till at last the whole room was lighted. He poured a large glass of wine for the Lady and a much larger glass for himself. He seated himself at the other end of the table, and laughed again as he cried:

"It all is as I dreamed. But who would have thought that the noble Lord Cecil and the brave Lord Gustro would have been so craven! Let's drink to our wedding, and then to the bridal chamber."

And he drank his drink in one swallow. But the

Lady Angelica took from under her gown a golden flask and raising it, she cried:

"I drink to you and your future, whatever it may be." And she drained the golden flask and sat very still. A mist filled the room and swirled widdershams in thirty pillars around the long oak table. When it cleared, there were thirty men between the Giant and the Lady.

The Juggler took his golden balls, and the man with the dazzling eyes looked hard on the Giant, and the Student took from his robe a Book and read the wise sayings of dead Gods backwards, while the Singer of Songs plucked his harp strings and sang of the brave deeds of brave men long dead. But the fighting men rushed forward, and on all sides started the battle. The Giant jumped back, picked a mace from the wall, and fought as never man fought before. He had two things in mind: to kill, and to reach the smiling Lady and strangle her with bare hands for the thing she had done to him. But ever between him and the Lady was a wall of men who, with steel and song and dazzling eyes, formed a living wall that could be bent and crushed but never broken.

For centuries after, in the halls of Walling, the blind singers of songs told of that fight while the simple folk sat silent and listened to the tale. No doubt as the tale passed from one singer, aged, to the next singer, young, it became ornamented and embroidered and fabricated into something somewhat different from what really happened that night. But even the bare truth-telling at first hand, as told in parts, at different times, by the Lady Angelica, was a great enough tale. For men fought and bled and died in that hall. Finally, the Giant, dying, broke through and almost reached the Lady, but then the Song Man tripped him with his harp, and the Wise Man threw his heavy tome in his face, and the Juggler shattered his three golden balls against the Giant's forehead, and, at the lastward, the glittering eyes of the Sleep-Maker fastened on the dying eyes of the Giant and sent him on his last sleep.

The Lady Angelica looked around the shattered hall and at the thirty men who had all done their part, and she said softly:

"These be brave men, and they have done what was necessary for the good of their country and for the honor of our land. I cannot forsake them or leave them hopeless."

She took the rest of the wine of synthesis and drank part, and to every man she gave a drink, even the dead men whose mouths she had to gently open to wipe the blood from the gritted teeth, ere she could pour the wine into their breathless mouths. And she went back to her seat, and sitting there, she waited.

The mist again filled the hall and covered the dead and dying and those who were not hurt badly but panted from the fury of the battle. When the mist cleared, only the Lady Angelica was left there, for all the thirty had returned to her body through the magic of the synthesizing wine.

And the Lady said to herself:

"I feel old and in many ways different, and my strength has gone from me. I am glad there is no mirror to show me my whitened hair and bloodless cheeks, for the men who have come back unto me were dead men, and those not dead were badly hurt. I must get back to my horse before I fall into a faint of death."

She tried to walk out, but, stumbling, fell. On hands and knees, she crawled to where her horse waited for her. She pulled herself up into the saddle, and with her girdle she tied herself there, and then told the horse to go home. But she lay across the saddle like a dead woman.

The horse brought her back. Ladies in waiting took her to bed, and washed her withered limbs, and gave her warm drinks, and covered her wasted body with coverlets of lamb's wool. The wise physicians mixed healing drinks for her, and finally she recovered sufficiently to tell her father and her lover the story of the battle of the thirty against the Giant, how he was dead and the land safe.

"Now go to the old man and get the other elixer," she whispered, "and when it works have the dead buried with honor and the wounded gently and wisely cared for. Then we will come to the end of the adventure, and it will be one that the Singers of

Songs will tell of for many winter evenings to the simple folk of Walling."

"You stay with her, Lord Gustro," commanded the OverLord, "and I will take the wise Homunculus in my arms and gallop to the cave and secure the elixer. When I return we will have her drink it, and once again she will be whole and young again. Then I will have you two lovers marry, for I am not as young as I was, and I want to live to see the throne secure, and, the Gods willing, grandchildren running around the castle."

Lord Gustro sat down by his Lady's bed, and he took her wasted hand in his warm one. He placed a kiss on her white lips with his red warm ones, and he whispered: "No matter what happens and no matter what the end of the adventure, I will always love you, Heart-of-mine." And the Lady Angelica smiled on him, and went to sleep.

Through the Dark Forest galloped Cecil, OverLord of Walling, with the little wise man in his arms. He flung himself off his war horse, and ran quickly into the cave.

"Have you finished the elixir?" he cried.

The old man looked up, as though in doubt as to what the question was. He was breathing heavily now, and little drops of sweat rolled down his leathered face.

"Oh! Yes! I remember now. The elixir that would save the Lady, and take from her the bodies of the men we placed in her by virtue of our synthetic magic. I remember now! I have been working on it. In a few more minutes, it will be finished."

And dropping forward on the oak table, he died. In falling, a withered hand struck a golden flask and overturned it on the floor. Liquid amber ran over the dust of ages. A cockroach came and drank of it, and suddenly died.

"I am afraid," moaned the little Homunculus. "I wish I were back in my bottle."

But Cecil, OverLord of Walling, did not know how to comfort him.

David H. Keller, M.D.
LIEUT. COL., U.S.A., RET.

BIBLIOGRAPHY

(Note: This bibliography includes the stories written under the Amy Worth nom de plume. Over 700 medical articles are omitted as being of no general interest to fantasy readers although they constitute the bulk of Doctor Keller's published work. Following the list of titles, is one of magazine names, accompanied by numbers referring to the titles given in the first part of the bibliography. Reprinted by permission of A. Langley Searles from *Fantasy Commentator*, Spring, 1947.)

TITLES
1. "Air Lines," *Amazing Stories*, January, 1930
2. "The Ambidexter," *Amazing Stories*, April, 1931
3. "Aunt Martha," *Bath Weekly*, 1895
4. "The Battle of the Toads," *Weird Tales*, October, 1929
5. "Bindings de Luxe," *Marvel Tales*, May, 1934; *Weird Tales*, January, 1943
6. "The Birth of a Soul," *The White Owl*, January, 1902

7. "A Biological Experiment," *Amazing Stories*, June, 1928
8. "The Bloodless War," *Air Wonder Stories*, July, 1929
9. "The Boneless Horror," *Science Wonder Stories*, July, 1929; *Startling Stories*, November, 1941
10. "Boomeranging Round the Moon," *Amazing Stories Quarterly*, Fall, 1930
11. "The Bride Well," *Weird Tales*, October, 1930
12. "The Bridle," *Weird Tales*, September, 1942
13. "Burning Water," *Amazing Detective Tales*, June, 1930
14. "Calypso Island," *Stirring Science Stories*, April, 1941
15. "The Cerebral Library," *Amazing Stories*, May, 1931
16. "The Chestnut Mare," *Scienti-Snaps*, April and Summer, 1940 (two parts); under the title, "Speed Shall Be My Bride," *Uncanny Stories*, April, 1941
17. "The Conquerors," *Science Wonder Stories*, December, 1929 and January, 1930
18. "Cosmos": chapter two, "The Emigrants," New York, 1933 (issued as a supplement to *Science Fiction Digest*)
19. "Creation Unforgivable," *Weird Tales*, April, 1930

20. "The Damsel and Her Cat," *Weird Tales*, April, 1929
21. "The Dead Woman," *Fantasy Magazine*, April, 1934; *Strange Stories*, April, 1939; *Nightmare by Daylight*, London, 1936
22. "Death of the Kraken," *Weird Tales*, March, 1942
23. *The Devil and the Doctor*, New York: Simon and Schuster, 1940
24. "The Dogs of Salem," *Weird Tales*, September, 1928
25. "The Doorbell," *Wonder Stories*, June, 1934
26. "Dust in the House," *Weird Tales*, July, 1938
27. "Eight, Sixty-seven," *Ten Story Book*, November, 1929
28. "The Eternal Professors," *Amazing Stories*, August, 1929; *Tales of Wonder*, Autumn, 1938
29. "The Eternal Conflict," *Les Premieres*, July, August, September, October, 1939
30. "Euthanasia, Limited," *Amazing Stories Quarterly*, Fall, 1929
31. "The Evening Star," *Science Wonder Stories*, April and May, 1930 (two parts)
32. "The Feminine Metamorphosis," *Science Wonder stories*, August, 1929
33. "The Fireless Age," *Amazing Stories*, August and October, 1937 (two parts)

34. "The Flying Fool," *Amazing Stories*, July, 1929; *Les Premieres*, July and August, 1937 (two parts)
35. "The Flying Threat," *Amazing Stories Quarterly*, Spring, 1930
36. "Free As the Air," *Amazing Stories*, June, 1931
37. "The Garnet Mine," *Ten Story Book*, November, 1929
38. "The Great American Pie House," *The White Owl*, April, 1902
39. "The Greatness of Duval," *Ursinus Weekly*, October, 1902
40. "The Goddess of Zion," *Weird Tales*, January, 1941
41. "The Golden Bough," *Marvel Tales*, volume I, number 3, (1935); *Weird Tales*, November, 1942; *The Garden of Fear*, Los Angeles, 1945
42. "The Growing Wall," *Science Fiction Quarterly*, Winter, 1942
43. "A Half-Century of Writing," *Fantasy Commentator*, Spring, 1947
44. "Half Mile Hill," *Amazing Stories Quarterly*, Summer, 1931
45. "The Headsman," *Ten Story Book*.
46. "Hands of Doom," *Ten Detective Magazine*, October, 1937
47. "Helen of Troy," *The Futurian*, January, 1939
48. "The Hidden Monster," *Oriental Stories*, Summer, 1932

49. "The Horrible Pantomime," *Scienti-Tales*, January, 1939
50. "The Human Termites," *Science Wonder Stories*, September, October, and November, 1939 (three parts)
51. "The Island of White Mice," *Amazing Stories*, February, 1935
52. "The Ivy War," *Amazing Stories*, May, 1930; *Les Premieres*, July, August, September, 1935 (three parts); *La Guerre du Lierre*, Saint Lo, May 25, 1936; *The Best of Science Fiction*, 1946
53. "I Want to Be an Author!", *Scientifiction*, March, 1938
54. "The Jelly Fish," *Weird Tales*, January, 1929
55. "Judge Not," *The Red and Blue*, November, 1899
56. "The Key to Cornwall," *Stirring Science Stories*, February, 1941
57. "Keller Interviewed by Himself," *Science Fiction Digest*, July, 1933
58. "The Last Magician," *Weird Tales*, May, 1932
59. "The Life Detour," *Wonder Stories*, February, 1935; *Startling Stories*, July, 1947
60. "Life Everlasting," *Amazing Stories*, July and August, 1934 (two parts)
61. "Lilith's Left Hand," *Helios*, October, 1937
62. "The Little Husbands," *Weird Tales*, July, 1928

63. "The Literary Corkscrew," *Wonder Stories*, March, 1934; *Startling Stories*, May, 1941
64. "The Living Machine," *Wonder Stories*, May, 1935
65. "Lords of the Ice," *Weird Tales*, October, 1937
66. "The Lost Language," *Amazing Stories*, January, 1934
67. "A 1950 Marriage," *Paris Nights*, December, 1939
68. *Men of Avalon*, (pamphlet), Everett, Pennsylvania, 1935
69. "The Menace," *Amazing Stories Quarterly*, Summer, 1928; *Ibid.*, Winter, 1933
70. "Menacing Claws," *Amazing Detective Tales*, September, 1930
71. "The Metal Doom," *Amazing Detective Tales*, June, and July, 1932 (three parts)
72. "The Mist," *The Galleon*, October, 1935
73. "Mr. Summer's Adventure," *Ten Story Book*, January, 1930
74. "The Moon Artist," *Cosmic Tales*, Summer, 1939; *Stirring Science Stories*, June, 1941
75. "Moon Rays," *Wonder Stories Quarterly*, Summer, 1930
76. "Mother Newhouse," *The White Owl*, May, 1902
77. "The Mother," *Fantascience Digest*, January, 1938
78. "The Mystery of the 33 Stolen Idiots," *Ten Story Book*, September, 1932

79. "No More Friction," *Thrilling Wonder Stories,* June, 1939
80. "No More Tomorrows," *Amazing Stories,* December, 1932
81. "No Other Man," *Weird Tales,* December, 1929
82. "One Way Tunnel," *Wonder Stories,* January, 1935
83. "On the Beezer," *Ten Story Book,* September, 1933
84. "The Parents," *Ten Story Book,* January, 1931
85. "The Perpetual Honeymoon," *Science-Fantasy Correspondent,* November, 1936; *Les Premieres,* June, 1938
86. "The Personality of a Library," *Reading and Collecting,* August, 1937
87. "The Pent House," *Amazing Stories,* February, 1932
88. "Phases of Science Fiction," *The International Observer of Science and Science Fiction,* November, 1935
89. "Phenomenon of the Stars," *The Mirror,* 1897
90. "A Piece of Linoleum," *Ten Story Book,* December, 1933
91. "The Pit of Doom," *Future Fiction,* February, 1942
92. *"Pourquoi," Les Premieres,* February, 1937
93. "The Psychonic Nurse," *Amazing Stories,* November, 1928; *La Guerre du Lierre,* Saint Lo, May 25, 1936

94. "The Rat Racket," *Amazing Stories*, November, 1931
95. "The Red Death," *Cosmic Science Stories*, July, 1941
96. "The Revolt of the Pedestrians," *Amazing Stories*, February, 1928
97. "Rider by Night," *The Fantasy Fan*, July, 1934
98. "Science Fiction and Society," *The International Observer of Science and Science Fiction*, January, 1937
99. "Scientific Widowhood," *Scientific Detective Monthly*, February, 1930
100. "Seeds of Death," *Weird Tales*, June, 1931; *At Dead of Night*, London, 1931
101. "A Serious Error," *Ten Story Book*, January, 1931
102. "Service First," *Amazing Stories Quarterly*, Winter, 1931
103. *The Sign of the Burning Hart*, Paris, 1938
104. "The Silent One," *The Red and Blue*, November, 1900
105. "The Sleeping War," *Wonder Stories*, February, 1931
106. "The Solitary Hunters," *Weird Tales*, January, February, and March, 1934 (three parts)
107. "The Steam Shovel," *Amazing Stories*, September, 1931

108. "Stenographer's Hands," *Amazing Stories Quarterly*, Fall 1928; *Tales of Wonder*, number 2; *Les Premieres*, January, February, and March, 1932 (three parts); *La Guerre du Lierre*, Saint Lo, May 25, 1936; *Avon Fantasy Reader*, Number 2, 1947
109. "The Tailed Man of Cornwall," *Weird Tales*, November, 1929
110. "The Telephone," *Ten Story Book*, January, 1932
111. *The Television Detective*, (pamphlet), Los Angeles, March, 1938
112. "The Thing in the Cellar," *Weird Tales*, March, 1932; *The Kensington News and West London Times*, April 10, 1936; as a pamphlet with "An Essay on Fear," a biographical interview, and two poems, Millheim, Pennsylvania, 1940; *Grim Death*, London, 1932; *The Coronation Omnibus*, London, no date
113. "The Third Generation," *Ten Story Book*, September, 1931
114. "The Thirty and One," *Marvel Science Stories*, November, 1938
115. *The Thought Projector*, (pamphlet), New York, 1929
116. "The Threat of the Robot," *Science Wonder Stories*, June, 1929
117. "A Three Link Tale," *The White Owl*, March, 1902

118. "Tiger Cat," *Weird Tales*, July, 1938
119. "The Time Projector," *Wonder Stories*, July and August, 1931 (two parts)
120. "The Toad God," *Strange Stories*, January, 1939
121. "The Tom-Cat Reforms," *Ten Story Book*, March, 1934
122. "The Tree of Evil," *Wonder Stories*, September, 1934
123. "The Tree Terror," *Amazing Stories*, October, 1933
124. "The Turn of the Wheel," *Ten Story Book*, October, 1930
125. "A Twentieth Century Homunculus," *Amazing Stories*, February, 1930
126. "Twin Beds," *Ten Story Book*, January, 1930
127. "Types of Science Fiction," *Science Fiction Digest*, March, 1933
128. "The Typewriter," *Fanciful Tales*, Fall, 1936
129. "A University Story," *Presbyterian Journal*, December, 1901
130. "Unlocking the Past," *Amazing Stories*, September, 1928
131. "Unto Us a Child Is Born," *Amazing Stories*, July, 1933
132. "The Valley of Bones," *Weird Tales*, January, 1938
133. "The Value of Imagination," *The Meteor*, March, 1933

134. "The Virgin," *Ten Story Book*, September, 1930
135. *The Waters of Lethe*, (pamphlet), 1937
136. "White Collars," *Amazing Stories Quarterly*, Summer, 1929
137. "Winning the Bride," *The White Owl*, March, 1902
138. *Wolf Hollow Bubbles*, (pamphlet), New York, no date
139. "Women Are That Way," *Ten Story Book*, October, 1931
140. "The Worm,"*Amazing Stories*, March, 1929
141. "The White City," *Amazing Stories*, May, 1935
142. "The Yeast Men," *Amazing Stories*, April, 1928; *Tales of Wonder*, Summer, 1937

MAGAZINES

Air Wonder Stories: 8
Amazing Detective Tales: 13, 70
Amazing Stories: 1, 2, 7, 15, 28, 33, 34, 36, 51, 52, 60, 66, 71, 80, 87, 93, 94, 96, 107, 123, 125, 130, 131, 140, 141
Amazing Stories Quarterly: 10, 30, 35, 44, 69, 102, 108, 136
Bath Weekly: 3
Cosmic Science Stories: 95
Cosmic Tales: 74
Fanciful Tales: 127
Fantascience Digest: 79
Fantasy Commentator: 43

The Fantasy Fan: 97
Fantasy Magazine: 18, 21
Future Fiction: 91
The Futurian: 47
The Galleon: 72
Helios: 61
The International Observer of Science and Science Fiction: 88, 98
Marvel Science Stories: 113
Marvel Tales: 5, 41
The Meteor: 132
The Mirror: 89
Oriental Stories: 48
Paris Nights: 67
Les Premieres: 29, 34, 52, 92, 108
Presbyterian Journal: 129
Reading and Collecting: 86
The Red and Blue: 55, 104
Scientific Detective Monthly: 99
Science-Fantasy Correspondent: 85
Science Fiction Digest: 18, 57, 127
Science Fiction Quarterly: 42
Science Wonder Stories: 9, 17, 31, 32, 44, 50
Scienti-Snaps: 16
Scienti-Tales: 49
Scientifiction: 53
Startling Stories: 9, 59, 63
Stirring Science Stories: 14, 56, 74
Strange Stories: 21, 120
Tales of Wonder: 27, 108, 142

Acknowledgements

All rights reserved. No part of this book may be reproduced in any form without the permission of Doctor Keller.

Life Everlasting, copyright, 1934, by Teck Publications for *Amazing Stories,* July and August, 1934. Reprinted by permission of Raymond A. Palmer and Ziff-Davis Publications.

The Boneless Horror, copyright, 1929, by Gernsback Publications, Inc. for *Science Wonder Stories,* July, 1929. Reprinted in *Startling Stories,* November, 1941. Reprinted by permission of Leo Margulies and Standard Magazines.

Unto Us a Child Is Born, copyright, 1933, by Teck Publications for *Amazing Stories,* July, 1933. Reprinted by permission of Raymond A. Palmer and Ziff-Davis Publications.

No More Tomorrows, copyright, 1932, by Teck Publications for *Amazing Stories,* December, 1932. Reprinted by permission of Raymond A. Palmer and Ziff-Davis Publications.

The Thing in the Cellar, copyright, 1932, by the Popular Fiction Publishing Company for *Weird Tales,* March, 1932. *The Kensington News and West London Times,* April 10, 1936. *The Bizarre Series,* 1940. *Grim Death,* London, 1932. *The Coronation Omnibus,* London. Reprinted by permission of Dorothy McIlwraith and *Weird Tales.*

The Dead Woman, copyright, 1939, by Better Publications, Inc. for *Strange Stories,* April, 1939. *Fantasy Magazine,* April, 1934. *Nightmare by Daylight,* London, 1936. Reprinted by permission of Leo Margulies and Better Publications, Inc.

Heredity, printed by permission of David H. Keller, M.D. *The Face in the Mirror,* printed by permission of David H. Keller, M.D.

The Cerebral Library, copyright, 1931, by Teck Publications for *Amazing Stories,* May, 1931. Reprinted by permission of Raymond A. Palmer and Ziff-Davis Publications.

A Piece of Linoleum, copyright, 1933, by Sun Publications for *Ten Story Book,* December, 1933. Reprinted by permission of Harry Stephen Keeler and Sun Publications.

The Thirty and One, copyright, 1938, by Postal Publications for *Marvel Science Stories,* November, 1938. Reprinted by permission of Martin Goodman and Manvis Publications, Inc.

8628